Also by Vicki Hendricks:

Miami Purity (Pantheon, 1995)
Iguana Love (St. Martin's Press, 1999)
Voluntary Madness (Serpent's Tail, 2000)
Sky Blues (St. Martin's Press, 2002)
Cruel Poetry (Serpent's Tail, 2007)

Fur People

Vicki Hendricks

Winona Woods Books
DeLeon Springs, FL

Winona Woods Books
ISBN: 9780615921723

All names of animals in this work of fiction are taken from dearly missed companions of friends and family, to honor and preserve their memories. A percentage of the proceeds will go to organizations that work hard with little funding to care for unwanted fur people.

Most locations in the novel exist in DeLeon Springs, Florida; however, the story is pure fiction. None of the events or conversations ever took place.

In Memory of Denise M. Fuciu, D.V.M
(December 2, 1951- January 21, 2011)
A dear, wonderful friend for over forty years
and
Purrsnickety ("Snickers") Hendricks
(January 20, 1991- March 17, 2011)
Smartest, sweetest, spunkiest, most beautiful kitty.

Hoping they are together.

Acknowledgements

Many thanks to the people whom I couldn't have done without and those who added fun to the novel:

Sharday for the use of Petey and Sweetie, Theresa for Choke the Chicken, Charles for Rafferty and Therm ,Woody for stories about cats; and Michelle for the lobster story.

My generous readers/editors: David Ash, Preston Allen, Patty Schwarze, Mary Anne Bennett, Betty Owen, Brian Sullivan, Ariel Gore, Susie Bright, and Aretha Bright.

Garry Kravit for a fantastic photo and Kelly Nichols for a wonderful animal-filled cover.

Brian Sullivan for technical work—well beyond duty—and Neil Plakcy for technical advice.

Jenny Feebeck for reporting on the Anna Twinney animal communication class.

Patty, Barbara, Ellen, Jason, and the rest of the Sugarmill Pancake Restaurant staff, for inspiring me over the years with the friendliness and beauty of DeLeon Springs State Park, as well as the delicious pancakes.

Finally, Willie Shields, who frequently used the phrase *fur people* many years ago.

"The animals of the world exist for their own reasons. They were not made for humans any more than black people were made for white, or women created for men"
—Alice Walker

Fur People

Chapter 1: Sunny Lytle

Fur—soft, musky, warm—Sunny's love of it, and the animal beneath, was physical and hardwired. To bury her fingers in the undercoat behind a shepherd's ears or tilt the snout of a dachshund and massage the silky groove between his eyes brought bliss. She'd tell anyone, fur people were her *people*.

She was pretty enough to be loved by young men her age, but she didn't need them. Mostly they lacked understanding. Now curled on the couch, amid purrs and dog snores, soothed by the luxury of fur, she drifted toward sleep . . . walks finished . . . cleaning done . . . food in the cupboard . . . In a dream, koalas and tiger cubs melded. She danced with upright deer and rested in the lap of a ragged grizzly.

Loud knocking jerked her awake. Cats' eyes opened wide, and a dozen dogs leapt up and sprinted, barks ripping through the apartment like a pack of firecrackers. Rufus, the huge shepherd, lunged to stand with his forepaws on the windowsill, his thunderous woof echoing. The orange tabby, Mr. Manx, sprang from Sunny's lap onto the coffee table, and Pancho, the hairless Chihuahua, stood shivering on the arm of the couch.

She dodged the commotion to peek out the window. "Shit!" The rent. On the porch the landlord was fingering his ring of keys. In the past, Sunny had always dropped the check at his office to prevent visits.

She opened the door a crack and flashed her sparkling smile. "Fred, I have my check. I just need to cash it."

His hand palmed the edge of the door as his foot wedged the crack wider. "Lock up those dogs and let me in."

No more secrets. She herded the big dogs and loud yappers into the bedroom, a couple at a time, struggling to think of a plan, failing. Pancho slipped back out and followed her, his nails ticking across the wood.

She opened the front door a few inches, wedging her leg to fill up the gap, but Fred forced the door wide and pushed past her, sending Pancho skittering. Sunny froze as Fred surveyed the visible number of cats and dogs and the rabbit. His eyes went to the bale of hay in the dining room, to the feed bag, and on to the rubber mat on the floor.

Gigolo, a miniature horse, was to be hers within the week. She bit her lip. Horse gear was the topper to get her evicted.

"What in the name of god? Are you nuts?"

"I've got the money, Fred. I'll just sign my check over so you can go."

He turned his head slowly, looking from one side of the room to the other, his jaw slack. He cupped his fingers over his nose and mouth. "It's disgusting."

"What do you mean?" She looked around, insulted. The fur people were well-fed and calm, the rabbit beans and fur balls minimal since she'd just swept. Clean food dishes and water buckets were lined up straight along the walls. Okay, the couch was soiled, but it was her property. Fred might not enjoy the smell of ferrets, but that was a personal problem. Nothing had been damaged. Nonetheless, she knew it was useless to argue, having been through it all in Cincinnati and again in Indianapolis.

Pancho screeched in his highest pitch. She picked him up, watching the landlord's face, still hoping for a break, and went for her purse. She'd been in Louisville less than six months, and the apartment complex was a good set up. Her place opened on the back side of the building facing a field and thick woods, quiet enough for visits from deer, and there was a fenced area off the kitchen where she could let the dogs out when she didn't have time for walks. Crack users on both sides ensured privacy. Why didn't Fred care about them? Her crime seemed nothing by comparison, but the cops would come to abduct the fur people and charge her with abuse, requiring a huge fine that she couldn't pay.

She offered her check to Fred, but he shook his head no. "I have your last month and deposit."

She thought he liked her, had caught him leering at her butt more than once, but now he was all business. "I'll get rid of the hay." She fingered her braid and offered her most wide-eyed, innocent face. "No horse—ever. Promise."

He stared toward the bedroom door, the muffled ruckus behind it. "This is pathetic. You can't keep all these animals here."

Her eyes filled and she wiped them with the back of her hand, spreading tears across her cheeks. Pancho moved up her shoulder to lick the salt. She tossed back her braid. "Just give me a day to clean up and get on the road." She set the tiny dog on the couch and started stacking food bowls, looking back at Fred with watery eyes.

"You need help, Sunny."

"I can handle it."

"That's not what I meant." He backed out the door, shaking his head. "If these animals are still here in the morning, I'll have to call the cops."

"How could you? They're my family!"

He spread his fingers, holding his forehead, as if his head might split. "Look—if you need me to drive some dogs to the shelter . . ."

She closed her eyes and shook her head hard, the long blonde braid whapping side to side, driving him back. Fred pulled the door shut behind him. If he thought she was crazy, that was fine. Make him damned uncomfortable throwing her out. Fuck.

She let the dogs back into the living room and collapsed on the couch, gathering Pancho into her lap. She had never intended to pack so many animals into the small apartment, and it wasn't ideal, but she couldn't help it. She was a magnet, drawing every boney, lonesome, injured, fluff-covered creature into her arms and her heart—every pampered pet, as well. She only had to gaze with yearning at a perky pup on a leash, and it would stop dead and turn longing eyes on her.

Life as an animal attractant required sacrifice, but she could live without nice clothes, TVs, computers, cell phones and IPods, the common comforts and necessities of most women her age. Her social life was full at home. She had never resented the lack of a career or living hand to mouth.

Sure, there were a few trips to the humane society that she should never have made, but she gave those animals life. She worked hard, tended bar as many hours as she could get, tried desperately to save money to start a rescue center of her own.

She looked around the apartment. Despite Fred and his world, she was proud of the freshly swept floor and tidy row of clean water buckets, the healthy fur-bodies spread or curled on every shelf, sill, floor, and piece of furniture. Sprawled near her feet on the wood floor were Rufus, his head the size of a breadbox, Schmeisser, another muscular shepherd; and Brindle, the blond lab-mix, swollen with pups. Their faces turned to watch her eyes, feeling her emotion, tails beating when she looked back at them with love. They shared the highest level in the dog hierarchy, after Pancho, claiming spots closest to her. The smaller breeds, Wookie, Devo, Willie, Sugar, Angel, Tulip, Gus, Duke, and Ginger were strung out head to tail, mostly resting against the dining room walls. Kiko, the Siamese, hopped up to settle near her, followed by Tazwell, the rex cat. Most of the cats had returned to napping on their shelves and tables.

Rosebud, the Dutch rabbit, wandered from the bedroom, and Pancho hopped down to follow, his nose to her black tuft of a tail. Panchy surely had dachshund in his ancestry, with short legs that made him barely taller than Rosebud. Sunny hoped he wouldn't get an erection. The last time, his hot pink arrow had grown longer than his legs and stubbed the floor like a kickstand, only allowing him to walk backwards. She'd had to dowse him in the sink.

"Mitter Manx," she called, baby talking her oldest orange tabby. He stayed on the windowsill eyeing her. Norton, the Scottish fold, held his post on the coffee table, gazing over the couch cats, as if amused. They didn't know enough to worry.

She took turns rubbing ears, then coaxed the dogs back to the bedroom and let the ferrets loose for a romp with the cats for their last night in the apartment. She loved to watch the ferrets slip under furniture and pop out some place unexpected. When the cats gave up, the ferrets continued to weave, bob, and roll, sparring with invisible opponents. Individual ferret boxing, she called it. Better entertainment than television. She hadn't owned a TV in years.

She thought of cheaper sections of Louisville, places less likely to call attention to her situation. Or heading to somewhere more forgiving. California. A job in a tourist area. Bear, her best friend—and lover—would help her out some, but it was too far, too difficult, and there would always be landlords.

She was stalling, trying to fool herself. She almost didn't dare think of one possibility . . . Jason. The only two-legger who felt the same as she did about animals. Leaving him had been a mistake.

A few weeks ago at the library, she'd had to duck behind the computer screen to hide her blushing and shaking, when she found his Facebook page. He hadn't changed. He was still living in her hometown, DeLeon Springs, Florida.

She hadn't sent a message, but looked up his address and phone number, just for the heck of it. After ten years, the odds were terrible for getting back together, but she couldn't let loose of her feelings. Now Fate was lending a push. It would be an adventure to go back home, a challenge. Moving everyone would require a huge favor from Bear, but she knew she could count on him, even though he would be unhappy.

She put the ferrets back into their crate and opened the bedroom door to get started on the packing. Ears perked up. She took Pancho into her arms and sat on the bed. His brow wrinkled and his eyes questioned as if he wanted to know what she was thinking. If dogs ever learned to talk, he'd be the first. She lowered him to the pillow. As she went to the closet, the big dogs tilted their heads and slapped their tails on the wood floor. Pancho stood on the comforter, half-turned away, and stared back over his haunches, as if he knew what was up, and that he wasn't going to like it.

Chapter 2: Rufus

Rufus' tail thumped. His eyes followed the two-legger from
the closet to the bed and back, his nose catching flowery bursts
freed from folds of cloth, and spicy, human scent loosened from
toes of shoes. Rufus remembered this behavior and what
followed—a ride in the vehicle, nose out the window . . . friends
and the old chewy pull-toy left behind.

He drew up his front legs and arched to a sit. The square
package, open in half on the bed, would go with his two-legger.
Nose near the floor, he whiffed. The new pull-toy was far. He
stood slowly, not to get attention, and followed the aroma of
saliva and hard red rubber indented by teeth. He stepped over the
stinking nipper, the shortest distance to the door. Pancho, the
nipper was called. Pancho, Pancho, day and night. The two-
legger was always barking for him, stroking, holding. A pad on
Rufus' hind paw grazed the nipper's thin ear. The nipper jumped.
A plume of hot male musk ascended. Nipper's organs were big
as his head.

Rufus found the new toy in the kitchen. Schmeisser had
gnawed it, the taint of his tongue still fresh. Rufus slid his teeth
around it, and loose-jawed, tossed it back until the loop hung on
both sides of his mouth. He carried it, jaunty, proud. As he
passed by Brindle, he slung down on his haunches, forelegs
extended, an invitation to grab an end in play, but she watched
without a flicker. He nudged her fragrant neck with his snout,
and she rolled and stretched out, huge belly bulging to the side,
pink teats long and ready. Soon she would birth Rufus' pups, and
they would grow solid and powerful.

His two-legger was back in the closet. Rufus leaped to the
bed and placed the new pull toy in the open package. He used his
back paws to scuff soft pieces of cloth together until they
covered the red loop. He hopped down under the window, resting
head on paws before she came back. She dropped another
armload into the package, pawed the clump he had made, and
uncovered the toy. She turned toward him. He closed his eyes.

All night, scurrying, clanging, banging, scraping. Things carried, things dragged. The male two-legger, the furry one, Bear, grunted and grumbled, poured heat and scent.

Richness from the kibble bag passing through the hall made Rufus' stomach lurch. But it was not food time. Useless to do the dance, start the whine. Then, still in darkness, his name was barked. He trotted outside and up steps to new smells among the old, including the pull-toy. Brindle lumbered to drop next to him and Schmeisser. Stinking nipper crept between, and others around, jostling for floor space. Rufus would not go alone this time. It was both good and bad.

Chapter 3: Buckaroo

Buck had spent the past two hours patrolling the sky, and he was dying for a cigarette and a beer, but the siege would likely go on until dark. He lay on his back on the cot inside the open tent, holding his foil-covered paper plate, ready for a deadly strike. He had doubts about the thin deflector, a primitive defense system, but it had worked to save his life again and again.

The clouds hung bruised and swollen, Cumulonimbus grumbling over DeLeon Springs. It was a lethal situation since Magnetoids loved to lurk up there. They kept their armaments cool in the mist, awaiting the chance to penetrate his skull and cripple his brain with vicious light rays, causing him blackouts and headaches. A particular frequency had been created to bedevil him. If he got zapped by several rays at a time or one high-beam, he would burst from inside out, like a frog in a microwave. He'd be flash-cooked into a pile of ash and disappear on a breeze. He often pictured it.

The rangers had cleared all squatters from the Ocala State Forest so he'd moved onto undeveloped property off a side road, near the entrance to the DeLeon Springs State Park. He was still deeper into the forest than Deep Woods Off could conquer, but in a convenient place for getting food and beer, and taking a swim in the spring if he wanted to rinse off. His tent was positioned among the trees, protected on all sides, with a clear opening straight above. Every blink of his eyes meant a risk that he would lack enough time to aim his reflector and send a ray ricocheting back into the clouds, so he had conditioned his eyes to blink only once per fifteen minutes. In the past hour, he had fought off three attacks, but he could still feel the tingling in his blood, hot wires through his brain. He was still in their sights. His eyes were tired and he was sweaty and mosquito bitten, as usual, but he couldn't move until the clouds rained out or blew away, or it got dark enough that the Mags couldn't spot him.

He'd drunk his last beer that morning and smoked his last whole cigarette. There were butts in the Altoids tin, for emergencies, but he had cash and planned to borrow Geordie's truck to buy cigs and put a case of Old Milwaukee on ice. If only the damned clouds would blow away.

Buck slapped a mosquito and jerked his eyes back to the dark heavens just in time to see the ray. "Fucker!" He lifted the plate over his face with a swift motion, tilting it forty-five degrees. "Gotcha!" There was never any sound, but the absence of burning pain in his head indicated that he had deflected the ray back to them. He held the plate still, counting buck . . . buck . . . buck . . . a . . . roo. Nothing. Sometimes there was a quick reload that discharged at the same angle. They were always watching.

Two years before, he had tried living inside a house with a girl. She was young, a nympho with big tits, and easy-going, but he had to take off for the woods again when he pinned down the source of his head pain—a big picture window in her living room. He thought he would be safe in a house, but the Mags must have glimpsed him through the window and he couldn't deflect the beams. He didn't miss her conversation or her soap operas. He did miss her pussy and refrigerator. Otherwise, he liked living on the loose, outdoors, and it was cheap.

Discovering the Magnetoids was the start of all his problems. He had explained their system of warfare to a few squatters before he realized he was putting other people in jeopardy with careless talk. Mags were always spying. A couple of his pals had disappeared, and he knew it was his fault. He did his damnedest to stop the carnage, but he couldn't tell if he was making any progress. Magnetoids seemed to reproduce faster than he could wipe them out.

He brushed a stray curl off his cheek. His hair had grown into a mane of blond dreadlocks. The color had always drawn attention from women, so he kept it long, even though it got in the way. His second wife said his light hair and blue eyes made her confuse him for an angel. He chuckled. She got over that confusion pretty fast.

It dawned on him that the Magnetoids probably had an on-going war with angels, since they shared the heavens. Why hadn't he thought of it before? Angels were generally blond! He tried to remember if he told any other blonds. He didn't have any blond friends now. Christ! All of them burnt to cinders!

Edges of gold appeared around some of the clouds and blue peeked through. The afternoon sun burned just out of sight. He might still get a break. He wanted to jack off while he waited, but today, busy as the sky was, he didn't dare move his hand that far from the plate. It was one small sacrifice, among many, that he made regularly in order to save mankind.

Chapter 4: Sunny Lytle

Sunny loved the air in central Florida, warm and sweet as puppy breath. Sun blazed into the camo-painted school bus, glistening on the four-leggers' coats in shades from coal black to milk white, making tongues drip, and sealing the young woman's sweating thighs to the plastic seat. November, and no sign of winter. Palmettos, cypress, magnolia, and live oaks against a brilliant sky; nature, out of control, just as she remembered. The red berries of Florida holly, green spiked bromeliads and powdery gray Spanish moss tangled along the sides of the road with branches and vines and moss. It was housing for lizards, rodents, and insects. The countryside hadn't changed over the ten years, and she realized she had missed it.

Up ahead, cumulus clouds were sculpted into a poodle. She glanced behind her to the nearest dog on the floor of the bus. "Look at that, Tulip—I mean, Gus. It's a good luck sign if I ever saw one."

She was dying to see Jason, but common sense kept her from driving to his house with a bus full of cranky animals. Her plan was to set up camp in the secret spot near the park where they used to smoke dope and hang out. Nobody would bother her there, and Jason would know exactly where to find her. She would wait to call until she was looking good.

A swath of humidity drifted through half-open windows to fill the bus, the smell of a piney hammock putting her right back into his arms. They had bought a tent together and hid out in the woods many nights, feeding canned sardines to the raccoons, cooking potatoes in the campfire, making love in their private place to the music of frogs, crickets, and the electric chirp of nighthawks. Once they heard the rattle of water as a male gator bellowed for a mate. It was beautiful.

She had never planned to stay in Cincinnati after giving up the baby, but her aunt was far easier to live with than her alcoholic father. She had finished her last year of high school, gotten a job, and moved out on her own with Miss Poodle, the hamster, the single animal her aunt had allowed. Ohio never felt permanent, even when she gathered a family.

The candy sweetness of blooming four o'clocks rushed through the bus with memories of swimming in the cool, crystal clear spring, sun-bathing, picnicking, and kayaking down the run. She remembered the day she found the turtle, tangled in fishing line, that bit Jason's arm. Freed, the cooter paddled deep into opaque green water, but surfaced to catch their attention, blinking its red eyes as if to say *sorry . . . and thanks.*

She worried that Jason's phone number might be outdated. Jason. Jason. Be there. Be there. She crossed her fingers on the steering wheel. They'd been inseparable, called twins for their blond hair—and love of animals—sentiment that people considered odd for a star quarterback. Why did she leave when it was obvious to everyone that they should be together? She hadn't wanted to force him into marriage and keep him from college, but if she had guts, she would have stayed.

The gas gauge caught her eye. The camper-bus had nearly bankrupted her, but she was almost in DeLeon Springs. She pulled into a Hess station and turned off the key, thinking two gallons would be more than enough. Dog commotion erupted from the back, all of them expecting a chance to stretch and mark and poop. But there was no place to walk. She pushed bodies back as she moved to the door—"Home soon," she told them— opened it a crack, and squeezed out.

As the pump clicked off, a car pulled beside her. The dogs were still barking and the woman driver looked up into the bus. She was frowning, a little too interested—the look of authority. County law enforcement? Humane society? There was no identification on the car, but Sunny had survived enough run-ins to develop a sense for officials and "do-gooders." She replaced the nozzle and hurried to screw on the gas cap.

The woman opened her door and came close, straining to see past the glare and into the bus. She smiled. "Your pals are desperate to get out of there."

Her smooth, friendly manner was expected. A professional type with gray in her short dark hair, glasses, silver earrings, an owlish look.

"They'll be fine. They're almost home."

The woman turned to the pump. "You live nearby?"
It was dangerous, being seen with the whole gang. "No."
"Oh, I thought I might be of some help—"
"No, thanks." Sunny started walking. "Gotta go."
She reached the bus door. Pancho's head slipped out. "Move, move!" She picked him up, pried open the crack, and squeezed in, pushing Tulip, or Gus? farther inside with her knee. She knew it. The woman had pegged her instantly as a problem. She was still staring, her arm frozen to the pump. Sunny started the engine and waited for a truck to pass. Ms. Hoot-owl scanned the windows, as if counting the heads of those standing on boxes or seats.

Sunny touched the gas, then braked for a leathery-faced guy with blond dreadlocks crossing in front of her. He took his merry time legging it slowly into the driveway past the wide bus window, pushing his curls aside, winking a pale blue eye and smiling, studying her. Bright white teeth were surprising above his faded clothes. She had forgotten the feel of a small town, sometimes creepy. If you remembered faces, you'd see them again. He finally passed, and she pulled out.

DeLeon Springs. Without the sign, she might have missed it. "Home, sweeties," she announced. She tried for more gusto. "Home!" The sweaty ferret on her lap looked up in understanding. They had come far and there was no means to go back.

She made the left turn a little fast onto SR 17 and glanced back into the bus. There was no upset, but the view in between appliances and camping gear showed several dogs, including Schmeisser, flat on their backs from the heat, heads lolling across others' legs and tails, all down the aisle. Mitter, Tazwell, and other cats mingled among them. Rufus and Brindle were wedged into the kitchen area where seats had been removed. Pancho rested his tiny head on Rufus' thick shepherd tail.

Pancho, nearly hairless, pink-skinned and scaly from a case of mange let go in a former household, was the Casanova of the group. He had spent much of the trip humping the butts of every species he could reach, and mostly Angel, the fluffy white cloud of a Westie. Angel's three-month-old pups, blocked off in back, wore coats the color of Pancho's sparse fur.

Sunny drove past a field with two horses, heads down, tails swishing. Her last visit to Kentucky Horse Rescue had been on a chilly autumn day, when the tall, sleek rascals were snorting steamy breath, flaring their nostrils, whinnying, kicking, and farting. Her plump little boyfriend Gigolo had trotted across his pen to see her. Solid mocha-furred stomach and broad withers, soft caramel face and huge long-lashed eyes—he had a body that begged to be hugged. With some luck, when she was set up in DeLeon, she could trailer him down.

She drove past The Outpost, the local bar where her father used to hang out. Lytle the Delight he was called by the other drunks, a sarcastic name. He had been hospitalized with liver problems even before she was sent to Cincinnati, so she didn't expect him to be alive. Communication had broken off long ago. She made the hard left smoothly onto Ponce DeLeon Boulevard. One good thing, Lytle had taught her to drive a semi. The bus was cake.

She made a left at the end of the road, passing the gate of the State Park. Her destination was isolated woods at the edge of state property, a place where nobody would bother her. The secret campground had always been cleaner than the real camping area over in the Ocala Forest where the Rainbow Coalition commune stayed. She remembered the old hippie guys always trying to weasel into girls' pants. They weren't as cute as weasels.

She wondered if the Rainbows were still there on Freak Creek. Likely. Probably still growing pot, selling braided palm trinkets outside of Walmart, and making their hallucinogens from Angel's trumpet. The flowers were a money crop that she used to snatch from people's yards to sell to the Rainbows, before she started to think about damage to the plants.

The old camping spot would be close enough to Spring Garden Lake to haul water, and she would be able to launch the kayak and paddle to the pancake restaurant in the park. It was nearly tourist season, so she might be able to get a job there, eat pancakes to save money, use the toilet and clean up at the sink in the ladies room until she could find a new place. She barely dared to hope for her wildest dream, but the thought kept her going.

She turned onto a gravel track with foot-high grass in the middle, Living Waters Road, and followed it for a quarter mile to a sign, *No Trespassing,* posted in front of a neglected fern field. *Agricultural Area, Pesticides.* That would keep normal folk away, but the sign was faded, and only patches of dark fluffy plumosa fern survived among weeds in the shade of the live oaks. Nobody had sprayed pesticides this season.

Sunny had loved the soft feathery plumosa on the fern farm where she spent her childhood. She remembered the tickle of fern on her cheek one morning, being wakened by her mother for school. Her mom often got up before dawn to start picking, so Lytle could sleep off his hangovers and not get into trouble. She hadn't thought much about her mother over the last few years. The memories were dim and confusing, from age eleven at most. Over the years Lytle had made her mother out to be insane, but Sunny knew it was his abuse that drove her away. Her mother never dared return home or let anybody know where she was.

She turned off on a path of packed sand alongside the fern field, following it past a tumbled-down cabin to the edge of the woods. Broken limbs and fallen trees from the last hurricane, two years earlier, ensured privacy, since nobody had cared enough to clear them. When the path ended, she was forced to drive over palmetto scrub, seedlings, and ferns. She pictured squished caterpillars and cracked beetle shells under her tires, casualties to her human needs—but the farther into the woods, the safer.

She picked a spot between two huge live oaks. A glint of light on moist leaves created jewels, encrusted parasols of diamonds and emeralds, shielding the bus from the hot sun. She had always loved the sprawling trees. They were spiders with rough limbs hard as concrete, sprouting ferns in their bent elbows and dripping Spanish moss like shawls. Alongside the bus, two limbs ran for twenty feet parallel to the ground, six feet high. She would throw sheets across the curving arms to protect the bus from the slanting afternoon rays.

She turned off the key and stroked the back of the ferret, Sula, still asleep on her lap. The short creamy fur was rich with oil, each hair sheer, sparkling like cellophane in the sun. She lifted the limp body and kissed the back of her neck, breathing in the rich musk. She set her inside the plastic crate with her albino buddy, Ajax.

Where to start? The bus was crammed. Fur people stretched and wagged and stood to look at her with lifted eyebrows, as if she knew what to do. She peered between the stacks and piles. For short-term living, the bus would be perfect once she cleared out the plastic furniture. There was a booth for eating and a built-in propane stove, plus her mattress. Lashed on top was a kayak, useful for getting into the park.

Originally Bear had given the bus a psychedelic paint job, but later decided hippie colors would draw attention from the cops, so now the shades of green and brown blended into the trees. Good old Bear. He had begged her to stay in Louisville, offering to help with rent. But he had a wife, Marci. His claim that Marci didn't care what he did seemed true, but Sunny had been uncomfortable since she found out about the marriage. Bear loved her, she knew, and that had kept her from breaking it off, but she was grateful for a way out. Bear offered to send a check to Florida if she needed money, but she didn't plan to get that desperate.

She stretched and lifted her cropped T-shirt to let in a breeze. The temperature and humidity weren't much lower than the peak of Louisville summer, but she would get used to it again. She would love it, especially if Jason came back to her.

Chapter 5: Rita McKenna

Rita chiseled dried diarrhea out of the corner of the concrete floor, then shot it with the spray nozzle. Daily interaction with dogs, and their unique personalities, kept her interested and cheerful at the shelter most of the time, but in the gaps between barking eruptions, the scrape of the putty knife on concrete echoed her loneliness. Six months of prison time had given her a special understanding of their isolation in tomb-like concrete pens with wire-fence doors. They were pack animals, as was she, without a pack.

She thought about the young blonde at the gas station with a busload of dogs that she'd seen on the way to work. So thin she could have been an adolescent, except for her weary face. The girl was not passing through—her evasiveness made that clear. Undoubtedly, a young hoarder looking for a place to squat. She would be found eventually and her animals brought in, adding to the thousands euthanized each year. Better than letting them suffer with disease or starve to death in a bus—she always had to remind herself that death was better. At least, the smaller dogs could get good homes. She would keep an eye out. If Rita reported the girl, it would make the surrender easier, friendlier at least. How did these people ever expect to feed so many? From the girl's looks, she couldn't even feed herself. A classic case. Yet, Rita knew the feeling, the desire to save them all. Love at an obsessive, clinically dangerous level, Rita knew all about it.

She wiped sweat off her forehead and dried her palm on her dirty shorts next to a smear of dog shit. She was inured to excrement, but annoyed at her sloppiness. She checked her watch. In a few hours she would be home with a glass of wine, the best part of her day. The Food Network and cheap shiraz—veggie chili or cream of mushroom soup. She didn't mind working hard for little pay. The animals deserved everything she could give them, but she could be doing much more if she were in charge.

She had put all the small breeds into cages, having been told to prepare every available pen. The crew was on its way with eight pit bulls seized from a dog-fight operation. Some might have to be put down. If so, she knew whose job that was.

She could barely fathom that she had been working at the shelter in central Florida for three months already. With a felony in her past and the loss of her license, it was the only animal-related work available to her, a great deal for the county, her expertise at minimum wage. She could do surgeries if Denise, the "real vet," was on the premises, but cleaning, worming and medicating had become her life, while Doc Denise saved lives. Rita was allowed to diagnose and prescribe, as long as she had no access to street-marketable drugs, but rarely was she given the opportunity to do anything that required the use of her brain.

Word was that Denise had sold a lucrative practice in Mill Valley. Still in her fifties, she was semi-retired and rarely worked more than a few days a week. In hindsight, Rita knew she should have done likewise and left southern Illinois to start her practice on one of the coasts, but she had married into a rural partnership, thinking love and the rewards of her profession were all she needed. But then love hadn't lasted long enough to test that theory.

She looked out at the parking lot. Silvery mirages, visible waves of heat, were still shimmering on the blacktop. October , and no fall weather in sight. DeLeon Springs, a legendary location of the Fountain of Youth, had seemed a romantic spot for starting over. At age forty-five, she knew country life best and thought physical work would be good for her. But there were few jobs, they paid little, and the cost of living was high in Florida.

After the years of dreams and struggles through school, being stripped of her license to be a doctor—for the rest of her life— was barely believable. She thought she had hit bottom five years ago, sharing the practice with her ex after the divorce, working every weekend to make the loan payments on her car, house, and half of the veterinary equipment, but it had been a false bottom. Involvement with Matt, a looker ten years her junior, dragged her into the pit. A dopamine addiction and daily orgasms replaced her heartbroken past. Snorting coke, taking X, sampling every insanity—selling Ketamine from the veterinary supplies easily fell into the mix. Matt recognized the time to split with a profit, but it took her months in prison to grasp his use of her. Now she imagined the pleasure of finding him, to run him over him with the car.

She heard the fence clank open and looked to see the first red-nose pit bull being led in. The ribs and the scars! She hurried in finishing the last pen so she could start filling bowls with water, opening cans of food, and gathering bedding. There would be disinfecting and stitching to do.

It was after eight and getting dark when she finished draining a dog's infected bite, swelled to the size of a grapefruit. In fear, even muzzled, he was uncontrollable, and the assistant had been needed to help bathe him and wrestle him down so that Rita could administer anesthesia in order to treat his festering sores. He was still under, his tongue flat on the metal table, probably the only few moments of his life when he had slept in securely. By unlucky birth, he was one of the several victim breeds identified as pit bulls, branded vicious since the 80's because of irresponsible humans.

She placed the gauze through the hole, made a knot to keep the wound open, and attached a wide plastic collar around his neck so that he wouldn't be able to pull out the wick. She was about to call the assistant to help carry the dog back to the pen when she heard the administrator, Jackie, coming down the corridor from the back, talking to Denise. Rita had left Denise a message over an hour earlier, asking for help, but she hadn't returned the call. The two women together meant bad news.

They stepped into the operating room. Dr. Denise had her shiny black hair up in a clip and was wearing a black shift and high heels that emphasized her tight calves, probably just come from a swanky restaurant in Orlando. Even in heels, she was several inches shorter than Rita's five-six, but small size contrasted with her personality.

"Sorry, Rita, I came as soon as possible."

Jackie clucked. "Rita, you shouldn't have wasted your time on that one."

"What do you mean?" She knew exactly what Jackie meant, but she wanted her to say it in front of Denise.

"Besides being half-mutilated, that dog is nasty. It will never be adoptable."

"He hasn't had a chance. If he's fed and comfortable, he'll be a completely different animal."

"I'm sorry," Denise said. "It goes against my feelings too, but we will have to put this big guy down. His chances for a home are non-existent."

"He's better off here than in the hellhole where he's spent his entire life."

Denise shook her head. "We're limited by the facility. You know the county won't pay for lifers. I hate it, too, but think about it. He would be locked up here, miserable until he died."

"I disagree. When he heals and his scars are covered by fur, and he gains confidence in people again, he'll be beautiful, a great dog for a farm or a ranch. Let's give him a few days."

Jackie crossed her arms. "You're not in charge here, Rita. Denise already made the decision and that's the way it goes."

Denise touched the sleeping dog's square head gently. "I've checked all nine dogs brought in today. This one and two others are the worst, by far. There's really no choice. We won't even have to wake him."

Rita huffed. She looked straight at Denise. "You won't be the one administering the shots, I take it."

Denise frowned. "I'm on my way home from a wake. You're in scrubs. I'll let you handle them."

Jackie held the door open and Denise followed her out.

Rita questioned her own sarcasm. She might have misjudged Denise. But as she readied the injection, she wondered if the woman had lied, just for effect. Denise had only lived in DeLeon Springs for a month or so longer than Rita, barely enough time to make a friend whose wake she would be attending. Rita hadn't known Denise to lie, but she didn't know Denise at all, only that she was the "real vet" and made all the decisions.

She put newspaper under the dog's pelvis in case of release and found the vein in his paw. There wasn't even a shudder, since he was still out, and his eyes remained peacefully closed. Still, it was a shame.

She needed control over her life. No one should have to follow orders like this.

Chapter 6: Sunny Lytle

It was dinner time and still hot. Sunny had worked all afternoon, attaching the sheets to limbs for shade, digging a latrine, scraping out a fire pit and ringing it with rocks and souvenir shells saved from a childhood visit to Daytona Beach. The shell pattern imbedded in the sandy ground gave a homey feel to the kitchen area. Jason would see that she had everything under control and hadn't come begging.

The little dogs were inside and the large ones tied with loops of nylon line stretched along the outside of the bus, so she could attach the leashes with separations between to avoid tangles. The dogs could go under the bus for shade, any time of day, and dig into the soft sand for cool napping. She kissed each head down the line, fluffy, stiff, downy, every kind of fur with its special perfume, then dragged out the bags of rabbit pellets, dog chow, and cat chow and portioned them out and filled soup bowls with water. The oily, pungent odor of skunk hung lightly in the humidity under the trees, and she drew in a luxurious breath. She wouldn't want to be sprayed, but skunk at a distance was one of her favorite smells, in the same league as horse manure, with a richness that clung to the lining of your nose.

Meat! She spun around. *Meat!* The sound came from close by, near the floor. All the cats had their heads down, crunching in their bowls of dry food. An actual word?—or the feeling of a word. She bent and stared into each cat's eyes, one after the other. Losing her mind. Had she hit her head lately? When she got to Mitter Manx he stopped eating and raised his head to return the stare. He was the oldest, smartest, boldest cat. She had promised him meat. She squatted and looked pleadingly into his eyes. He looked away. With disgust?

She held out her hands. "I'm doing the best I can."

Mitter crunched.

Did they think she had an unending supply of meat and was keeping it from them? "I don't have anything! I need money to—" She laughed, stood there laughing at her ridiculous pleas . . . as if they could understand paying. She couldn't stop laughing, recognized a touch of hysterics—pressure driving her insane.

She pulled herself together and handed out the rest of the bowls. When she set down Willie's, he showed his teeth in a smile, his pleased expression. He'd learned it from Tamper, one of her guys confiscated in Indiana. She lifted Willie's chin and kissed the top of his nose. "We miss Tamper, don't we, baby?" He always smiled when she fed him, no matter if it was kibble or meat.

She thought about her own dinner, her staples: Ramen noodles or pasta, but didn't feel like cooking. In the cooler, American cheese and butter in sealed baggies and a milk jug floated in cold water. Ice was going to be a problem. She nibbled a slice of American on white bread, thinking she might invite Jason for dinner the next night. He always liked her grilled cheese. She piled up sticks to make a fire since she didn't have propane for the stove, set up a card table and chair, stacked one orange crate on top of another, and stowed her small collection of pans and plastic dishes. She carried out the two remaining gallons of spring water and put them on the table.

Rufus caught her eye, reminding her of the rubber pull toy he had personally deposited in her suitcase. She chuckled, got it, and placed it between his paws, petted his head as his tail wagged. Life was good.

Last, she unfolded the lounge chair and covered it with a sheet, her spot under the trees. She poured the rest of the milk into a coffee cup and sat down. Time to find a phone and call Jason. Her stomach clenched. She shut her eyes and pleaded with the universe, tightening every muscle in her body, as if the harder she squeezed, the more likely that Jason would still love her.

She couldn't get to the bicycle without a complete unloading, so she shouldered her backpack and started walking. The dogs whined, but she was too nervous to be slowed down by sniffing and peeing. If there was still a payphone at the old Mini-mart, it would be a fifteen-minute walk.

Her breath caught as she spotted the phone on the back wall inside. Her shaking fingers dropped the quarters on the dirty tile, and she punched the wrong buttons twice. The phone rang and rang. It rang until the voice mail picked up, a male robot voice.

This possibility hadn't occurred to her. "Jason? It's Sunny . . . Lytle. I'm in DeLeon." What could she say? "I'm here . . . for a while." She felt ridiculous, wondering if she had the right number, or was putting her heart through a wringer for a stranger to hear. "I don't have a phone. Call you back." She hung up, shaking. At least it wasn't a turn down. Or a woman.

By the time she reached camp it was almost dark. Her hands, neck, and legs were bitten and she was exhausted. Not the first night in the woods she had dreamed of. Even a little creepy. She gave good night kisses and ear scratches and lay down on the lounge, hoping Pancho wasn't getting chewed up with so little fur. A skeeter buzzed past her head, the scout for an air force, no doubt. She dragged herself up, put on jeans and a long sleeved shirt, and sprayed Skin So Soft on her neck and patted some on her cheeks. It never worked very well, but she didn't think any animals had been harmed in making it. Sleeping inside the bus would be too hot if she closed the windows, and the skeeters were already in there. She unfolded the sheet and covered her head creating a sauna with her own breath. It was almost intolerable. "Sharp as a rat turd," she said, an expression her father loved to use to describe her. She'd seen enough rat poop to know it wasn't sharp at all. Mouse poop, that had a point to it.

Chapter 7: Jason Cox

Jason was peeling potatoes at the sink when he noticed the blinking light on the answering machine. His wife, Deb, had been home all day, but she never answered calls while she was working. He glanced at her. She'd brought the laptop into the kitchen so she could supervise while he cooked, but she was concentrating on technical reports, her blue eyes scanning the screen while she took notes without looking. Beauty and expertise. She was still a wonder to him.

He knew how to make killer desserts from his grandmother, but his repertoire of dinners was limited, so the evening's lesson was on country fried steak, green beans, mashed potatoes, and gravy. He enjoyed cooking, but it was late to start an elaborate meal, and his feet hurt after a long day at work, toting pancake batter. But he'd promised. Money beat effort, and Deb brought home the big bucks. Making dinner was his payment toward the mortgage until he could finish his computer degree—a long way to go, and getting longer since he'd taken the last two semesters off.

As directed, he cut the potatoes and put them in a pot of water and laid out the cube steaks on wax paper. He got into the pounding, watching the slices of meat flatten and spread into sticky slabs with holes.

Deb looked up, "Okay, that's enough. You don't want to shred them. Now pour on the buttermilk and let them soak—in the refrigerator—while you snap the beans."

He followed instructions, rinsed his hands, then took the opportunity to punch the code into the phone to get the message. Heat rushed into his neck and face when he heard the voice. Sunny? In DeLeon Springs?

He fumbled the receiver into hang-up position and sat down on the closest chair. He boosted Wootsie, the oldest dachshund, onto his lap.

"Have you snapped the beans?" Deb looked at him over her laptop screen. "Problem?"

"A blast from the past." He wasn't sure how much detail to give. In five years, Sunny had never come up in conversation. Now didn't seem the time. "There was a message from an old friend, a girl from high school. She's in town."

"Should I be worried?"

He rolled his eyes to make it harder for her to read them. "I just never thought she'd turn up back here."

"She dumped you?"

"No, moved away."

"Guess you really scared her. What's her name? If you want, give her a call. We can get that pork roast out of the freezer for Sunday."

Deb liked to entertain as long as Jason did the cooking, but her interest seemed above normal. He hadn't ever heard this many words out of her in the midst of a project. He was glad Sunny hadn't left a number. "I don't think she has a phone."

"Not even a cell? What's her name?"

"Oh, Sunny. "Maybe she'll call back—or we'll run into her." There really wasn't much chance of that, since they rarely went anywhere together. He would rather talk to Sunny the first time by himself. His ear started to itch. Was she talking about him? He wondered if she still had her long blonde braid.

"Earth to Jason."

"Huh?"

Deb was pointing at a wet newspaper in the doorway. "Good puppy, good boy." The weenie pup, Spike, had peed where he was supposed to. "Would you get that before you start the beans? I'm way behind on this article."

It was her dog and her turn to get off her ass, but he lowered Wootsie to the floor and got the Windex and paper towels. He folded the newspapers and stuffed them into the can and sprayed and wiped the tile. Sunny . . . the feel of her fragile body in his arms. Never thought he'd hear anything. He'd tried for a long time to find her. He remembered her roosters and the pygmy goat he hid for her in the back field.

Chapter 8: Sunny Lytle

A crack of lightning startled her awake. The wind had picked up, and the mosquitoes were gone, but she could smell rain on its way. With only the beam of the flashlight, she struggled to put the dogs inside, getting soaked on the last two trips. Finally, in the dark, she swept what she could of dirty, wet sand down the steps, and brushed off a spot on the mattress to curl next to Brindle's damp furry back. The music of frogs drowned under hard drumming rain on metal, and she couldn't stop the tears trickling into her ear.

Mitter walked across her chest and licked her cheek. His sandpaper tongue hurt and she gently nudged him off. She needed a Bear hug. She missed Bear, his husky body, silky gray hair covering most of him. It didn't hurt that he looked more bear than man—even his face, nearly covered with bushy eyebrows and a full beard—but his caring was what she missed most. He'd warned her about staying alone in the woods, and hadn't wanted to lend the camper, but she'd been thinking of Jason, remembering freedom and fun. She wore Bear down, until he figured out a plan for her to "steal" the bus from behind his barn, leaving her old Toyota. Since the wife, Marci, ignored his car hobby, she'd never notice a swap. She would be thrilled, he said, if the camper disappeared from the face of the earth.

Sunny wiped her eyes on the sheet. Moving to Florida had seemed the answer to all her problems. She would never love Bear like he loved her, and it was wrong to be with him. Now, one night in the woods, alone and responsible for everybody, and she wanted him back. She remembered that she had forgotten to put the title of the Toyota into the glove compartment, as promised.

Again, in the night, she was awakened, this time by a strong odor. Not urine, diarrhea, or vomit. She opened her eyes. The mattress was empty except for Mitter. The rain had stopped, and moonlight glowed on fur, dogs huddled in a semi-circle facing the cleared corner. She heard words—or felt them—or dreamed them.

Mine! Mine!
No! Mine!

Sunny strained to see, moving only her neck. Brindle was in the center of the group, licking down low, on something blocked by the huddle. Sunny recognized conflict in the posture of Pancho and Rufus. She wasn't dreaming.

The stare-down lasted only a few seconds. Rufus stretched out his front legs, yawned and settled on the floor. Pancho strutted off, and the circle opened, showing five scrawny pups, two of them tan, with heads too big for their bodies, and three larger dark babies, one still attached to the placenta. Three from Pancho and two from Rufus? She chewed the inside of her lip, yearning to pick the tiny babies from the wet newspaper and cuddle them to her chest, but held back. Brindle finished eating the afterbirth and curled on her side for the pups to nose in.

She shut her eyes. Maybe she'd heard "radio sounds," as she called them as a kid. She never knew if they were real, but sometimes in bed words seemed to come from a TV or radio announcer, almost out of her range of hearing. She always thought it was her father with the television volume low, until one night she got up and found the TV off, nobody home.

She watched the pups nurse and Rufus look on from a respectful distance. They were innocent and natural. It was her responsibility to feed them, and she would manage. She always had. It was just a bit rougher now.

Chapter 9: Sunny Lytle

Sunny awoke to a rough scrape to her eyelid. Mitter Manx had licked it. "Mitter." She stared into his gold eyes, then sat up and scratched her scalp, itchy with no-see-um bites. It was already light. She turned toward the back of the bus. There they were, five little ones, nursing. She must have seen the babies through half-sleep and blended reality into a dream.

The day was fresh, pine in the air, a minor cold front having blown away the humidity. Trotting with the dogs through the woods, she barely broke a sweat. She knuckled down to feeding and cleaning in good spirits, thinking that she would try Jason again in the evening. Meanwhile, a possible job at the pancake house was just a short paddle away. She felt lucky. They were bound to need a waitress for the upcoming tourist season.

She stripped and dowsed herself with a chilly bucket of water dragged from the lake, slipped on a loose cotton dress, braided her hair into a thick pigtail, and found her baseball cap. She took a long drink of water, trying to calm her stomach, ate the last slice of cheese and bread. If she couldn't get free pancakes for lunch, she had two dollars left for something.

She climbed up the welded ladder on the back of the bus and unhooked the ropes that fastened the kayak to the roof. The plastic boat hit the ground with a rumble and bounce that startled the pack into barking mania, but the sand was soft and the kayak survived without damage. She dragged it to the shore, lizards darting from her feet, some like tiny dragons with armored necks and wide nostrils. She remembered Jason prying two lizards off her earlobes. She had heard you could wear them as earrings, and it was true—they held on for hours, till Jason pulled them off. Now she couldn't imagine herself being so cruel.

She maneuvered past a parade of huge green and yellow and orange grasshoppers the size of birds emerging from their nesting hole. Lubbers. It was all coming back.

Near the water, movement caught her eye. A tiny lizard had clamped onto the tail of a large dragonfly, and the bug took off, lifting the baby lizard into the sky, legs dangling. In hopes of a full belly, the little guy had put the bite on a monster. Would he drop when his jaws tired, or eat his way up until they both fell? Nature's endings were rarely happy.

She shook herself, loosening the chills, like cats shed pain, and dipped the paddles. Wherever there was fresh water in Florida, there were gators. She remembered an attack, a woman, on alcohol or drugs, lying comatose near a canal. Nice juicy legs and dangling arms to tempt any gator. And the snorkeler who happened into a gator's territory.

It wasn't long and her dress was plastered to her stomach from water dribbling off the paddles, but she was nearly there, and exercise had warmed her. She paddled past the docks, an empty tour boat, and paddleboats to launching area. Canoes and kayaks on racks, just like in the old days. She adjusted her braid as she walked, already smelling bacon, and turned onto the concrete bridge that divided the gators from the swimmers in the circular pool of the spring.

The rock underneath had been rebuilt since last time she was there, but the manmade waterfall looked natural, streaming with lime-green eel grass under the glassy water. Could it be true that two million gallons of water flowed from the spring boil into the lake every day? She wondered where she had heard that. Maybe dreamed it.

She remembered otters barking at kids in the pool area. The slinky mammals probably still walked across the concrete like they owned the place. Of course, they did own it.

She'd lost track, but it must be Sunday with such a crowd. A lifeguard sat in his chair watching over screeching kids with rafts and tubes and Styrofoam noodles, and a group hovered outside the restaurant. She crossed her fingers as she passed the wooden sign, Old Spanish Sugar Mill Pancake House. That last summer, she and Jason had tried to get a job waiting tables, but they were too young. It was her dream job, the restaurant being close to the spring and screened, instead of air conditioned, almost like being outdoors. She could check for otters, maybe swim during her lunch break.

The smoky, salty smell of bacon hung thick outside the door, and her stomach became an empty shell. She hadn't eaten bacon for eight years, but always had to fight the temptation, regardless of her love for pigs.

People blocked the path, waiting to get in, and the loud speaker announced for the Buller party to take their table. She slowly pushed the swinging door and stepped inside. The place was packed. She glanced around, not eager to explain herself to anybody from the past. She twitched. A woman at the first table resembled the owl-lady from the gas station. Could be. The woman looked straight at Sunny. No reaction.

The place hadn't changed, black griddles built into each varnished table, rough wooden walls covered with antique photos and postcards, a fireplace, the mill wheel visible through the window straight ahead. The gift shop nook past the cash register was still stocked with wildlife jewelry, figurines, and animal puppets, same, same. She loved it.

Servers in Sugar Mill T-shirts moved fast, emptying tables, taking orders and carrying ceramic pitchers of pancake batter. A waitress passed by with small dishes of pecans, blueberries, bananas, and chocolate chips balanced on her forearm. Sunny's stomach contracted. Pancakes with pecans and chocolate chips were her favorite. A curly-haired redhead—Barb, by her nametag—was working the line of people at the cash register, calling names over the microphone.

Sunny followed Barb's suggestion and took the application outside to a picnic table. Having no phone was going to be a problem. She printed the names and dates for the last three bars where she had worked and gave Trotters' number as a recommendation. She'd left without giving notice, but the owner liked her, and she could rely on Bear to explain the emergency.

Barb scanned the sheet. "Forgot your contact information." She handed the paper and pen toward Sunny.

She had thought it out and it wasn't a lie. "I'm staying with friends right now, looking for my own place." The furs were her only friends.

"Okay. Check back Monday-a-week," Barb said. "Patty's on vacation and she'll want to interview you."

A week. Sunny's stomach rubbed against itself.

Barb was watching her. "Wait a sec." She turned and went into the kitchen. Sunny became riveted on bags of homemade chocolate chip cookies on the counter, the sweet smell. She thought of buying a bag, but it was luxury that would use up the rest of her money. Snatching one came into her head.

Barb held out a foil packet. "I made a BLT by mistake. Would you like it?"

She stiffened at the B-word, but her mouth filled with saliva and she put out her hand. It was early for lunch and she wondered if Barb might really have made the sandwich for her. She swallowed instant saliva. "Thanks. Really nice of you."

"Come back next week. I'm pretty sure we'll need somebody."

Sunny stumbled through a group of people toward the door. She couldn't eat it, bacon. Visions of pigs, their last squeals, bloodbaths, dismemberment, orphaned piglets, all the suffering to produce these strips came into her mind. Yet, it was a shame to waste the bacon when the pigs were already dead.

She had reached the door when she heard a scream.

"Snake!"

People scooted from their benches and ran. Those at the closest table leapt up and backed into Sunny, pinning her against the ice cream cooler. As Sunny tried to see between the bodies, Barb pushed by with a broom. "Just a black snake. No problem."

The dark shape dangled, part of it curled on a shelf above the table. "Get up on a chair and knock it down," Barb called. A husky blond stood with his back to Sunny, looking up at a corner shelf as Barb passed the broom into his hands. He pushed a chair close, stood on it and swept across the shelf toward the snake. A rusty pie pan hit the floor and the reptile dropped down after it. Someone screamed. The guy bent over and disappeared behind the table, then backed out, sweeping the snake toward the door.

Sunny glimpsed his face. Jason! *Her* Jason! He had put on weight, mostly muscle. What was he doing working at the restaurant? He had gone to college to learn computers. She called to him, but he didn't hear. As he opened the door, his left hand caught sunlight, a wedding ring . . . Sunny leaned against the cooler to keep steady.

Jason pushed the snake outside and people reclaimed their seats. She watched him through the window as he swept the coiling reptile toward the grass. She ran out, down the walk, hoping he wouldn't see her red face smeared with tears.

"Sunny!" His voice came from under the trees, and the breath went out of her, but she didn't look back.

"Sunny, wait!"

She put on speed, across the concrete bridge and through the grass, not stopping until she reached the kayak. She set off and stroked several times before risking a look. He was on the dike, gripping the rail and staring in her direction, his face still as sweet as she remembered. The stretch of water between them widened, but the wedding ring still glared at her, seeming to draw power from the cruel sun.

She paddled a good distance, and glanced behind her again, recognizing his shape, the wide torso and small waist. He kicked at something, then walked toward the restaurant. She put the paddle between her legs and stared ahead into the lake, letting the current carry her, drifting into the weeds.

She looked into her backpack, found a napkin, and blew her nose. Bacon aroma filled her next breath. *Eat the damn sandwich. The whole world can go to hell.* She unfolded the foil packet and lifted the whole grain bread, biting into smoky, salty crunch, tangy mayonnaise, fresh lettuce, sweet tomato. Despite the deliciousness, swallowing took three hard tries.

She calmed herself and opened the bread slices on her thigh to pick out what was left of the crunchy strips and wrapped them in the foil. She would save it for the big boys and Brindle, and a bite for Pancho. They needed it. She put the sandwich remains together and stuffed most of it into her mouth. Smoky flavor had soaked into the mayonnaise, and the bread with lettuce and tomato was delicious. She wanted more bacon. She wouldn't do it. She licked her fingers and slipped the foil envelope into the backpack. The fur guys would love her for it, and she needed all the love she could get.

Chapter 10: Pancho

Pancho was the dog most likely to run, yet less suited to freedom than any other canine. Tiny and delicate, he suffered from separation anxiety and boredom. He awakened from a nap. Sunny gone. His nostrils opened wide, searching, capturing scents of rotted vegetable matter, sweet blossoms, and unfamiliar fur. His three-inch legs stirred with wanderlust. A newly familiar smell of salt and grease carried in on a breeze, bringing saliva to his mouth. He did not know the source of such deliciousness.

He went down to the window in the bus door and perched on his back legs, clicking his nails against the glass. He clawed at the rubber flap and pushed his paw between the doors. He could not squeeze through and lacked strength enough to force the doors farther open. He scrabbled and pushed until he was worn out, stopped to rest, then scratched and nosed his snout into the crack, his tongue hanging outside the bus, feeling the breeze. It was as far as he could get. He pulled back.

A fresh scent beckoned to him from inside. It was the enticing whiff of a female in heat, and he responded, the only intact male in the bus, six pounds of muscle, the king. Recent attempts to mate had failed, but now the pheromones played another enticing game. Not the day to escape. He leapt back up the steps, picking through the scents, sorting for the one. A combination of saliva, feces and urine hung like mist, with ferret musk overpowering all, but Ginger's lure from where she had settled above him on the driver's seat was easily separated.

His foreskin slid back as he came close, and the wisp of breeze from forward motion caressed the hard pink point that yearned to slide into the space under her tail. Her perfume was less gamey than rabbit, more delicate than Labrador.

He hunched down, took aim, and sprang onto the seat, landing in the small space next to her thigh. Her eyes had been closed, but startled by the jolt, she leapt to her feet, wedging her rear into the steering wheel.

His posture sent signals and she responded with a tilt of her hips, but angled herself more toward the window, requiring him to stretch his neck through the wheel and over the steering column to push his nose closer to the source. He took a deep snuff of erotic female essence with a touch of feces, a brew that closed his eyes in ecstasy. His organ rubbed painfully against the hard rippled wheel as he stretched, squeezing his body through one section until he had her head between his paws.

Her body relaxed with the contact and she turned her rear in his direction on the seat. She was ready. He grasped her sides and rose over her back, gripping with his dewclaws, until his thin-haired thighs locked over her rounded, curly-furred rump. His hind end pumped until he was paralyzed with the satisfying surge.

As his instincts returned he tried to pull out, but his organ was locked tight. His weak back legs collapsed on the seat and his tongue fell out of his mouth into her curls.

The males on their leashes outside began to bark, but he was not positioned to see. He pulled and twisted, excited, wanting to know what was happening, his feet scrambling on the seat, turning his body until he was lined up end to end with Ginger. The more he pulled, the harder and more painfully his organ was squeezed. The voice of the pack turned joyous. He was missing something good. He joined in, yipping and whining.

Sunny opened the bus door. The concentrated aroma of grease and salt triggered his saliva. His stomach felt empty again. He could not see the meat, and still, Ginger would not slide off.

"Panchy, you're such a stud. Don't tell the other little guys I gave you this." Her hand came around to his mouth and he devoured a tiny morsel from her palm. Ginger stretched to get a piece.

"You like bacon?" Sunny stroked his head. "You do, don't you? You too, Ginger? Yes, bacon." The word became associated with the rich flavor on his tongue and the aroma in the breeze. The world of bacon beckoned to him, but he was still stuck.

Chapter 11: Jason Cox

It was a mystery to Jason how the two wiener dogs could breathe under a heavy quilt, but that's how they slept every night next to him. He rolled over, and over again, on the Tempur-pedic, adjusting and re-adjusting the hardness. It was supposed to provide comfort to both individuals separately—probably his wife's definition of a perfect marriage—but not a chance with Buddy between his legs. Debbie looked comfortable enough, lightly snoring, facing Wootsie on the other side of her pillow. He knew she wouldn't like it if he made Bud jump down—bad for their backs to jump—and if he woke the little one, Grouper, there'd be lots of whining and hopping around until he could get him tucked under the covers again.

Jason's back was always sore and his tired feet pounding from work. He was worn out, but his brain ran in half-sleep cycles. Sunny, her blond braid bobbing just out of reach, Sunny running away. He woke fully and realized that she still looked exactly like the last time he'd seen her. It didn't make sense, her paddling down the run as if she was afraid to talk to him. Then why had she called? He rolled over and put his arm around Deb. Nice to have a wife to cuddle, to save him from memories leading nowhere. He wondered if Sunny was camping in the woods in the old spot. Must be.

"What's the matter?" she turned over to face him. Wootsie leapt over her shoulder to settle between them.

"Can't sleep."

"So you have to wake me?" The clock showed 3:00. "You always sleep. I'm the insomniac."

"Feet pounding. Back aches." He knew she wouldn't buy it. She could always read him. "At least I'm not snoring, keeping you up."

"Except you woke me." She raised her head and braced it with her arm. "Did she call again? Sunny?"

He was startled, not having figured that Deb would remember the name. He pulled the covers up to his neck. "No. "

"What then? What's going on?" She turned on the lamp.

She could often read his mind. There was no reason to keep secrets, unless he was planning something. He wasn't. "She came to the restaurant this afternoon—but it's got nothing to do with not sleeping."

"Why didn't you tell me?"

"Forgot. I didn't even talk to her. I think she was looking for a job."

"You didn't say hi? Kind of rude."

He wasn't sure where this was headed. "She was leaving. I yelled, but I guess she didn't hear me."

Debbie was looking into Wootsie's ear, picking around. "Is she going to be working there?"

He petted Wootsie's behind. "I don't know." Her question made him realize that he'd been hoping. "Nothing to do with me."

Deb yawned. "Maybe I can go back to sleep." She rolled over, leaving Wootsie between them, and turned out the light. Jason pulled up the quilt and rolled to his other side, lifting a leg over Buddy, so the two dogs were in the middle of the bed. The AC was turned way low, big electric bill coming soon. He closed his eyes. The blond braid started bobbing.

Chapter 12: Buckaroo

Buck checked the sky through the tent screen. He'd slept late, but been lucky. There wasn't a puff of white in view and the air had cooled. He unzipped the door. Everything outside was soaked. At least he could afford a real tent instead of sleeping in a crappy lean-to or under a tree like most of the outdoor crew. He took a swig of water from the jug and spit it out the door to rinse his mouth. He needed a beer. He reached into a plastic milk crate, got an orange and a knife and took them outside to his flat rock, where he peeled off the skin and cut segments, eating as he worked. He had cash for a couple of six-packs and a carton of smokes, and by now his disability payment should have been loaded onto his debit card. He could pick up his prescriptions to sell for extra beer and cigarette money for the month. He remembered the book of food stamps he'd gotten in trade. Too bad they wouldn't buy his kind of staples. It was easy to eat cheap so he didn't need much in the food category.

He had carved some small figures of manatees, otters, and gators, and he put those into his backpack along with the food stamps, in case he could sell something, and took his reflective plate for emergencies. He slipped on a long sleeved shirt and jeans and stuffed his T-shirt and shorts in the backpack to rinse out at the Mini-Mart restroom on the way home.

Beth and Geordie let him use their address for mail, and he could usually borrow their truck if he replaced the gas, so he cut through the neighborhood to pass by their house. Sometimes Buck helped with heavy work or weed-whacking for cash, but today he hoped to make a fast stop.

He stepped out of the woods and spotted Geordie on the roof in long sleeves and a wide-brimmed hat, replacing shingles. Buck ducked back into the foliage. He took the long way around the house, cut through to the next street, and walked the three miles to Winn-Dixie. It was worth calling a cab to haul his beer and ice.

He checked with the cashier to make sure his benefits had been loaded to the debit card, then grabbed a cart and headed up the pet food aisle on his way to the crackers. For camouflage, he threw in a sack of cat food and one of litter. That way he could snack while pretending to shop. He chose Cheez-Its and went to the refrigerated section for a cold Coke, not planning to pay for anything, except the beer and ice, unless he got caught.

He stopped at the deli section and picked up a package of Genoa salami, wrestled open the re-sealable plastic, and shoved a few slices into his mouth. Perfect accompaniment for Cheez-Its. He'd love a beer right now, but if he got spotted with open alcohol, they'd call the cops.

The store was nearly empty, so he took his leisure, wandering through the produce section, trying a bite of a nectarine—sour. He tossed it into a garbage bin. Strawberry, umm, good. He placed a quart of them on the seat of the cart and bit one after the other off the stems, as he worked his way down the dairy aisle toward the heavy cream.

He was spritzing mouthfuls of whipped cream alternated with berries when a scrawny blonde with a backpack stopped her cart to stare at him. She had an unkempt, outdoorsy look, a crooked braid and a spatter of mud on her calf. Late-twenties, sweet thin face with high cheekbones. She was definitely braless under the T-shirt, and the baggy shorts seemed like they could fall off without help.

He removed the cream nozzle from his mouth and licked his lips. "Take a picture."

"Huh?"

"You the store detective?" He waited, thinking he might get a laugh, but she huffed. No sense of humor. Didn't matter. She was cute enough, even while irritated. Her blue eyes were wide and unblinking, with that deer-caught-in-the-headlights look he loved in women.

"I'm just waiting for you to get out of the way."

He bowed with a flourish of his hands, and pushed the cart so it rolled all the way to the end of the milk case and bumped into the egg section. "All yours, girlie."

She turned away from him and chose a half pint of whipping cream.

He watched while she fumbled at the pour spout with her grubby fingernails, trying to coax the waxy cardboard to bend open.

"Somebody's gonna see you." He stepped closer and stuck his hand out, happy to see it wasn't any grimier than hers. "Here, let me do it." She was so thin, he realized he would almost rather feed her than fuck her—at least, feed her first.

She handed him the carton.

He popped it easily and pulled out the spout, expecting a "Thanks," but she turned to the shelf and gulped the cream. She got most of it down before stopping to breathe, then tilted the carton to finish and dropped it behind the half gallons of milk. She wiped the mustache with her hand.

"You're gonna get fat drinking all that cream."

She glared at him.

"Jeez. It was a joke."

"You don't know a thing, dirty old Rainbow."

He pursed his lips. "Well, that's nice, after I helped you out."

She looked down at the wheels of her cart. "Sorry. I'm sorry. I'm having a bad day—a string of them."

"I'm no Rainbow—not that old either. It's just this beard—" He fingered it, feeling the coarse gray in the blond. "My name's Buck, short for Buckaroo."

"You ride broncos?"

"I did. Long time ago."

She pointed at the bag of Friskies in his cart. "You have cats?"

"No. I just—no."

She nodded and smiled. "It was nice meeting you, Mr. Buck." She looked toward the toothpaste aisle.

He grabbed the side of her cart to stop her, but she turned and walked, leaving it behind, and he realized she wasn't buying anything. There was a half empty jar of honey and a gnawed block of cheddar nested among rolls of paper towels and toilet paper.

"Wait a sec. I think we can do each other a favor."

"I doubt it."

"A business deal."

She paused, and he waited for a woman with a kid to pass by, then stepped closer. She smelled musky. *Ooh, baby.* A little movement in his jeans. He put his hand on her arm. "I've got food stamps that I can't use for beer."

"I don't have any money."

"Oh." This would seem to give him leverage. "We might be able to work something out."

She laughed. "I'm not that desperate."

One front tooth had a small chip, but her teeth were pretty and white. Probably hadn't been homeless for long. "No, no. Nothing like that. I'll give you the food stamps that I can't use. Then when you have money, I'll probably be broke, and you can buy me some beer. It'll be like a savings account for me, and you get to take home some groceries." He grinned. His own teeth were good too, hereditary luck.

"What I really need is some Fancy Feast and a bag of dry dog food—a box of Milk Bones . . ."

"Dawg food? Oh, man. We can do better than that."

"Not for me. I have a lot of hungry fur friends at home."

"Fur friends?" Strange, but sweet. "I don't know if food stamps work for those, but I think I can charge them on my card."

"I don't know."

"Look, I have money and plastic. It's fine. Come on." He showed her the emergency three twenties in his pocket.

"I might not be able to return the favor."

"You stock up. I'll be right back."

Her eyes looked even brighter blue. She turned the cart toward the pet food aisle.

"Be right back. In three shakes of a lamb's tail. I have to check something." He gave her his most angelic trust-me look and took off down the aisle. It was getting toward afternoon, and clouds could appear fast. He walked through the electric door and did a quick 360. Damn, a dark build-up in the west. He shook his fist at the largest looming cloud. "Give me a fucking break!" Where did those mother-fuckers come from and why were they always after him? A teenaged boy passed by staring. Who cared? He put his hands on his hips and faced the sky. "Leave me alone, assholes!"

There was definitely no time to get laid, unless she jumped him behind the dumpster, and that seemed unlikely. He'd have to call the taxi right away. He hurried back inside and grabbed two six-packs of Old Milwaukee and headed to the dog food aisle. She was reading a label. She'd taken the paper products out of the basket and put in some cans, a small bag of kibble, and a couple of boxes.

He put the beer into her basket. She was worth the whole emergency fund. "Thought you said 'fur *friends*.' Don't pass up the free offer. Get the economy sizes."

"Nothing's free."

"Today it is."

She paused. "That's nice of you, but I can't carry the big stuff on my bike."

"We're taking a cab."

"I can't—"

"They'll stick the bike in the trunk. Really. C'mon. We've been farting around too long. I have an appointment. Where you headed?"

That took her some thought. "Near the recreation area, a house on Ponce DeLeon."

No way, a house. "Great. Only a few miles, right on my way. Get more pet food and some shit for yourself. Just do it fast. I'll find a pay phone." He started to walk. "Meet you at the checkout."

"Not pet food. They're family, not pets."

He looked back at her and nodded. "Dawg food, cat food."

He'd finally gotten her to smile. "That's cute," she said. "The way you say dog."

"A little Mississippi left in me." The chick was screwy, but he could go with it. He backed down the aisle. "Dawg, dawg, dawg."

He called the cab and went to the check-out to meet her. Not there. Might have tricked him. He took a trip back past all the aisles, just in case she was still shopping. There she was, way back by the deli. Damn. The clouds outside were building. Her voice was at a high pitch and hands flying for emphasis. A big man in an apron leaned against a lobster tank, saying something and looking amused.

"You're mean!" she yelled. She turned and jerked her cart toward the last aisle and took off in a run.

"Sweetie!" Buck caught up. Her face was redder than sunburn. "Do I need to have a word with that idiot?"

"No. It's useless."

"What's his problem?"

She sniffed and said nothing. When they reached the checkout, he helped her unload. She had piled in the pet chow, as well as cartons of Parmalat milk, a tub of margarine, bread, an unopened stick of cheddar, water, and a large bottle of store brand vitamins. No meat. She needed some. Maybe she'd been dying for a lobster, but thought the price was too high.

He did a quick calculation and figured he could afford a small one. He wanted to cheer her up more than anything, even though he could see the clouds outside moving closer, his life hanging on a moment. "Look, I'm in a rush, but if you want a lobster, I'll run back and get you one."

She stared at him. The cashier was watching. They were blocking her register.

"Just say the word," he told the girl. "No problem."

"Thank you. You're sweet. But . . . I don't have any place to keep a lobster right now. I was just trying to help. There's a big lobster bully in the tank picking on the little ones, beating them up. I told the manager they need to be separated."

"Oh?"

"He acted like it was a joke! Like I'm a joke. He told me— 'Don't worry. I'll cook him *first!*'"

Buck bit his knuckle. The cashier was tuned in, raising her eyebrows, and he was afraid she would laugh.

The girl stared toward the deli. "It makes me sick. First they're tortured in that little tank—and next thing, boiled alive."

He nudged her shoulder, but she wouldn't look him in the eye. "Listen, sweetie," he said. "They don't feel pain. They're like big bugs."

She jumped, as if shocked. "Haven't you ever heard them? They scream when they're dropped into the boiling water!"

"That's air escaping from their shells."

She flashed him a look that meant he was completely crazy. "They have nerves, don't they? They feel pain."

"No. I swear. It's true." He felt a tap on his shoulder and turned.

"You don't dive, do you?" A sturdy brunette next in line was talking to him. "Scuba dive?"

His nostrils flared. "No."

"If you did, you'd know how smart they are. I've seen them sit in a hole with a moray eel, just waiting for somebody to stick a hand in there."

"See," the girl said.

"Florida lobsters don't have claws to defend themselves, so they need friends."

He put his hand on his hip. "Ma'am, the ones they sell here are from New England."

The woman lifted her purse like a shield.

Buck stepped in front of the girl and took out his wallet. "No time to waste." He handed over his twenties rather than deal with the plastic. She was still staring toward the back of the store. Strange girl. He didn't believe she lived in a house. He would soon find out.

Chapter 13: Sunny Lytle

She waited in the taxi while Buck stowed the groceries in the trunk and wedged the bike on top of them. She wasn't comfortable with him, but for the sake of her family she had to take a chance. He had muscles and looked nice under the dirt, dreads, and beard. His body odor was light and his big gray eyes soft and deer-like with thick blond lashes, more like a buck's than a Buckaroo's. He seemed truly generous, but no way was she going to lead him to her camp so he could sneak up on her later, even with good intentions.

The trunk wouldn't close, and the driver shook his head, but Buck said something, and they headed off with the lid flapping.

"You never did tell me your name," he said.

"Sunny."

"That your real name?"

"Yeah, Sunny Lytle."

He chuckled. "Sunny Dee-light-el."

She blushed, heating up the sunburn, and turned toward the window.

"Nobody ever said that before?"

She shook her head. "You living over at Freak Creek?"

"No. Told you I'm no Rainbow. Spring Garden Ranch Road. The rangers moved everybody off the campsites in Ocala. Garbage was piling up."

She turned back to him. He smiled, showing pretty white teeth. "You have a job?"

"Not a regular job. I'm an artist." He smoothed his mustache. "I get money from the government."

She wondered how that worked, in case she could get some, but it wasn't the right time to ask. They turned on to Ponce DeLeon, and she thought of a house down the road to claim as her stop, one with thick bushes where she could hide her stuff while she made trips back and forth to camp.

Buck turned to look out the back window. "Holy shit! Stop! Stop!"

"This isn't Spring Garden," she told him.

The taxi stopped and Buck fumbled with his money and threw a twenty into the front seat. The meter showed twelve dollars. He put a hand on her arm. "Get the change. Gotta go. Where can I find you?" He shouldered his backpack as he stepped out.

She wasn't sure she wanted to see him again, but she did owe him. "I'm supposed to get a job at the Sugar Mill—"

"I'll find you. Give your fur family a pet for me—I mean a hug. Tell em Buck treated dinner."

"Petting's okay—just don't call them pets."

He was out and motioning to the driver to wait. He disappeared behind the taxi and emerged in a run with his six-packs, turning into a patch of woods between houses, not even slowing down. Whatever. It worked for her.

She directed the taxi driver to take a left at the park gate, and got as close as she could to her path through the woods. She kept the six dollars change, leaving two quarters for a tip.

The driver helped her unload at the edge of the fern field. "You live here?"

"My house is farther back, but there's no road. I'll be fine."

She waited until he drove off and picked up the two plastic bags, one of Kennel Ration and Fancy Feast and the other of her food. She hung them on the handlebars of the bike and left the twenty-pound bags of dog chow and cat chow and two gallons of water in the bushes for later trips. The sky rumbled and she looked up. A thunderhead covered the sky above her.

As she got close to camp, she heard a whimpering noise coming from the other side of the bus and followed it. A gray and black fur bundle tossed itself back and forth, a small raccoon, tangled and panicked, caught in an accidental trap. She dropped the bike and bags to the ground. She had hung the cat food in a net bag on a tree limb to discourage bugs, never thinking of a disaster like this.

He would bite her if she grabbed for him, but he was in pain. She yanked down a sheet, dropped it over the little bandit, and wrapped it tight to stop his squirming. She picked into the sheet carefully until she felt the foot. She stretched out the body, held the torso to the ground, and peeled back the sheet. The whole foot was through the webbing, each toe caught, and the ankle worn raw, to the bone.

She worked at the foot, wincing with the rough operation she had to perform, until the leg was free, then carried the wriggling bundle, soft tail batting her thigh, in search of the First Aid kit. He would pull off any gauze, so she slathered on Neosporin and hoped for the best. She squeezed him into an empty cat carrier, sliding out the sheet as she closed the metal grill. Instantly, he mashed his nose to the grate and started clawing at the plastic molded bottom. She dropped in a handful of cat food, but he ignored it, manic with fear.

Now what? Would it be better to let him go and hope he was well enough to escape predators? If his wound got infected, he'd die in terrible pain. Words came back from her father. "There are plenty raccoons." Plenty of everything. Like Goldie flushed down the toilet, and Guinea, who mysteriously disappeared. He squealed for lettuce every time the refrigerator door opened. It annoyed Lytle when he went for a beer.

But she couldn't listen to Lytle—or blame him for the injured raccoon. She got some water and dribbled it into the cage. No interest, just digging at nothing.

Lightning cracked in the distance. The sky had blackened and the wind picked up, blowing sheets onto the ground and rattling the leaves enough to start the dogs barking. She used to enjoy thunderstorms when she lived inside.

Chapter 14: Sunny Lytle

It was a scramble to haul the bags of food and gather the dogs, but she managed, and only a few dogs got wet. Rain hammered the roof as she made space to feed them all inside the bus, and she figured she must have picked the rainiest November on record to live outdoors. When she'd finished dishing out the food, and they all seemed satisfied, the rain had stopped. She tied the big dogs outside and walked the little ones a short stretch, trying to keep them out of the tall weeds so they wouldn't get soaked. She was dog-tired as always by the time she'd toweled off all the legs and bellies, and she curled onto the mattress. Dog-tired, what did it mean?

Pancho watched her from the end of the mattress. If he could talk, surely he'd say thanks for the nice meal. "Come over here, little pal."

He turned and walked to a round bed and plopped down facing away from her. She closed her eyes.

She woke, not knowing why. The night was black. Nothing to do but go back to sleep, but thoughts wouldn't let her. Jason, a married man. It didn't jive with her expectations, but she guessed he'd grown up and changed. What did he think of her running away at the restaurant? She should have spoken to him like an adult.

A sudden rip of barks from outside chilled her. She held her breath, listening, hoping they would stop. They weren't used to the woods. Every raccoon, possum, and armadillo set them off, and she never knew what kind of critter had wandered by. After the wave ran through the pack, they'd usually settle down, but this time the excitement turned to throaty growls.

She heard voices, two men getting closer. There was a beam of light flashing through the trees. She was scared.

The dogs were going wild, tied to the bus, helpless. She should have kept Rufus inside, so she could let him loose, but little guys were all she had, the size men called "drop-kick dogs." She rose up to a crouch and peeked out the window. She could barely make out two figures, one holding a flashlight, running it over the dogs. Why didn't they just keep going? The beam started to travel, and she took a breath but sensed that the men were not moving away. They were headed around the far side of the bus, to avoid the tied dogs. In seconds they'd be at the unlocked bus door, letting out the little guys and trapping her inside. She lunged and got there first, pushed the door open, jumped down and closed it behind her. She stood straight, arms at her sides.

The one with the flashlight stopped. "Wha's this?" The beam blinded her, then moved over her T-shirt and shorts. "Mmm, mmm."

She could barely see their outlines a couple of feet in front of her, but the voice was young, and slurred. Recognizing drunkenness was a skill she'd learned at a young age. She wished she had a gun, not to shoot, just an empty gun to scare away rowdy young guys beered out of their minds. "What the hell do you want? Get out of here!"

The other guy stuck his hand into the light and touched her hip with a beer bottle. "Look a here. Nice li'l puss in the woods."

"Doesn' sound too nice. But with a little coaxin' . . . Some sugar, sweetheart?"

She pictured his mouth puckered in a foul kiss. The din had settled some, but snarling and growling came menacing from the other side of the bus. "They'd like to tear you up," she said. "Move along before I open the doors and let the big ones out."

"I don't believe she has any big ones in there. D'you, Jeremy? I think we seen the big ones all tied up."

"I got a big one for her." They both guffawed. Jeremy pushed her aside and she glimpsed his features. Only a few inches taller than she was, probably younger, a spider tattooed on his neck. "Hand me the flashlight," he told the other guy. He shone it into the bus. Both of them peered through the glass doors.

Now was her chance to dart into the blackness where she knew the path, and they would never catch her. But she couldn't leave her family with possible torturers. The thought brought strength. Jason had taught her how to show the horny old Rainbows that she was serious when she said no. She shoved the back of the closest guy, all of her weight into it, cracking his forehead on the glass, following with a hard smack to both ears, like smashing a bug in flight. She dodged as he yowled, flinging out his hands before he stumbled backwards into the weeds, shock and loss of balance toppling him. She would not have flattened an innocent bug, but this smack felt solid and good.

The flashlight had hit the ground and gone out, and Jeremy stumbled and fell into the heap of his friend. She was already past them, running.

The assholes wouldn't stay down for long, but it was enough. In seconds she had untied Rufus, and he led her back around the bus. There was crashing in the bushes as the jokers tried to navigate around the trees in the dark.

"Stop right there!" she shouted. The barking settled some and she healed Rufus.

"Fuck, lady. We're goin'," Jeremy yelled out. "We can't remember how we got here."

"We wouldn't a hurt ya," the other one whined nasally.

Bloody nose, she hoped. "What are you doing here?" she yelled. "This is private property." They didn't need to know whose property.

"Trying to find a shortcut to Glenwood. That's all."

She could believe it, but wanted to be sure they wouldn't remember how to get back, so she followed them with Rufus at their heels, directing them in a long haphazard pattern to take them way down the road when they came out of the woods. There was dim light from a lamp post at the corner. They were boys, still in their teens, wearing long T-shirts. The baggy crotches of their pants were near their knees. No wonder they could barely walk. "Don't you ever come back to bother me, punks! Rufus will be waiting."

"Don' worry." His forehead was split and blood was dark on his lips and chin. They turned and walked down the road toward Glenwood, their shoulders drooped. She wouldn't worry much about them coming back, but there might be others.

She patted Rufus and ruffled behind his ears. From now on he would sleep in the bus at night.

Chapter 15: Sunny Lytle

At dawn she lay on the mattress with her eyes closed, hoping to sleep a little longer, trying to ignore meows and Mitter Manx and Cali tromping across her chest. If she didn't move, there was a chance they would go away. More likely Mitter would lick her eyelid.

She had been enjoying a dream about a piglet, a Vietnamese pot-bellied, small and gray, with a heart-shaped pink spot on his back. Jason was there, feeding it a bottle, scratching its rump. A friend in high school had raised a huge pig that loved Burger King and would knock the girl down and take away her Whopper and fries.

Rufus gave a single bark and the others picked up on his energy and started the morning commotion. She yawned. Her legs didn't want to move—they'd had a workout. She hadn't realized camping would be so much work: walking, feeding, watering, poop-scooping, hole-digging, dog-washing. The basics took hours. Not counting personal needs—clothes-washing, bathing, cooking. But she damned sure wouldn't let it beat her. As soon as she got work, she would start saving for an apartment, or maybe gas money to get back to Louisville.

It was after noon when she finished everything, bit off a chunk of cheese and dragged the bicycle through the weeds. She didn't dare put all her hopes on the Sugar Mill. She had already applied at all the nearby bars, except The Outpost, besides trying the two Mexican cafés, the Dollar Store, Mini-Mart, and feed store, among other small shops. She would take any kind of work. She wondered if the county animal shelter was still open. It was the job she was best suited for, if she could avoid the sadness. She knew she couldn't rescue them all—she could try.

It was a sweaty five-mile ride. She parked the bike behind a bush, hoping nobody would steal it. She needed a lock, among so many things.

The tangy scent of puppies wafted from inside as she opened the door. There was no one at the counter, but the door to the next room was ajar. When she peeked inside, deep barks and high-pitched squeaks rippled from end to end, echoing down the concrete hallway in welcome.

"Anybody here?" She wiped sweat from her face with her wrist.

"Yes?" A woman with glasses and short salt and pepper hair stuck her head out and started down the corridor. A widow's peak gave her a heart-shaped face like a barn owl. Sunny turned and ran.

"Can I help you?"

She struggled with the door knob. The woman was next to her. "What's . . . ? Oh."

Caught in a lie, no way out. "Can you use some help? I'm a total animal lover."

The woman smiled and waited a few seconds for the noise to settle. "I remember you and your busload. I wouldn't expect you have time to volunteer."

She shook her head. "I need pay."

The woman gritted her teeth. "Sorry."

Sunny managed to open the door.

"Wait. Please. Let me get your name, just in case." She introduced herself as Rita. "I'm the only paid assistant right now, but you never know . . ."

They always wanted a name. "I'm Sunny. I have to go."

Rita smiled and motioned toward the next room. "Come with me for a second."

The best bet was to get out fast, but she felt weak and thirsty, and the ride back was long. She followed the cool corridor in a haze, wondering if there was a lesson coming. A pen filled with sickly puppies taken from an irresponsible hoarder? Or interrogation? She'd played their games.

Rita led her into a kitchen and motioned her to a chair. "We have food left from a volunteer lunch yesterday. Are you hungry?"

She admitted she was.

Rita brought out a can of Coke and a white carton and uncovered a plate of thin-sliced ham. "Help yourself." She handed Sunny an index card and pen, a paper plate and plastic spork package, and set a bag of buns and a jar of mayonnaise on the table. "Bring me your contact information before you leave. I have to get back to work on the pens."

"Thanks." The door shut. Sunny stared at the food. Not much there she would normally eat, but she broke off a piece of bun and stuffed it into her mouth. The more processed the food, the more easy it was to fool herself since it has no resemblance to anything living. When she opened the carton, the smell of mayonnaise and onion completely overcame her. There was only a quarter of the container of potato salad left so she didn't bother to use the plate. She drank most of the Coke straight down.

She fingered the card. Her address? Tenth oak from the road? There was no job available. No way was she going to give her location to the authorities. She dropped the card into the empty potato salad container, tossed it into the trash, and rolled up some thin slices of ham to take for her fur guys.

She was heading out when she heard scrubbing from the back. It was too rude to take off without a word, so she followed the sound to Rita on hands and knees on the concrete floor of a pen.

"Thanks very much."

Rita smiled. She seemed sad and tired looking up from the floor, not smart and in control—an old Cinderella, who'd missed getting the prince. "Can I help? In return for the lunch?"

Rita stood and handed her the scrub brush. "I'd love a break from this, if you don't mind. My knees have had it."

Sunny took the brush, dipped it into the bucket and went to work, smelling the clean scent of bleach.

Rita came back with the hose and squirted out a pen on the opposite side. Sunny's knees ached within minutes, but furry faces watched her through the fencing with loving eyes.

Rita shut off the water. "I appreciate your help for these guys."

"It makes me so sad to think about them."

"I know. It's overwhelming."

"Not always." Sunny hoped to skip the lecture. "I plan to open my own rescue someday, so this is good experience for me."

"I see."

"I'm used to hard work. I have it all planned out."

Two women came down the hall, a short one in scrubs and a large one. The large one stared. "What's this?"

"This is a new volunteer." Rita introduced Dr. Denise, and the tall woman with her as Jackie, the director.

Jackie turned to Rita. "As a former veterinarian, you think you should be running this place, but you don't. You just can't let people in here and put them to work when you're tired."

Sunny stopped scrubbing.

Rita's face blazed. "If you had been here, Jackie, I would have asked first. We need all the help we can get today."

"Jackie," Denise said, "maybe we can—"

Jackie shook her head. "The girl isn't prepared to see those dogs—" She turned to Sunny. "You need to leave. If you want to be a volunteer, come back in the morning and we'll set up hours."

Sunny stood and handed the brush to Rita, trying not to think about what she shouldn't see. She started down the hall, hurrying past several dogs, as the women watched, but she had to stop and surrender, just for a second, to the round eyes of a shiny black mutt. Her hand was small enough to reach him through the chain link fencing, and she put her palm on his smooth satin head. His love shot through her and into her chest like a current. She sagged against the fencing, light-headed and distant from the concrete and metal.

She heard Dr. Denise speaking to Rita, her voice drifting from farther than a few steps down the hall, a question asked in surprise.

"Such a connection," Rita answered. "I was afraid Chuckie would sink his teeth into her arm." She called out, "Sunny, please, wait."

She straightened, torn from the dark eyes and shared bliss. She realized that the strength of love had dwindled in her own fur family. She never got such a good feeling from them anymore. "I'm supposed to get a job at the Sugar Mill Restaurant, but I'll help out here if I can."

Rita raised her brows above her glasses. "Hope to see you."

Sunny ran the rest of the way to the door.

Chapter 16: Rufus

Rufus' tail pounded the dirt. Pancho, the nipper, was tied outside near him. Nipper, whose sticky body would sprawl over Rufus' limbs or tail or wedge against his stomach. Nipper, who on hind legs often poked his nose into Rufus' anus. Not a quick friendly snuff, but a nose-nudge into the dark flesh, startling. Worse, the nipper would scramble underneath Rufus' tall haunches to lick the most tender part. The plan was to flip the runt's body onto his side and pin him with a foot, hard enough to make him screech.

The nipper hunched on the far side of his leash-range, chewing a dewclaw, just a lick beyond Rufus' outstretched neck. Likely, he waited for the big dog to shut down his tail flagging, close his eyes, and breathe light and even. Then he would squirm and press bare skin against Rufus' stomach, leaving a grease spot for Rufus to lap off.

Today the nipper was wrapped in pup scent. Not all the pups were Rufus-blooded. The nipper had boosted himself to Brindle's pink flesh and claimed it.

Rufus flattened his tail, closed his eyes. His nose worked to pick up the least motion of the nipper moving closer. It did not take long. His slit eyes gazed through lashes until he launched, using his snout to flip the small body. Pawing, he put pressure on the gut, almost enough to burst the nipper, and pinched the long furred organ under his nails into the grit. The two-legger was nowhere near to catch the ribbons of throaty squeak or come running to punish Rufus with harsh tones and make him cow .

He held the nipper until screeching dribbled into whines. The nipper eyes, round and bugged, focused. There was understanding. Slowly, Rufus hefted the paw and dropped it on empty dirt. The nipper hopped to all fours, shook, still whining. Rufus nudged him back to where he would lie down and lick and make himself better.

Chapter 17: Sunny Lytle

She got back to camp during the hottest part of the day, gulped a cup of water, and took Pancho with her up the steps into the bus, ignoring the eager greeting of the outside dogs, wanting to sleep and never get up. She hadn't had a good night's sleep since she arrived. The atmosphere was steamy and tinged with ammonia, but discomfort melted away when fur people gathered around her, and she fed them bits of ham. Clue licked Pancho's mouth after the tiny guy swallowed. A dog kiss, Sunny was certain, not only looking for meat flavor. She had the "beautiful feeling," as she called it, stroking their fur. Their health and happiness meant more than the pig's.

Staying anonymous in the small town would be hard, and she regretted that she couldn't trust Rita. She dropped into the mattress, just for a minute among her pals. She was starting to drift when she picked up a low-level rumble, the far off radio voice at first. Then words happened again.

Walks! Walks!

She froze. It was like a consciousness overlapping hers—or maybe her thoughts on another level. She looked for Mitter, but he wasn't in sight. Pancho was asleep on Angel's bed. The words seemed to come from everywhere.

She crawled toward Pancho, focusing, trying to penetrate his tiny brain. *Are you saying something, Panchy? Panch?* He looked innocent, but she knew he always longed for attention. She reached for him and jerked her hand back. Touching his skin brought his need for love to an emotional level she could barely stand. She braced herself and stretched her arm toward him again.

Panchy, come to me.

He opened his eyes, stretched his legs out in front, and released a squeak. He stepped onto the mattress and moved close to her face, sniffing her breath. As she cuddled him, the sensation overwhelmed her body, and goose bumps told her this was real, not a weird manifestation of guilt, not her own loneliness.

She took turns putting her hands on the other four dogs inside. Discomfort came through, hunger, itching and burning of fleas on butts and limbs, bladders stretched tight with urine. The words of complaint were superficial compared to the feelings, just a boiling over of the physical. She remembered something she had been told about elephants, that they could talk with subsonic vibrations using their feet. She had imagined it in their bones, the buzz of live music close up. Not like this.

It was natural, the connection she always thought she should have with every living creature, but this was too intense, a terrible miracle, fed on desperation.

Normally, she didn't give them lunch, but she hurried to portion out each bowl. They hadn't been getting enough. "Please, say it's okay," she pleaded with Pancho. "Tell me you love me."

She stood up, wobbly, and collected leashes to take the first group out to empty their bladders. After some legs had lifted, she felt relief. She trotted them along on a run between the trees. The sensitivities were torture, but the knowledge powerful. She could take care of her own, and maybe others, use the ability toward a good purpose. It might even mean money. People wouldn't mind paying her a small fee, a tiny portion of what the vets charged, to know whether an animal needed to be treated. Fees would put meat in their bowls every day.

The idea sounded insane, but she had no other prospects for the afternoon. She changed into clean clothes, still plagued by the flea itch, and took off on the bike to the strip mall.

It was a long ride, but she was excited. PetSmart. A hateful name, but a great place to find dogs with their people. In Indianapolis she had lucked into a Halloween party and become the center of a licking frenzy with Underdog, a bumble bee, the devil, and Tinkerbell.

There was a bench near a patch of clumpy brownish grass to one side of the store, and the garbage can overflowed with pooper bags—a popular spot. She would have time to talk to the people while the dogs nosed around. As she sat waiting, she noticed that the flea itch had gone away. Distance from the pack might have something to do with it.

She read the names of veterinarians painted on the glass. She would try to catch people before they took their animals inside for unnecessary treatments.

A woman got out of a car and set down a golden brown Pomeranian with a fresh haircut, its body buzzed short except for a mane and a tuft on the end of the tail. She was a delicate little girl, skinny legs clipping along in triple time, but head low, rather than in proud Pom posture. The woman gave her a few seconds to sniff the edge of the grass then tugged her leash. "C'mon, Tiny. We're in a hurry."

Tiny hunkered down and tried to use her weight to counter the leash. The lady pulled her past Sunny toward the door.

Tiny, sweetie, what's the matter? Sunny leaned forward and touched the furry round forehead with her palm. Busy straining, the dog didn't care. Sunny's skin prickled with the connection. Nudity! Tiny missed her swishy skirt of shiny fur.

Sunny stood up from the bench. "Ma'am, I have to tell you that she doesn't like that haircut. Hates it, in fact. She's vulnerable. She'll be cold inside the store."

The woman put one hand on her hip to stare. "Really?"

Sunny recognized sarcasm, but there was nothing to lose. "I get direct feelings. I'm trying to start a business to help people and their beloved companions. Would you consider giving me a small donation? I have a lot of hungry animals to feed."

"I don't think so." The woman tossed her short curls, bent down to pick up Tiny, and stepped closer to Sunny. "You're telling me you're psychic?"

"I don't know what it is."

The woman laughed. "Tiny was walking with her head down, like she wanted to hide. Pretty obvious."

"But I got the feelings from inside her—telepathically."

"Well, don't worry. We're here to buy her a sweater."

"Oh?" Sunny sat down on the bench, already anticipating itchy fabric with her own irritated skin. "She needs a nice soft fleece." She smoothed Tiny's mane. "Do you, maybe, have a dollar or two for a hungry fur family?"

The woman chuckled. "Fur family. Well, it's original. You look like you need a good meal, too." She dug into her shoulder bag and came out with a ten. "Go crazy."

It hadn't worked how she expected, but she wouldn't refuse a gift at this point. She thanked the woman, regretting she couldn't be more helpful.

After a few minutes, the woman came back out carrying the little Pom wearing a leopard print fleece. She waved and Sunny waved back. Everyone was happy, and the money was great—but begging was a means she had hoped to avoid.

She was toting up possible purchases for the ten dollars when an SUV pulled up. A tall, middle-aged man opened the hatchback and held the leash for a male greyhound, black with a white star on his chest, to climb out. Odd. The fur guy was slow and didn't seem up for an adventure. Greyhounds usually had two speeds: asleep and forty miles per hour.

She rushed to meet them as they stepped onto the sidewalk. She put her hand on the dog's flank, despite the owner's stare. A terrible stretching, cramping pain in her stomach nearly bent her to the ground. There was the taste of rotten eggs, a yellow burn through her torso.

She swallowed hard and straightened up. "Sir, your dog's stomach is ready to burst!"

"What?" The man stepped back.

"His whole body is in agony from being so full."

"That's ridiculous. He's hardly eaten in two days."

She grabbed the collar to keep them both there, and put her hand to his side, preparing for the pain. *What is it? I'll help you. What's the matter, boy?* Cramps like knives, guilt underneath. "It's awful." She clutched at her stomach.

"If you're trying to get business for Pet Smart, more likely you'll scare people away."

She barely managed to choke out the words. "I'm a private person. I want to help him."

"Oh, I get it, looking for a tip. Good luck." He lifted her wrist from the dog's collar, rolling his eyes, and led the dog inside.

She watched through the glass as they walked down the aisle, her guts still twisting. She concentrated on the pain, keeping it going. She needed details, knowledge. She opened the door. "Sir, sir!" He had ducked behind a cat toy display, but the dog was too big to hide. She ran to get closer.

"Go away before I report you to the manager."

She knew shapes, inedible objects, and strong guilt. "He's got . . . toys. . . I don't know . . . He's afraid he'll be punished. He swallowed toys."

The dog's head dipped lower. "Toys?" The man frowned. She thought he paused slightly to think. "He was lonesome."

"We don't leave Ace alone unless he's caged."

She shook her head. "He's a rescue, right? He's used to training with a pack."

The man looked down at Ace and she knew that she was correct, but for a greyhound it was an easy guess. The man put his hand close to Sunny's face and waved. "Good bye."

He was making fun of her. She blocked the aisle. "Please, take him right to the vet. He'll die!" The dog wouldn't make it one more day.

"Sweetheart, move so I can get to the Eukanuba."

She considered arguing, then turned and ran outside. Stupid asshole. She sat on the bench, gritting her teeth while the pain ebbed, feeling useless. Finally, they came through the door, the man carrying a big sack of food, the greyhound dragging behind. She wanted to scream that Ace would never live to eat another meal, but she tried to sound reasonable. "It's an emergency."

The man ignored her.

Ace. She tried to reach in more deeply. *Ace? Ace?* She swiped her hand across his stomach as they passed by. "Stuffed animals! Could he have eaten some?" It seemed odd that nobody would notice torn up remains, but why else would this detail come into her mind? "Furry things, like the rabbit he was trained to chase?" Could her seeing dog toys in the store have planted the idea? She didn't think so. She felt the impossible number of fourteen stuffed animals packed inside her—inside Ace.

The man kept walking, but glanced back. She watched the car until it was gone and pain diminished. She wiped her eyes and said a prayer to St. Francis. Maybe she had stirred a recollection, and Ace had a chance.

The late afternoon sun seared her forehead and cheeks. Sweat soaked her clothes. She wanted to be home under the trees with her family, giving them the love and attention they deserved, not watching idiots let their best friends suffer. But with another ten bucks she could buy kibble for a week.

A hairless Chinese crested came by, a plump package of joy and energy, dark brown with pink spots on his back, a few white hairs on the tip-top of his head. The lady brought him close. Sunny stroked his back, warm and smooth as a loaf of pumpernickel right out of the oven. She recognized a doggie smile. Thank god.

She had just sat back on the bench when a dark-haired, bearded man climbed out of a white pick-up, coaxing somebody on a leash. The smooth chocolate head of a Doberman appeared, but the dog wouldn't budge. It was too hot to leave him in the truck, and the man hefted the dog to the ground. He handed him the end of the leash and the dog took it into his mouth, holding it like he was taking himself on a walk, staying by the man's side.

From a distance she thought the dog was fat and that made him sluggish, but as they came closer, she knew the old guy was sick. The man walked slowly next to him, as if escorting an aged parent, allowing time for each stiff-legged step. They stopped on the grass, and even in his weakness, the dog was proud enough to lift his leg.

Sunny stood and moved toward them. The man came close, the dog following slowly. "He won't hurt you. He enjoys being petted."

She wasn't sure the dog could enjoy anything, but she put her hand lightly on his back to see what was inside him. His whole body seemed tight, weary, his chest especially, the pain of stretching like Ace's belly, but everywhere. Her breath felt short and she knew he had hardly any room for air, yet he was happy. Deep feelings of contentment and love kept his legs moving. *Baron.* The name flowed from nowhere.

Another case of bloating? She wasn't sure if she could trust herself. It didn't seem likely, and her diagnoses of good mental health might have been set up by the man's kindness.

"Good boy," she told him. She wanted to give him a hug, but it might hurt. She looked up at the man. "You gave him a happy life."

He was taken aback, just for a second, as if she'd guessed the end was near. He rubbed behind the dog's ears. "Yeah, he's the best. Aren't you, old buddy?"

She was too sad to make her prediction.

"He doesn't have much time left. Congestive heart failure."
He patted Baron's head. "We had to stop for food. He usually
likes to go in for a sniff."

They walked slowly, and she realized that this man might be
receptive enough to believe in her—if the dog's name was
Baron, she could prove her ability. But there was no point.
Nothing could be done. Her chest ached and she would burst out
crying if she tried to talk. Better to let them get home as soon as
possible. She got on her bike and took off.

Chapter 18: Sunny Lytle

It took willpower not to call Jason from the Mini-Mart on the way home. She should apologize and ask about his family, but she knew she'd cry if she talked.

Long walks and canned meat for dinner made the furs more content, although there was still some grumbling, and she had sympathy itches and discomfort throughout her body when she touched any one of them. She had to force herself to show affection. The new sensitivity was a curse.

The big boys didn't like being tied and they were hot. The smaller guys in the bus were crowded. The whole setup was bad and starting to feel more permanent. Maybe there would be a job at the Sugar Mill, but nothing was as simple as expected, or as much fun.

She cooked up spaghetti with grated cheese and took it a short distance away behind a tree for a minute of peace. She had to find somewhere else to live. The bus was uncomfortable, unsafe, and on the way to unhealthy—almost as bad as living in the trailer with Lytle after her mother left. Almost. She couldn't remember how long they'd lived there—long enough to make the next farmhouse seem huge. Lytle hired Mexicans to do all the picking, and he stayed drunk for days at a time. The ferns grew lush in green houses and under trees, and so did the illegal vegetation that explained their new wealth. She was old enough to understand the extra usefulness of the semi he rented for fern deliveries, but never let on that she knew anything, and happily stayed away as much as possible, out with Jason all hours, day and night.

If Lytle was still alive, she couldn't avoid him forever in such a small town, and she was uneasy thinking about it. But she was an adult now. Things would be different. It might be best to look for him instead of being surprised, try to make up, forgive.

She finished her spaghetti and felt refreshed. It was a good time to look for Lytle, before she lost her courage. Her aunt had complained about his cheapness, that he never sent enough money for Sunny's keep, but she wondered if he might give her a loan now. It didn't seem too much to ask for a long-lost daughter. If not, she would be satisfied to have faced him.

She chose Rufus for the walk to The Outpost, Lytle's old hangout. The shepherd outweighed her by at least forty pounds, but never pulled, and she liked to feel protected. As they walked, she put her hand on his head and felt pure joy in movement and inhaling of new scents, itches drowned by contentment. She let him dawdle in the warm, humid night so they could both enjoy the sweet heavy scent of trumpet flowers hanging along the road. Angel trumpet was poison if you took too much, and nobody knew how much that was because the chemical varied in each plant, but she'd been lucky. She used it several times along with her friends, swallowing small pieces of cigarette-pack paper soaked in the juice, tripping into vivid fantasies. The drug was more potent than cow mushrooms and not so nasty tasting. She remembered panic, waking up nearly blind, one of the less enjoyable side effects, lasting for a few hours. Before she met Jason, she drank and smoked and did everything she could to escape her home life.

A car coming toward her seemed to slow. *Damn!* She didn't want to be recognized. She stepped behind a bush and bent down, as if studying something in the grass, and called Rufus close. The car was small and white, a Corolla or something similar—like Rita was driving at the gas station. There were a zillion of those, but she held her position as it passed. From the back, the driver looked to be a woman with the right kind of hair. It might have been a close call. The last thing Sunny needed was to give away her location.

It was dark when she got to The Outpost. Live hillbilly rock blared from behind the building. She led Rufus through the parking lot and off into the weeds around the side. In back there was a short wall surrounding tables and a dance floor, a scruffy band on stage and a beer-guzzling, cigarette-smoking crowd. Burgers sizzled on a grill, making her mouth water, even though she didn't want any. This was a new addition since she had been there. Probably too loud and lively for Lytle.

She walked Rufus to the front and tied him to a post a short distance from the porch steps. It didn't make sense that every grubby old asshole in the world was permitted in bars and restaurants, and Rufus wasn't, but she knew she wouldn't make it through the door with him. She patted his head and gave him a kiss on the snout, trying to communicate that he didn't want to go in there anyway, but he followed her till the leash was taut. He stood whining, as if she couldn't feel what he wanted in every cell of her body.

As she opened the door most of the men turned to look. The tables were nearly empty, but the bar was full and the noise from the back came through. She could see most of the guys seated on barstools, but she walked to the end to make sure, half relieved and half disappointed that Lytle wasn't there.

A young bartender called to her, "What can I get you, babycakes?"

"I was just looking for somebody—Lytle. Know him?"

The guy gave a short laugh and looked past her. She turned. Chills. Lytle was closing the men's room door, easy to recognize, his beard stubbly and his thin gray hair slicked back in a pony tail. He was shorter than she remembered, and stooped, wearing a ratty T-shirt and dirty jeans. Still looked like a bum.

His surprise turned into a grin, showing blood on his lip. He wiped across it with the back of his hand. "Well, if it isn't my skinny little girl come back looking for me!" He came toward her with his arms out, limping slowly, but not staggering.

She'd planned to try for a hug, but the booze and cigarette smell drove her back. She touched his arm lightly, staying away from the blood on his wrist.

She smiled. "Yeah, it's me." She lowered her backpack onto a chair at the nearest table and sat down.

He was holding something in one hand, and he picked a beer bottle off the bar with the other and sat down across from her.

"So, you missed your old pop. I knew you'd be back one of these days." He yelled toward the bar. "Get me a Coke and another Bud Light, Ray."

"I don't want anything." She crossed her arms. "How are you?"

"Falling apart, that's how I am." He tilted his palm and something small and hard rolled onto the table. "Just yanked this sucker out with my fingers. It was bugging the shit outta me."

Sunny swallowed. It was a molar with blood on the roots. He hadn't changed a bit. "Maybe you'd feel better if you stopped drinking."

"You joking?" He laughed and choked, and she figured it was blood from the tooth. "Drinking is the only thing makes me feel any good at all." He pointed at the beer. "Course, I wouldn't be drinking this Lite shit if I had a choice."

"What do you mean?"

"Health issues." He finished off the beer. "How the hell are you?"

Ray brought the drinks and she sipped from the plastic cup. "Fine. I moved back here—for a while."

"That's nice." He took a long drink of beer. "You seen your mother?"

Her breath caught. "She's here? In DeLeon?"

"I don't know where she is. I thought you might a seen her."

"Oh. No." She shrugged off the disappointment. "Never." She couldn't think of anything else to say. "I'm short on money. I was wondering if you could give me a small loan."

"Jesus, the first thing out of your mouth after ten years is gimme, gimme? I thought you were going to invite your old man over for dinner."

"I don't have money for dinner." She looked into his bloodshot eyes. "I need it bad or I wouldn't ask. I'll pay you back as soon as I can."

"I've heard that somewhere before." He rolled the tooth under his finger on the table. "I only got a couple of these molars left." He took a long drink off the bottle. "Mouth keeps filling up with blood."

She looked into her Coke and sipped on the straw. The crushed ice sparkled. She concentrated on how beautiful it was and how good it tasted.

"Where are you living? You and that football player back together?"

"Jason? He's married." She got the words out with a short catch in her voice. Lytle likely knew that information. The question was punishment.

He flicked the tooth toward her. It rolled to the middle of the table. "There you go. Don't say I never gave you nothing."

She put both hands on her lap, determined not to lose control. "It was nice to see you. I better go. My dog's outside."

"Just one dog? How many turtles and rats and squirrels you got at home?" He slapped the table and laughed.

The bartender was watching. She whispered, "Can you just lend me a hundred? Please? I haven't been able to find a job and I can't—pay my rent."

He took a pack of cigarettes out of his shirt pocket, tapped one out and lit it with a Bic. He blew smoke out the side of his mouth where a few teeth were missing. "Let's see." He took his wallet from his back pocket and cracked it open, tabbing through a thick wad of bills with his finger, lingering. He handed her a twenty and snapped the wallet shut. "Money's tight these days."

It was better than nothing, but his stinginess made her angry. "You ruined my life! I just need a little help!"

He laughed. "I never runed your life. If it's runed, you done it yourself."

She grabbed her pack and headed for the exit. "I'll pay you back."

He stood up with his beer as if to follow her out. "You on drugs? That why you need the money?"

She opened the door and turned halfway. Lytle reached for her arm, but she jerked it clear. "Don't touch me. Rufus will take a bite out of you."

All the men had turned on their barstools.

"Sunny, gimme your address. I'll bring you some money next week when I collect a payment."

She stood her ground, unblinking. Unexpectedly her eyes filled up and her throat tightened. Expectations had run deeper than the need for money.

He waved her away. "I'll find you." He shuffled back toward the bar.

Chapter 19: Rita McKenna

It was almost nine when Rita got home. She tried to counteract too many cups of coffee with a glass of wine, but it didn't work. Her feet still pounded during the second glass and her stomach felt jittery. At midnight a downpour rattled the leaves and she had to close the windows. Thank god, tomorrow was her day off.

She watched the rain in the glow of the parking lot light, unable to let go of the day, the past, or a future that lacked opportunity. Most of her life had been spent doing exactly what she was supposed to, working harder and living smarter than most people, reaching her highest goals. Yet all that counted for nothing—a few months' mistakes, the result of heartache—and years of learning and skill turned to waste. Reminding herself that other people's lives were worse, much worse, didn't make her feel any better.

Animals had it worse. And Sunny. Was it Sunny on the road with the big German shepherd? Rita should have stopped to find out, done something. Right now the girl would be sleeping in the bus, probably no dinner, mosquito-bitten, maybe soaking wet from rain pouring in. And the dogs—likely to be full of parasites and not current on vaccinations.

She would make a call in the morning, discuss the case with Maria, the field worker, and ask the rangers to check secluded areas near Ponce DeLeon large enough to park a bus. Or, if Sunny was telling the truth, she might be working at the pancake place. Rita could find her and set up a time to talk about reasonable options before the law got involved.

Chapter 20: Buckaroo

A green corrugated roof blocked the sky above him. It was daylight, but Buck didn't know what day. His head ached. He was soaked and cold, lying on a hard bench with a graffiti-covered wall beside him. The bus stop.

He'd forgotten to buy cigarettes.

He dragged himself up enough to check the sky. Some light cirrus, nothing Magnetoids could hide in. The two cardboard six-packs were turned to sludge, bottles fallen out on the ground. Not a one with beer left in it. He couldn't remember drinking more than one or two. The fucking Magnetoids had hit him pretty good. The last thing he remembered was being stuck on his back in the field volleying rays all afternoon. Somehow he survived and took cover.

He lifted his plate from the concrete. Mush. He wondered if it had gotten wet, and that's why he couldn't return the shot.

His backpack was open on the ground, the clothes in it soaked. He was stiff and tired and didn't want to move. As he stood, a sharp pain jabbed through the back of his skull. A wonder he was still alive. He slung on the backpack and headed toward his camp. He thought about the girl at the Winn-Dixie. Skinny, odd, but a real cutie. Sunny.

His stomach rumbled and he figured he hadn't eaten anything since breakfast the day before. The girl said she worked at the Sugar Mill. It would be nice to eat a huge pile of pancakes with bacon and good coffee, and watch her work, maybe get in a little conversation. He'd never been to the place, heard about it from Geordie. He still had a twenty left in his pocket. Wet, but it would spend.

Back at camp he dried his hair and put on a clean shirt. His hands were shaky. He got the pickle jar out of the cooler and took a whiff of dill juice. Yep, he could smell it, good and strong. Passed the test, as always. He had a lot of diseases, so he was told, but Parkinson's wasn't one of them. If only there was an easy indicator for manic-depression and schizophrenia. He'd heard those words tossed around for years, but never seen any proof. They all wanted to prescribe drugs. Fine. He had a use for them.

By the time he arrived at the park, a few cars were lined up to pay the ranger. The posted walk-in fee was only a dollar, but it didn't cost the county anything for him to walk through the park. He'd walk carefully. He stood behind a car until the ranger was busy counting out change, then dashed to the other side of the guard building and entered the exit. The restaurant was down the hill, but he could already smell bacon.

"No shoes, no shirt, no entrance. No wet bathing suits." He checked himself, noting all the requirements—just a little sandy, and his jeans damp. He even smelled good, having had a rinse.

"Barbara," according to her tag, a saucy redhead, looked surprised when he requested a table for one by a window, but he had beat the crowd, and she seated him in a far room with a wide view. He could see the lake and—if he stretched his neck—three directions of blue sky. Each table had a griddle, and he realized he was going to have to pay to do his own cooking.

Barb brought him his place setting and coffee, took his order, and flipped the switch to turn on his griddle. He fingered the metal pie pan—red, white, and blue speckled enamel—more substantial than paper plates and easy to cover with foil to create reflective qualities.

People started to fill up the tables fast. The cute chick, Sunny, didn't seem to be working.

Barb delivered Buck's order, his own pitcher of batter, small dishes of peanut butter and bananas for doctoring the pancakes, and two sides of bacon. He took his time cooking up one big cake at a time, then smearing on the peanut butter and trying out the combination with honey and molasses.

He kept tabs on the sky. Clouds were likely to come from the west, and everything was bright blue and clear in that direction. He got up once and stuck his head out the screen door to take a look south, and it was clear there too.

When he got back, a group with a woman in a wheelchair, holding a dressed monkey on her lap, had come in and sat at the big table across from his. The critter was wearing a diaper and little red vest that said "Service Animal." He scrunched his nose at it and clucked his tongue, but the monkey was unwrapping the paper napkin from the silverware and didn't pay any attention. Buck was on his last few bites, but he asked for more coffee so he could hang around and watch. He was surprised a monkey was allowed into the restaurant, since he himself barely made the qualifications.

When the bananas and blueberries were served at its table, the monkey's eyes zeroed in, but it didn't make a move. Buck felt sorry for it, forced to sit and salivate. The husband took care of pouring and cooking the pancakes while the monkey stared.

The man cut bite-sized pieces for his wife and set the plate in front of her and the monkey. The rascal went to work feeding the woman bite after bite, getting no reward, all those banana slices sitting right there unguarded.

The repetition started to get boring, but then the monkey held back a piece of pancake when the woman opened her mouth. Buck laughed out loud. He was on the monkey's side. The monkey faked her out two more times. Buck could barely control himself.

The woman cursed and Spunky Monkey showed his teeth and made a huh-huh sound. He held a bite touching her lip and dripped syrup on her blouse, then whipped the bite away. Buck couldn't stop laughing. *Go, Spunks.* Some other people stopped watching the monkey and stared in Buck's direction. He was used to it. Still, he was done eating, and he didn't want to wait and see the monkey get disciplined. Buck bowed as he left the table.

At the register he asked the red-head if Sunny worked there. "Skinny blonde."

She closed the cash drawer and looked at him. "Nope."

A waiter, pouring coffee behind the counter, was watching over his shoulder, suspicious. Nobody was likely to give a straight answer. He'd just have to come back for another breakfast and see if Sunny was around. He hoped Spunks was a regular.

He walked past an empty table on his way out and saw a semi-clean pie-pan amidst the leavings. It would hold up during any storm. He snatched the pan and headed out the swinging door.

Chapter 21: Rita McKenna

Rita went to the counter to give her name, expecting a wait, but "Ellen," a sweet, old-fashioned-looking server, took her to an open spot in the second room. Rita took a careful look around. There was much activity, but Sunny didn't seem to be working.

The homey atmosphere was enough to make the trip worthwhile, and Rita could always make the phone call when she got home, if necessary. It was uplifting to get out of the house. She ordered whole grain batter, blueberries and pecans.

A paraplegic woman a few tables away had a service monkey—squirrel monkey? Rita had never seen a service monkey, or heard of one. After a few minutes it was easy to see why. The monkey would aim a bite of pancake at the woman's mouth, and when she opened up, he pulled back. Syrup dripped onto her ruffled neckline. The monkey gave her about one bite out of three. The angrier the woman got, the fewer bites of pancake made it into her mouth. The monkey rocked back and forth on the arm of the wheelchair and let out a sound that Rita interpreted to mean pleasure.

The woman cursed aloud and a homeless-looking man with bright blond dreadlocks burst out in a laugh. The woman's husband, engrossed in his pancakes, paid no attention at all. As the monkey continued his antics, the scraggly fellow got louder and louder. Rita glared, trying to give him a hint, but he wouldn't look her way. Finally, he finished and left.

When the husband wiped the woman's lips and rolled her out, she was fuming and red-faced, with the monkey on her lap eating a slice of banana that he had snatched. The drama was over, no physical injury, but Rita knew that the monkey would continue to get more aggressive as he aged. Even at his small size, he was fast and strong and could inflict deep bites—nothing like chimps, but still serious. She'd learned about chimpanzees when she toured the Great Ape Retirement Center over in Wauchula. Most had been used for films and commercials, but once they reached adolescence they became unreliable and ended up caged and lonely in basements. Only a lucky few were able to be rescued. She suspected that this small monkey was a teenager showing his oats and wondered what would happen to him eventually.

Ellen came by and asked if there would be anything else.

"Does a woman named Sunny work here?"

Ellen picked up the pie plate and silverware and crumbled the placemat into the pan. "No. Sorry."

"I thought she started last week."

"No. We could use somebody."

Rita finished her coffee and got up to pay. A blond waiter was at the empty table, sweeping at the monkey's mess on the floor. He looked up and caught her eye. "Funny thing. You're the second person asking for Sunny today."

"I thought she worked here."

"Are you a friend of hers?"

"I'm a vet at the Humane Society. She stopped in to volunteer. I just wondered . . . Do you know where she lives?"

"Not really."

He seemed to be holding back something. She noted the name on his tag. "Jason, I was thinking that if she needed a ride, it would be worth it for me to pick her up and take her over there. We can't pay, but we offer lunch—"

He picked up the bus tub of dishes and rested it on his hip. "She loves animals. That's for sure."

"Can you give me her phone number?"

"I doubt she has a phone."

"Does she live nearby?"

"Probably."

She wondered if he had been warned not to give out information. "Okay. Please tell her that I stopped in, if you see her."

Rita paid at the counter and dropped a tip into the plastic jar. Now she wondered if the girl was all right. Maybe it hadn't been Sunny with the dog. She couldn't think of anything to do. She walked to the bridge over the spring and stood breathing in the beauty of the park, delaying her return to the empty apartment and laundry. Live oaks draped in festive sweeps of Spanish moss shaded the grassy lawn, a romantic setting. She had read that two million gallons of pure water forced itself through the spring each day, flowing into the pool, down the lake, eventually joining the St. Johns River, ongoing for thousands of years. Whether it had the capability to bestow longevity was questionable, but its own eternal vitality was enough to earn the name Fountain of Youth.

She crossed the concrete bridge to watch the water churn over the rocks and ripple the eel grass. A green heron, maroon back shining in the sun, landed on a water hyacinth, and in seconds, darted its head into the water and snared breakfast. It reminded her that she was due a visit to Woodruff, the wildlife refuge, where she had seen sand hill cranes and black-bellied whistling ducks for the first time, along with a ten foot alligator. Birding in the Midwest had been an interesting pastime, but Florida's many large species could be enjoyed without binoculars.

She was standing unprotected in the sun, and sweat dripped from her hairline down her back, but she rested her elbows on the rail to relax for a few more minutes, watching tiny fish below the cascade of clear water. Just in case there was magic in the "fountain," she made a wish. She needed change—maybe a friend.

She turned to leave. The waiter was leaning against the trunk of a tree. He came toward her. "I know where you can find Sunny."

"Yes?"

"I saw her out the window a few days ago, paddling away in a kayak. She's probably camped on the south side of the lake. That was our spot when we were in high school."

"Camped?"

"I never saw Sunny paddle for exercise." He gave her the driving directions. "If you find her, tell her Jason says hi."

She shook his hand and introduced herself, saying she would give Sunny his regards. A wedding band glinted on his finger, but from his earnest tone, Rita guessed they'd had a relationship.

He went back inside and she paused, thinking about her sandals and shorts, wondering if it was a good idea to trek through the woods where there were likely to be swarms of mosquitoes, red ants, and possibly poisonous snakes, but she wanted to see Sunny's set up.

"Can you believe that monkey?" A big man with a ruddy complexion stood next to her, grinning, his eyes crinkled with fun. "It was a first for me."

"He needs psychiatric help." She hadn't noticed this man in the restaurant, but he had obviously seen her.

He introduced himself as John, a friend of the owner, and put out his hand. "You must be new in town. I would remember your sparkling eyes."

"Fairly new." She gave her name and put her hand into his large one, feeling herself blush.

He was around her age, possibly trying to pick her up. It had been a long time since a man had approached her and she was flattered, but on guard. Despite the heat, he was dressed neatly in a button-down shirt and light slacks.

"Do you know Patty?" he asked. "The owner."

"No. This is only my second time here."

He wasn't her usual athletic type, but then "her type" had never been good for her. It occurred to her that she had never found a man who was truly good for her. "I have to go."

"I was hoping you and Patty were friends so she would vouch for me. Can I walk you to your car?"

It was a rhetorical question. He walked beside her across the gravel road and across the wooden walkway. She couldn't ditch him without being rude.

"Patty and I belong to the same antique car club." He took a card from his pocket, reached down to her side and pressed it into her hand. "Are you interested in cars?"

"Not really. I'm a veterinarian." Immediately, she wondered why she had given out the information, and if she should revise to *was a veterinarian.*

"Should one exclude the other?"

She snickered, and he took it as encouragement to chat about himself and his job as they walked up the hill. By the time they reached her car, he had her convinced that procuring vintage cars for films was a fascinating occupation. He claimed insider knowledge of the stars. Sylvester Stallone had a huge head that photographed well, and Antonio Banderas was a skinny chain-smoker.

"I'd still like to meet Antonio," she said.

"Ah, he's not smart enough for you. You'd rather have dinner with me." He pointed to a shining black convertible. "Look. Right by yours. We were meant to meet."

It glistened next to her powdery beige Corolla, a sign that they had nothing in common. "Sure you can't fix me up with Antonio?"

"Come to dinner tonight—any night—and we'll give him a call."

She looked at her watch. "I have to go."

"Give me your cell number. I can show you all the hot spots in DeLeon Springs."

She smiled. Cell phones couldn't get a signal in her apartment, and she saved money doing without. "I don't think I'll ever have that much time." She held up his card to acknowledge that she could reach him if she wanted.

He took her hand into both of his. "Seriously. Just for fun. Call me."

She nodded in a non-committal way, waved goodbye, and got into her car. He followed her out through the gate. When she turned right he kept going straight. The attention had brightened her day, but she wasn't ready to take a chance.

3

Chapter 22: Rita McKenna

Per Jason's directions, Rita pulled off the road south of the park where the blacktop ended. The underbrush looked scratchy and was sure to be full of mosquitoes and chiggers, probably banana spiders too, the size of her hand, lurking in the palmetto scrub. It didn't seem possible that Sunny lived in there, yet the waiter seemed certain.

The bugs were as she expected, and she slapped and ducked her way in the direction of the lake. She was ready to turn back when she saw something white hanging from a tree. A sheet—two sheets—draped over branches. There was the bus barely visible through the foliage.

A sharp bark set off an uproar. A half-dozen dogs turned toward her, straining on their leashes. Yapping exploded from inside the bus. More animals than she had expected. She would have to put in a call and get the county system into action.

"Hello? Sunny? Are you there?" She couldn't hear anything except the dogs. She walked between sheets to a fire pit ringed in rocks and shells. An orange crate served as a table, holding a gallon of drinking water, and a cup sat beside an old lounge chair. Sad, how the girl was living, and all the dogs. They looked healthy so far, but it couldn't last. There were shallow holes under the edge of the bus that the animals dug, trying to keep cool. She walked around the side. The doors were open an inch and she pushed them farther and called, "Sunny, are you there?" The cacophony of high pitched yaps drowned her voice.

She wondered if the girl might be sick and unable to yell above the noise. She pushed hard and the doors opened. A Chihuahua and a Westie were the first two in a pack of small dogs that came wiggling to greet her. She bent to pet and block them until she could reach the handle to close the door. As she climbed the two steps, she smelled cats. Several well-used litter pans were at eye level on stacked boxes.

A few cats looked up from a dirty mattress. The arrangement attested to how well dogs and cats could get along. There was a rabbit in a hutch, a crate holding two ferrets, and a raccoon inside a carrier. Partial bags of dog food, cat food, and rabbit pellets took up the tabletop. A jar of honey, a bottle of oil, and some boxes of dry pasta sat on a shelf with a few pans and cups. There were discarded single serving containers of Parmalat milk in a trash can. No refrigeration. No ice. No running water. Rita walked to the back and saw five puppies and their Labrador mother cordoned off by large boxes.

The dogs outside started to bark. There she was, Sunny, racing though the scrub holding on to four leashes, as if towed by sled dogs.

Rita called through the open top of a window. "Sunny. Remember me?—from the shelter."

The girl opened the door and dogs pulled her inside. Barking and yipping, they plowed into Rita, knocking her down onto the mattress.

"No! Back! Back! Be good!" Sunny strained to hold them. They choked and slobbered. They were licking, not biting, but Rita pushed them off, trying to sit up as paws scratched her legs. A huge shepherd licked her face. Sunny backed him off.

"Sorry, I couldn't hold them. Take Rufus and Gus—would you?—while I tie the others."

Rita accepted the leashes of the German shepherd and the schnauzer that stood panting with his paws on her knee. She sat down on the edge of the booth and the schnauzer jumped to her lap. "Good Gus. Nice guys, good boys. Good Rufus." She petted them and looked at her dirtied shorts and shirt.

Sunny came back to take the dogs and Rita followed her outside. The air felt amazingly cool by comparison. The girl tied the dogs and took a drink from the gallon of water. She looked near anorexia in the cut-offs showing her thighs. "This camper's private property." She took another drink. "You're trespassing."

"I'm sorry. I thought you might be hurt."

"I'm fine. You need to go."

"Could I have a drink, please?"

The girl held out the jug. "Just don't spill it. Drinking water's like gold when you have to carry it this far."

Rita took two sips and put the gallon back on the orange crate. She told Sunny that she'd been to the Sugar Mill and that Jason had sent his greetings. The last part seemed to knock the girl off balance. "The waitress told me they need somebody," Rita said, hoping to be the bearer of good news.

"Really? I wasn't supposed to check back until tomorrow." She sat down on a plastic chair. "You're not going to turn me in, are you?"

In a way, she was. "Turn you in?"

Sunny motioned for her to sit on the lounge. "To the police— for living here. I know I must be doing something illegal."

"The police? No—I was concerned when you didn't come back to the shelter. I can give you a ride, if you want to have lunch and help out. Jackie has some hours open." She felt dishonest, but the girl would run at any mention of bringing help. She was sure of it.

Sunny shook her head. "I have to get a real job." She pointed at the dogs racked out for their morning naps. "These guys are about out of food."

Rita swatted a mosquito on her arm and wiped off the blood spot.

Sunny cringed. "Ouch!"

"Bugs love me."

"I meant, poor mosquito."

Rita met her eyes. Sunny was dead serious. This was a level of empathy way beyond anything she could imagine.

"Sometimes at the shelter we get donations of dog food brands that don't fit our dietary requirements. I can check tomorrow. It's better than nothing."

"Are you a lesbian?"

"No." Rita touched her short hair. She'd never heard that before. Being homosexual would have saved her a lot of trouble.

"Not the haircut. I'm wondering why you'd track me down, hike through the woods, get your nice shorts trampled, and still offer me food."

"I see." She chewed her lip. "I guess I wanted some company on my day off. I'm an animal lover like you—almost like you—I know you need help."

"I'm not doing a very good job."

"It's hard on your own. That's why there are organiza—"
Sunny shifted her gaze to the ground. "They're murderers."

"It's far from a perfect system. Believe me, I know. But it's the only system." She touched Sunny's shoulder. "Maybe that's why I'm here. I need to do something good. I became a vet to do good, but I failed."

Sunny pointed toward the bus. "I know how you can do some good. I have a raccoon with a damaged ankle. Won't eat."

"Let me see him."

The girl went into the bus and brought back a crate. The raccoon was scratching wildly. Rita knelt on the ground and peered inside, seeing the kibble, and asked if he'd had water.

"I gave him some, but I couldn't tell if he drank." She knelt beside Rita. "See his ankle. It's a mess."

Rita tried to take a look, but the animal was a scrabbling blur of movement, stressed to the limit. It was lucky she'd come when she did. "He can't stay in here. It's probably doing him more harm than good."

Tears gleamed in Sunny's eyes, making them more childlike. The girl meant well, as they all did.

Sunny stood up and turned her back, holding her hand across her eyes, her shoulders shaking. "I can't do anything right."

Rita took a chance and put her arm around her. "You might have saved him from predators."

"It's my fault his ankle got torn up in the first place."

Rita motioned around the camp. "You have quite a set up here. You're amazing, living here with nothing, except your principles. I admire you for your determination."

"Everybody's all bitten up and not getting enough food. Now I'm fucking killing a raccoon."

Rita was careful to avoid asking any questions. "I assume that you plan to get a place to live."

"I didn't expect to be here more than a day or two. I just want to give these guys a good home—but I'm as bad as . . ." She wiped her cheeks with her wrist and forearm.

"That's what I've always wanted, too, to rescue every animal that needs help, and I had the advantages—parents who supported my decisions and took out loans to help pay my way through vet school."

"So what was the problem?"

It wasn't easy to answer. "I didn't charge enough and got into debt. But in the end, it was much less noble—in fact, completely selfish." She stopped. "I'll tell you about it some time—if you really want to know."

"I never had the money for college, but anyway, it would've been a waste."

Rita shook her head. The poor girl. "I'm sure that's not true. You have spirit. That's what's important."

Sunny grabbed the corner of a sheet and wiped her face. "I used to."

Rita looked into the crate at the skittish raccoon. He needed antibiotics. She offered to take him to the Wild Animal Rescue.

"They won't kill him?"

"Sunny, they love animals. That's why they're a rescue."

"I guess you better get going then. He's probably dehydrated."

Rita wasn't sure she had gained any trust. She didn't dare make other suggestions. "Are we friends? Do you mind if I come for a visit?"

"Okay. I do need his carrier back."

Rita picked up the crate, nodding. "I'll bring him back when he's well."

She started off through the weeds, ducking a spider web on a branch.

"Rita?"

She turned. Sunny stood with sad, pleading eyes, and beyond her, the multitude of dogs strained on the leashes, hoping for something.

"Next time I'll make sure they don't jump all over you."

"That would be nice." She made it back to her car with gritty feet and itchy legs. The situation was hopeless, but now she couldn't make the call. If Maria and her crew came out, it would be instant betrayal, turning her sympathy into lies. She would have to figure out something else to do.

She opened the door on the passenger side and picked up John's card from the seat, then set down the raccoon crate. His dinner invitation felt more tempting. Getting cleaned up for a nice meal and enjoying some light conversation seemed deserved.

Chapter 23: Sunny Lytle

Finally it was the day she had been told to return to the Sugar Mill. Kiko rode on her shoulder while she did chores. The small Siamese liked to suck her earlobe, attached like a baby to a nipple, sometimes slurping and nipping. He hung on while she moved and bent, his soft body against her neck, a live fur collar, the feel of love from his innocent heart. Still she was worried. If the job fell through she was lost.

As she measured out kibble, she could sense their stomachs growling, and the word *meat* ricocheted back and forth inside her skull. Cats rubbed against her legs and dogs nudged her, but she was careful not to touch them with her hands. Purposeful contact seemed to jazz up all the itching and burning in her body. She felt sad, but needed her wits for the day.

She took her vitamins and ate a slice of white bread with honey and strained a pan of buggy water through a thin cloth— no survivors. She hoped to see Rita about the raccoon, pick up some donated food, and get to the Sugar Mill by mid-afternoon when it should be less crowded.

She slid a plastic bag filled with plastic bags onto her handle bars to carry canned food and started off on the long ride. She stopped at the Mini-Mart to use the restroom, and slurped water at the sink. Next time she would bring an empty jug. On her way out, the pay phone drew her like a magnet. There was change rolling around in her backpack and she thought of calling Jason to see if a woman picked up. That would be plain stupid. She should call Bear on his cell phone. He would be happy to hear from her, and although she didn't want to ask for money, she was desperate.

He picked up. "Sunny! Where are you?"

She already felt bad that she called. "In DeLeon Springs."

"I've been worried. I thought I'd hear from you sooner. You okay?"

"Mostly." She asked him if he'd found her car behind the barn.

"It's sitting there with an expired license. I had to make up a story for Marci since I couldn't sell it."

"I'm so sorry!" She told him she'd remembered it the first night in the woods. She would find it and mail it.

"Never mind. It's yours. You can pick up the car when you bring the bus back."

"Really?" He was so good to her. If only sex wasn't involved, or a wife. "I'll do that soon. It'll be nice to have my car."

He asked if she had an apartment, and she summed up her rotten luck, including the raccoon story. "It hasn't been as easy as I expected."

"How'd the bus run?"

"Great. Drove fine. Except it really sucks up the gas—just like you said." She took a breath. Her minutes were ticking away. He always made it so easy to ask for anything, and it wasn't right, but there were so many counting on her. "Any chance you might loan me a little money till I get paid? I should be starting work soon."

"You know I don't loan. Your fur guys are my favorite charity. Where should I send the check?"

"Oh, that's a problem." Stupid. She hadn't even thought about it.

The minutes ran out then. She hung up. She had no more money, stood staring at the phone.

It rang. "Bear?"

"Sunny, you worry me, living in that bus. How about if I bring you cash? I can stay a few days and help you find a place."

"You would do that? Drive all the way down here?" Her luck was turning. "Bear, I'd love it!"

"I haven't been to Daytona in a long time." He asked if she would stay in the hotel with him.

"Would I! A hot shower!" She knew what came with it, but it didn't matter by now.

"Hot shower? What about your favorite bear? Just give me a few days or a week to set it up."

"A week?" She tried not to whine, but a week in the bus was like a month anywhere else. If she held out that long, she wouldn't need the money. She told him to call her at the Mini-

Mart and gave him the number, setting the time for noon on Saturday.

"Or you call me," he said, "in case you have to work or something."

It wasn't quite a full week to wait for the news. She did look forward to burying herself in his husky arms, his human fur, and forgetting her world of pain. "You're the sweetest. I can't wait for a big Bear hug."

Chapter 24: Buckaroo

It was a blinding blue day, the wide pallet of sky dabbed with only a few splotches of bright white clouds, one of many clear days to come in the winter season. Buck could roam without fear. He had borrowed Geordie's pickup and was driving back from Winn-Dixie with a load of beer and groceries when Sunny made the turn onto Ponce DeLeon on her bike.

Man that girl was thin—but pretty. Hair like wheat, lighter than his. She had plastic bags hanging from her handle bars, looked more homeless than before. She was trying to duck him, turning away, as if there was something interesting in the woods. He pulled next to her, almost blocking her path.

"Need a ride?"

She stopped and slid off the seat, but wouldn't look at him. "I'm headed the other way."

"I see that, but I'm in no hurry. Take you wherever you want." He had beers on ice in a Styrofoam cooler next to him, and he flipped off the top and held up a six pack of Old Milwaukee. He plucked a bag of Ruffles out of a sack and showed her. "Ranch style."

"No, thanks." She shook her head. "I don't drink beer."

He offered water with the chips.

She stood pondering, so he put the truck in park and hopped out. He took the handles of her bike and gave her an expectant smile.

"Okay, I guess. Take me to the animal shelter."

He hoisted the bike onto the bed and cleared a space on the seat for her. She reached into the cooler for a piece of ice, holding it near her lips. "Do you mind?"

He noticed she had acquired some tan and looked good in it. "Take all you want." She crunched, and he tried to remember what he'd heard in his youth about girls that ate ice. Horny? Didn't seem to fit. More likely thirsty.

He followed her directions and pulled up near the building under a tree. She jumped out and started for the bike. He yelled after her. "How long are you gonna be? I can sit here in the shade, drink a beer, have a smoke."

She scratched at a bite on her arm. "I'm not sure my friend is here—let me check."

She went inside and he popped a tab. He'd only lit up and taken a few swigs when she came back out.

"No luck. My friend's off today, and my raccoon's somewhere else."

His first thought was rabies. "Your raccoon?"

"Not mine. I found him—hurt. Anyway, animals don't really belong to people."

He checked the sky. Beautiful. He offered to let her see his camp, have something to eat.

"Not now. Just drop me at the Sugar Mill, if you don't mind."

"Oh, yeah. You work there?"

"Hope to. I need the money."

Yet another chance for him to be magnanimous. "This is your lucky day. I'll drive you over there, and if it's a no-go, I'll take you someplace else—till we find you a job. I've got a half tank of gas in this truck and I only need to leave it with a quarter."

She seemed to be deciding. He knew she was going to be a hard nut to crack, but the best ones usually were. Sooner or later, she'd be all over him, wanting to move into his tent and cook, like the last one. He'd worry about that when the time came. "Look, it's nice to have somebody to talk to." She didn't move, so he touched the gas.

There was no line at the park entrance. He drove through the gate and handed over the five-dollar car fee at the ranger station, wincing inside. She promised to pay him back with her first tips.

He followed the drive under the huge limbs waving lacy Spanish moss. There was blue sky all around. "I love these trees," he told her.

"Me too. I built my camp—" She stopped.

Finally, truth. "Your camp?" He tried to say it lightly, interested, not like he remembered a lie.

She explained that it was short term until she made rent money.

It was a common tune, but he didn't understand it. The world was his in the woods. "Been camping for years. Can't stand walls."

"I like walls—and especially a roof."

No matter what she said, they had a lot in common. He drove down the hill to the restaurant and backed into a handicapped spot so he could gaze at the spring and sky. "I'll wait here. You let me know if you're leaving or staying."

She opened the door and hopped down. He watched her ass in the shorts, what there was of it. She would have a great shape if she put on a little meat. She pushed open the wooden door and went inside, and he turned to the spring head and lit a cig. The green cavern had always fascinated him, too deep for eyes to penetrate, but somehow glowing under the surface, teasing with its power. The beards of moss on the branches overhead shifted in a breeze. He glimpsed the edge of a cloud and stretched his neck out the window to look overhead. A thin ruffle of cirrus, no way for brain-zappers to ruin his day.

The door opened and Sunny came walking out, head down, weaving a little, like she'd had a few shots of booze. But they didn't serve alcohol. Bad news, he figured. She walked to the side of the truck and disappeared.

"Sunny?" He opened his door and darted to the other side. She was on her face in the grass. He crouched and lifted her head. Her eyes were closed. He scooped her up like nothing, a wisp. Her hair smelled like the woods, and he felt the twitch of a stiffy. Sometimes he disgusted himself.

Her eyes opened. "What are you doing?"

"Getting you off the ground. Did you want to stay there, sweetheart?"

She squirmed in his arms and he lowered her legs to the road, but they wouldn't hold her. He kept an arm under her shoulder and moved her toward the door of the truck. She let him boost her up and dropped her head back on the seat. He asked when she last ate, and she mumbled something about bread.

"Well, my guess, you blacked out from starvation or dehydration. I'm taking you back to camp where I can feed you some lunch and keep an eye on you."

He thought she would object, but she closed her eyes. He got a water, cracked the lid, and pushed it into her hand. She drank half of it, screwed on the top, and closed her eyes again.

She was asleep when he pulled in next to his tent. He turned off the truck. She raised her head and looked around. "Sorry, I don't get much sleep at night."

"You're welcome to crash on my cot. I'm gonna cook up some hot dogs."

Her face went pale again and he raced to the other side of the truck in case she was going down.

"None for me." She slid to her feet and walked to his plastic chair and sat.

He frowned to show irritation. "Beggars can't be choosers."

"You said chips. A few of those will be fine."

He started to wonder how much trouble he was in for. "Are you one of those anorexics?"

She shook her head and stood up. "No, there are a lot of foods I would rather not eat. I'm sorry. I'll get my bike and ride out of here."

"Stay where you are." He squeezed her shoulder in a friendly way and asked her if she got the job.

"Oh, yeah! I almost forgot." Her face lit up and she smiled. "They were hoping I'd come back."

Man, was she pretty with her teeth showing. He kissed air. "Sweet! Let's celebrate." He got the groceries from the truck, opened the Ruffles bag, and handed it to her. She needed more than that to keep her alive. He set the half bottle of water near her. "Sure you won't have a beer?"

She shook her head. She took a handful of chips, then handed him the bag. "The pay will be just in time."

"A little late, if you ask me, unless fainting is normal for you. He took some chips and passed them back, told her to work on those for a while. "I'm going to boil a hot dog."

She swallowed. "I'm fine. It's the fur people I worry about."

He winked. "The furpees, huh?" He knew he was clever. "I'll have these ready in three shakes of a lamb's tail." He took a pack of hot dogs from the cooler, got a pan, and lit up the propane stove. She was munching, but still looked strained. He asked if she was feeling okay.

She insisted she was. "I know it sounds silly, but these were living potatoes once upon a time, like most everything we eat. I eat as little as I can."

"You don't eat vegetables or meat? What does that leave?"

"I eat vegetables—fruit and grains, too—but I feel bad."

"You need to get over that."

"I don't know if I should or not." She was staring at his tent, covered with fronds on top to camouflage its bright green from the Magnetoids.

"Rain protection. My water repellency is shot."

"Good idea." She motioned toward the stove. He had mounted it on some concrete blocks, so sand couldn't get into the food. She told him she had a stove, but no propane. She didn't cook much, except spaghetti.

"Hey, I got some spaghetts. Angel hair—cooks fast, saves on the gas. I'll put a pot on the other burner."

"Got any Parmesan cheese? The shake kind?"

He made an internal note to get some. "Butter and salt and pepper okay?"

Her face lit up and he went to work on it, finding the pasta and filling a pot with water. He cracked another beer and handed it to her. She looked up at him and then took a sip and handed it back, making a face. "It tastes the same as when I was in high school." She wiped her lips with her hand. "Bitter."

He drained half of the beer and belched a good, long one.

"Get any on you?" she asked.

What was she was talking about?

"Whatever you brought up. Never mind. It was a joke."

He faked a chuckle. She pointed at his beer. "My father's an alcoholic. It's not like I never saw beer before."

"Oh, yeah? I guess I'm an alcoholic too—and a drug addict when I get the chance."

She chewed her bottom lip. "You're not mean enough for an alcoholic, I don't think."

"Not mean, but I've heard crazy." It made him sound honest to admit it.

She laughed. "No problem. I know I'm crazy, but that's better than being like the rest of them."

He added salt to the water. "The rest of who?"

"Normal people."

"No worries there." He looked up and was glad to see her smiling. He crouched and put a match to the gas and set the pot of water on the burner. Suddenly, a lot became clear. *The last name, Lytle.* "Shit!"

"Burn yourself?"

"No. I know your old man. I've drank with him at The Outpost."

She huffed. "He's a buddy of yours?"

"Acquaintance." He would never have connected her with greasy old Lytle. He wondered how much he should say. He couldn't stand the jerk-off, would like an excuse to knock his lights out.

She said she'd gone to see him. "I thought if he was still alive, he might have changed." She crossed her arms.

"He was raisin' hell as of a month or two ago." Buck pulled a chair over to Sunny and took her hand. "I'll make sure Lytle doesn't bother you."

"How could you do that?"

"A warning. He knows I'll kick his ass."

He put the angel hair into the pot and got out the butter. She was sipping from the water bottle, looking worried, and he didn't like knowing that nasty old Lytle was her father.

He checked the sky. Still clear, thank god. He wasn't ready to explain about Magnetoids.

Chapter 25: Sunny Lytle

Her stomach had been grinding for hours, and when she finished her serving of buttery angel hair, she was full and sleepy. She hoped Buck wasn't going to try any moves.

He sat on a stump, stuffing his mouth with a quarter of a hot dog and bun at each bite. He swallowed and took a swig of beer, reached for the chips. "You have a lot of animals, huh?"

She picked a stray strand of pasta from the plate.

"All your groceries? All that dawg food?"

He was milking his drawl, she knew, for her benefit. "You could say that."

"Dawgs especially, huh?" He belched a deep rumbler.

"Add a little flour to that and make gravy."

"Huh? Another joke? Sorry, I don't agree with what you call "manners." Asking to be excused for natural acts. It's part of the reason I live out here."

She set her plate down on a flat rock. "What's the other part?"

"Nature. Freedom. No taxation. I'd be out West in the mountains if it didn't get so damn cold."

She knew he was keeping something back. He had a lot of money to choose living in the woods. She told him she wanted a big farmhouse, a barn, and a chicken coop, everything comfortable for fur people.

"They're the furs and we're the skins?"

"Yes and no. I'm a fur person, too, because I love them—furred, feathered and scaled. I'm not that crazy about humans."

"Then I'm a fur person, too. You eat eggs?"

"No." She considered how far to go. He was more accepting than most people. "I have a special relationship with chickens. When I was a teenager, I had a rooster who loved me, I mean really, really loved me. Fricken."

"Fricken chicken? Ha!" He laughed and fell off his stump onto the sand.

She laughed along, reaching out to brush sand off his back, realizing he was a little drunk. "Guess the other chicken's name."

"Chicken Little? Chicken Delight-el!"

"Nope—those would've been good though. Choke."

"Choke the chicken? Oh, god." He bellowed and put his arm on her shoulder. "You're one funny gal."

They had been Lytle's names. "I also had Alice and Attila, but they were more ordinary." He was sputtering beer. She told him he'd have to stop laughing if he wanted to hear more.

He moved his stump closer to her, wiped his eyes, and took out a cigarette. "Please tell me. I want to know how a chicken shows affection."

"Better than most people, I'll tell you that. I got them as chicks, and they all turned out to be roosters. Right off, Fricken thought I was his mom. Choke would go off with the others, pecking in the dirt—until Alice and Attila disappeared. Then he got more possessive, too, but still not like Fricken. Fricken never left my side if he could help it."

He grunted, said it was inconvenient.

"You're wrong! It's wonderful to be loved that much." She felt herself turning red and picked up the potato chip bag.

"Pets are a lot of trouble."

She ignored the P-word and took a few crumbs. "He'd greet me happy as a dog—come running when I got home from school, and if I wasn't careful, follow me inside. Lytle didn't allow him in. When I cleaned, he would watch me walk from one room to the other with the broom or vacuum and follow me window to window. Every time I looked out, he'd be staring at me with his neck stretched, desperate for me to hold him."

"That's creepy."

She looked Buck in the eye. "You've probably never been loved like that." The words made her remember that she hadn't given Jason the chance.

"People have better ways of lovin' . . . mutual ways." He handed her a clean, folded rag from his pocket. "Here, wipe your snot-locker."

She took the cloth and wiped her eyes first. "Sex, huh? I knew you'd say that. Yeah, sure. That's always meaningful."

"It works for some of us."

She couldn't resist telling him the rest. "Fricken did that, too."

He squinted and his nose wrinkled up. "How was it?"

She had to laugh. "Great!" She let the word hang for a second to keep up the tease. "He would hold onto my arm, fluff up and quiver, and stare into my eyes. I could feel the love oozing out of him. Then he'd drop a little . . . gob . . . on my arm."

"Ack!"

"It was proof of his feelings."

"You're one crazy chick." He rolled his eyes.

She could tell that he was enjoying her story. "Fricken was one of a kind. One time he spurred Lytle in the calf—deep. Trying to protect me."

He asked her what had become of the roosters. Unexpectedly, bitterness welled in her stomach and she couldn't answer. She looked off into the woods, trying to let go of the image of a stewing pot.

"Roosters are pretty tough to eat."

He'd read her easily. "Yeah. He probably just ran off."

Buck went to the tent and brought back sticks and logs and layered them in a neat square for a fire. He chuckled to himself and kept mumbling "Fricken Chicken."

He had that way of talking to himself like street people, but the campsite was organized and swept, much neater than hers. He smelled better than she would expect, too, not being near water, but she still wasn't going to spend the night. The sun had dipped below the trees, painting streaks of light and shadow across the camp. The dark would come fast. She asked for a ride back to the bus.

"Too bad you have to go. It's going to be the first cool night, a beauty—all the stars you could want. Plenty wishes waiting for you up there, little girl."

At the gravel road she asked him to let her out, afraid he would be hard to get rid of if she let him follow her to camp.

He looked into the pitch black woods. "You live back there?"

"Yeah. It's fine." She was wishing she had Rufus with her.

Buck turned off the ignition. "You're going to have to trust me." He got out and came around to her side of the truck and opened the door. He promised to do whatever she wanted, except to leave her on the road.

Once they started dragging the bike through the brush without a flashlight, she was glad for the company. Soon the weather would be getting cooler, and it might be nice to have someone to sit with around a fire. But now that she had a job, she wouldn't be staying there much longer.

Chapter 26: Sunny Lytle

She had dragged herself up at four-thirty in order to do all the feeding and walking, to make it to work by six-thirty. *Get used to it*, she told herself.

There was no sound in the weeds. "Woohoo, howdy-do! Good morning Mr. Alli Gator!" She kept up the chatter, not wanting to catch anyone off guard. She launched and paddled, waiting to dip her muddy feet quickly when she was well away from the bank. She was wearing her prettiest blouse, in case she saw Jason before she changed into a Sugar Mill shirt. She should be ashamed for trying to look good for him. Hadn't she learned her lesson with Bear? Apparently not, since she had called him again.

She went around back to the screen door as she had been told, stopping to pet a cat. She was a few minutes early. Light flowed from the kitchen into the parking area and the sounds of pans clinking and two women's voices sounded cheery. Meeting a few ladies—making friends—might be okay, as long as none of them got nosey.

She stepped inside and a woman turned and introduced herself. "I'm Patty, the proprietor." Her short hair glistened with red highlights under the florescent lights, and dangling glass earrings picked up the color. Her voice was chipper, her eyes round as a puppy's.

Sunny followed her across the kitchen to supplies, the dishwasher, convection ovens and a huge refrigerator, and she met a server named Ellen, who took her to a large metal table and demonstrated how to portion pecans. Sunny went to work scooping pieces and lining up small dishes on a tray. Easy work. She wondered when Jason would show up. She tried to concentrate on her job, but every time the door opened, she took a quick breath.

Patty brought out six new Sugar Mill T-shirts, and Sunny was headed toward the restroom with one when Jason walked past. He was tying on an apron, looking down. She couldn't control her smile.

Patty motioned, "Sunny, this is—"

His eyes caught hers and his face glowed.

"I guess you know each other."

Sunny was still grinning, paralyzed.

He blushed. "From high school."

Patty put her hand on Sunny's shoulder. "Okay, time to get to work. We've got a tour bus on the way."

Jason brushed past her, fingers touching her arm, and Sunny's gulp of air was audible. He turned back and grabbed her in a quick hug. "I forgot how much I missed you."

"Me too." It was a lie. She knew exactly how much. She wanted to curl up on his lap and live there.

"Talk later," he said.

She nodded. She didn't want to relive the past, her mistakes, but he deserved an explanation. She turned to follow Ellen into the dining room, re-imagining his hug.

The morning went fast with learning table names and the menu, racing to wipe up spills, and busing dishes. Her feet were pounding in the flip flops, but the pace was exciting, and atmosphere nicer than bars. No rude drunks. Before noon, she was already taking small tables of her own.

Jason flashed a smile when he zipped past her, and she tried to return it in a distracted way, but she knew she wasn't fooling him.

"Meet me outside for a break in ten minutes," he said.

Her heart jumped. He must have been keeping track of her tables to know that she had time.

She sat at the picnic table near the spring. Jason came out the side door and down the wooden steps, carrying a mug of coffee.

She wanted to escape and, at the same time, throw herself on him. She stood up. "My break's over."

He caught her hand as she tried to scoot from between the bench and table. "No, you don't. Sit down, Sunny. I saw you come outside less than a minute ago." He turned red, and she remembered how easily he blushed.

It was time to get it over with. "Okay."

He let go. She sat down and clamped her hands between her thighs.

"What was it?" he asked.

She squeezed out the words, "A boy."

"I heard. Just wanted to be sure." He smiled sadly and looked down, picking at a splinter on the edge of the table. "You gave him up."

"No choice."

He smacked the table the flat of his hand. "What the hell does that mean? I would've married you! You never gave me a chance. I didn't even know you were pregnant till you were gone."

She blinked and a tear rolled out. She told him how her aunt in Cincinnati offered to take her in and set up the adoption. "It was the only thing to do." There was more to it than that, but she couldn't sort it out herself, the old feelings, duty and regret.

"Your father's sister? I knew Lytle was behind this."

"I wanted to go. You were leaving for college, remember? You didn't want a baby."

"Yeah, well, I might have. –I only stayed one semester."

"Why? You were so excited." She remembered it clearly, the tests, paperwork, waiting for the letter, picking out a bedspread for his dorm room.

"I lost the scholarship—too much partying, old story."

She wondered if that was the real reason. Maybe he didn't want to leave DeLeon Springs after all, and her head was too messed up to see it.

"I deserved to know. You decided for both of us."

"One person has to decide." She covered her face with her hands and wiped her eyes. "I know. Now I know. I don't expect you to forgive me. I can't forgive myself." She sniffed and touched her wrist under her nose. She pointed to his hand with the wedding ring. "You're married. Everything's good." She swiped at her cheeks. "So that's that."

He let out his breath in a burst, and stood. "Yeah, that's that. If I'd known you'd come back, I would've waited—even this long. I asked your girlfriends, but nobody knew how to reach you—or they wouldn't tell me."

"Nobody was that close." Not as close as he was, she wanted to say.

"Me and your dad went at it one night at The Outpost. He wouldn't give me any information. Like you just disappeared."

Jason ran a hand over his hair. "I'm still in love with you, Sunny."

She struggled against the ache to reach for him. She wanted to brush her palm across his head, feel the thick, short hair, like fur. "Don't say that. Your wife wouldn't like it."

He put his hand over his mouth and it slid down his chin. "I won't say it again." He stepped over the bench with one leg. "You'll like my wife. Debbie. She'll be around on Thanksgiving."

Sonny could barely whisper. "Any kids?"

"No." As he moved away, he kicked over the bench and turned to set it back up. He looked into her eyes. "Just the one."

Chapter 27: Bear Hansen

Despite guilt and the fear that Marci was suspicious, freedom inspired a lead foot on the gas pedal of Bear's rebuilt '65 Mustang. He had decided to surprise Sunny and arrive at the Mini-Mart on Saturday instead of calling. He couldn't stand the thought of her skinny body going without a decent meal for several more days—not that she ever ate right—and since he got the idea into his head, he was feeling desperate to see her.

He had pretended his interest in going to Florida was for the Antique Car Show in Daytona with a friend. His buddy George invented travel details that Bear could never have managed, but Marci knew something was up ever since the Magic Bus had disappeared, and his depression was tough to hide.

He had abandoned most of his projects for dozing in front of the TV, left rotten pumpkins on the vines and the gutters packed full of leaves. With the first good freeze, ice would build up and crack the metal off of the eaves. He knew it. Marci knew it. She was not a nagger, but she had mentioned that he was smoking more weed and eating less at meals. His beer gut, nearly gone, proved it.

He wondered if she'd known about Sunny all along and either didn't care or wouldn't admit it to herself. Marci didn't have time for him anyhow. She worked at the hospital all day, exercised at the gym in the evening, and volunteered at hospice most weekends. They only saw each other for a few dinners per week, and she went to bed early. He couldn't remember the last time they had sex or when the intervals in between got long. He thought about the first time he laid eyes on Marci's dimples and freckled cleavage—and a waist he could put his hands around. She was still the most attractive woman his age that he knew. It wasn't a lack of passion on his part that had put space between them.

He usually ended up staying late at Sunny's apartment at least once a week, pretending to be at the bar, and a few times he had fallen asleep and didn't sneak in until dawn. He was sure Marci was awake, but she never questioned him. Besides that, there was all the dog hair and cat fur adhered to his clothes. He tried to brush it off before he went inside, but it was impossible. He took up the chore of vacuuming after Marci commented that the canister was full of fur. Coarse black German shepherd hairs and fluff from dogs' undercoats and cats. He told her he'd been wrestling with George's Doberman, but Marci wasn't blind—or stupid—probably just couldn't put clumps of fur together with the idea of his having an affair. Or didn't care enough to wonder. Before she had time to contemplate specific hairs, he had adopted Kelly, a black lab mix with a streak of white on her chest, and now they had plenty fur of their own rolling around in the corners.

He hated lying to Marci, but Sunny had sounded desperate. He hoped to convince her to come back to Louisville and get another apartment. He could pay first and last month rent. It wasn't so much the sex—he was worried about the girl.

He cut west off I-95 through Ormond Beach and headed south to DeLeon Springs, passing by countless acres of forest and small county roads where Sunny might have taken the camper. It was nearly dark, and she would be alone back there, in the tangle of trees where nobody could see or hear.

At first sight, DeLeon Springs wasn't much of a town. Where was the spring with barking otters . . . and turtles lined up with their backs shining like silver? Manatees and alligators? The legendary Fountain of Youth?—that's what he needed most.

He passed the Mini-Mart, noting its location, and kept driving south on U.S. 17. Used furniture, beauty shop, Dollar General, ice cream store, gas stations, a hardware store/

Laundromat combination. Small businesses and strip malls. Spring Waters Inn. Pretty place and right on the highway. He was beat.

He carried in his suitcase and switched on the TV. He had put off talking to Marci because he felt guilty. He told her he had trouble getting a signal earlier and now was having a beer with George. "We'll be spending the day tomorrow at the car show. I'm not sure the phone will ring."

She didn't question any of it. Their daughter and grandson had joined her for lasagna, since the son-in-law had to work late. Bear's mouth watered thinking of the gooey cheese and rich, meaty tomato sauce. The conversation seemed too short, so he detailed the perils of traffic in Atlanta and construction and rain through Jacksonville.

"Be careful—and go easy on the beer," she told him.

It was her standard line, and he had the feeling she was reading e-mail during their conversation. After he hung up, he felt worse about the lies, but went straight to bed, tired enough to put everything out of his mind.

He woke up early, refreshed and excited about surprising Sunny. He took a shower and put on clean clothes and combed his beard. He was starved. He remembered that Sunny had raved about the best pancakes in the world in a restaurant in a park. He figured there would be bacon and eggs, too, although the girl never mentioned them since she wouldn't touch the stuff. The desk clerk told him it was only about a mile down the road, the Old Sugar Mill Pancake House. He followed the directions and arrived at the park entrance to find a long line of cars. The sign said it cost five dollars per car, just to get inside. He was going to hand it over until he saw another sign saying that the wait was an hour and a half. *Hell, no!* He'd seen a Denny's little bit south. Who would pay to make their own pancakes and wait hours to do it? Lots of people apparently.

He was waiting inside the Mini-Mart by quarter to twelve, but at one o'clock Sunny still hadn't shown. He hung around, reading labels for an hour, and questioned the guy at the register three different times, until asked to leave. He bought a magazine and sat the rest of the afternoon in the car, listening to the radio and burning gas to run the AC. Just in case she had gotten her days mixed up, he spent half the day Sunday. In the afternoon he drank some beers and watched football, and called the two nearest hospitals. If she was sick or hurt in the woods, nobody could find her. He should have never let her take the bus with such a crazy plan.

Monday morning he started to doubt himself. It was stupid to drive all the way to Florida without getting directions. She was probably fine, got a job and decided not to bother him. But after such a long trip, he wasn't giving up. That afternoon he headed down the highway, stopping for beers at likely bars where she might work, but no luck. People didn't want to answer his questions either—probably thought he was a dirty old man when he described her.

He passed Quality Taxidermy. Nope. Although, he could picture Sunny latching onto a stuffed skunk or raccoon—she loved the smell of skunk. In fact, she loved animals so much, he sometimes wondered if she kept any in the freezer. He had never investigated.

He saw a veterinary office, but Sunny had no training and had never worked at any type of animal facility. Too horrified about the pain and death, he figured. DeLeon Springs itself was mainly on 17, but there were probably a hundred retail stores stretching the eight miles to Deland. Family Dollar, hardware, groceries, feed stores, strip malls full of rinky-dink shops, and a Super-Walmart—a long bike ride, but he knew Sunny could do eight miles if she had to.

In his limited time, it was impossible to check all those places. Bars were the best bet, and there were plenty more to keep him busy, especially since he felt obligated to order a beer each time.

He woke up with a hangover on Tuesday, sun glaring through his eyelids. He dragged himself to the window to make sure the car was outside. He'd told Marci he would be home for Thanksgiving, but that was only two days away and would mean leaving with nothing accomplished. He'd missed one Thanksgiving in the last forty years, on a hunting trip when the roads were covered with snow—this one would be tougher to explain.

Chapter 28: Rita McKenna

She felt energized by the cooler, drier air of her first cold front in DeLeon Springs. Temperatures in the eighties and high humidity in November were not unusual according to the locals, but she had given up on ever feeling comfortable again. Now without fear of working up a sweat, she happily began a full morning of cleaning ears, clipping nails, and expressing anal glands.

She put the last pooch back in his pen at one o'clock and washed her hands to take a lunch break. As she set a cup of vegetable soup into the microwave, the outside door opened in the next room.

"Is Rita in today?" It was Sunny.

"Yes, but I think she's busy," Jackie said.

Rita stuck her head into the office. "I'm having lunch. Want to join me?" She motioned the girl into the lunch room.

"I came to find out about the raccoon."

"Oh." Rita had forgotten it. "Sunny, sorry. He was set free. I know I told you I'd bring him back, but he healed fast and the Wildlife Rescue people released him without telling me."

"You promised."

"I did mean to bring him back to his territory." She tried to touch Sunny's shoulder, but she dodged the contact. "He'll find friends. Don't worry. They said he scampered off like brand new." Rita tried to break the grim mood. "It's nice of you to visit."

Sunny explained that she had gotten the job at the Sugar Mill and this was her first day off.

Rita pulled out the cup of soup. "Let's celebrate! I have more in the fridge. It's homemade Veg Head Chili from the Food Network. Yum-o."

"Already ate." Sunny sat down.

Rita sensed repulsion. The girl probably disdained beans. Rita suggested that Sunny stop by her apartment later to meet her two new Siamese kittens.

There was a flicker of a change. "Sure."

She finished her soup and put Sunny to work brushing dogs. It was a start.

When they pulled up at the apartment, Sunny looked at the pool. "I wish I had my bathing suit."

Rita warned her that the nights had been cool. "The water isn't heated, probably pretty chilly."

"I used to swim in the spring year round, and it's always seventy-two."

Rita carried the kittens from the bedroom and dropped them on Sunny's lap, then found shorts with a draw string and a T-shirt that had shrunk. The kittens played, swatting each other and bounding over Sunny.

Rita came out of the shower and found the kittens alone. She went to the window. Sunny was standing in the shallow end, doing something with her hands on the surface of the water. Every rib was visible through the T-shirt, and with her tiny breasts she looked more like a twelve-year-old than a woman in her twenties. She had a little muscle. She was picking tiny leaves or something from the water and putting them on the concrete.

Rita set out some bread to defrost. She figured Sunny would stay for dinner, and there was still more chili, or grilled cheese. She played with the kittens and turned on the TV to catch the news, and when it was over, put the chili in a pot, made the sandwiches, and set the table. She sat down with a book in her lap and looked out the window. Sunny was still in the pool.

Hoarder was such a pejorative term for a person sacrificing her own needs and struggling to care for animals that no one else wanted, but it was the word the county used, and the newspapers. Then again, some of those animals would never have been conceived if Sunny exercised good judgment. There had to be some way to reach her. Living by herself in the woods was dangerous. Rita looked out at the pool again. The girl had to be frozen. What was she doing?

Rita took a beach towel and went out. She could see Sunny shivering from twenty yards away.

"What are you doing? You're a popsicle."

"Almost done. There were all these beetles floating on their backs—" She paused to wipe her nose. "Most of them were still alive, but they couldn't get out." She placed one gently, belly side down, on the edge. Its thin brown legs took hold and it limped away. "I rescued some bees too. I was afraid they'd sting, but they just crawled up my arm until they got their bearings. Some of them dried their fuzzy faces with their arms, just like a cat bathing. I never realized how cute bees can be."

Rita showed her the fluffy towel.

Sunny held up one finger, then moved to a last scrambling bug, putting the flat of her hand under the beetle until it fastened on, then raising it out of the water to deposit it on the side. "Bees have a social system just like ours. I don't know what kind of system beetles have." Her teeth chattered and goose bumps stood up on her arms.

Rita shook her head. "I don't know either. Come on out. You're going to get sick."

"You sound like my mom—I mean like a mom. I don't really know how mine sounds." Sunny walked up the steps, her lips almost as blue as her eyes, and her fingers shriveled, but her face all smiles. "I never did get to swim, but that's okay. I can swim at the spring if I ever get time."

Rita gave her the beach towel. "Get right into the shower and warm up, while I heat the chili."

"No chili for—"

"Just taste it. I'm not taking no for an answer."

"Okay, *Mom*."

She held the door to follow Sunny inside.

The grilled cheese was keeping warm in the oven when Sunny came out with her hair combed back and face shining.

"I forgot how nice a hot shower feels. My hair is actually clean."

Rita told her she was welcome at any time.

Sunny grinned. "I might take you up on that when it gets down into the forties."

"I wouldn't mind if you slept here till you got enough pay checks to rent an apartment." She knew that could be forever, unless she did something to help.

"I feel guilty as it is, leaving the animals while I'm at work."

Rita tried to put it out of her mind, the dogs tied to the bus. She served up the grilled cheese and a half cup of chili. "Pure vegetarian. I don't eat meat, only seafood." She waited for Sunny to try it, but the girl stared into the bowl as if counting the beans. "Mama Rita says eat."

Finally, Sunny put a spoonful into her mouth and swallowed it, seemingly straight down.

Rita held back her comment on the need for chewing and rested her elbows on the table. "What if we took a few of the fur family to the shelter, a few puppies? It's so crowded in the bus. I would be there to give them plenty of attention and the best treatment. You could visit whenever you wanted, and I would make sure the right people adopted them." From Sunny's look, Rita knew she had gone too far.

Sunny put down the half of grilled cheese that she'd started to nibble. "No. Sorry." She pushed her chair out. "Thanks for the dinner. I'll take the grilled cheese with me so it isn't wasted."

Rita reached for her hand and held it. "I'm not going to kidnap any of your children. I'm offering to help. You must be having a terrible time keeping them all fed and clean."

"It's not fair to them—that's what you're saying, like people always say. You don't understand. They're family. You don't give up family when money gets short."

"Okay, enough said. You can come here any time you want. I won't do anything against your will. I promise. I was just giving you an option."

"I've heard it all before."

"I like you, Sunny, and I also care very much about animals. You have to admit I must know a few things, being a vet."

"You're not a vet anymore." Sunny gasped, as if trying to inhale the words. "I'm sorry!"

Rita drank her tea. The girl was striking out in fear. Her belief system was anchored in distrust of authority. "How's your chili?"

Sunny sat back down and picked up her sandwich. "I am sorry. That was mean."

"Apology accepted."

Sunny turned the bread around, picking at the cheese that had oozed between the toasted slices. She pointed at the chili. "Wonder how those beans felt when they were ripped out of their skins."

Rita looked into her bowl to keep from rolling her eyes. "Is that why you don't chew? To lessen the pain? That makes no sense."

"I know. I just feel better not chewing."

"Sunny, I have years of education in animal physiology and chemistry, and some botany. I can tell you that beans don't have a nervous system. They can't experience feeling of any kind."

"Plants react to light and music—they must sense things."

Rita rested her chin on her hand and looked over the rims of her glasses. "This will interest you—in Switzerland there's a law protecting all creatures, including the rights of plants being prepared for eating, to preserve their dignity."

"We need laws like that."

"I interpret it as not wasting." Rita took a bite of chili and chewed well to demonstrate normal mastication. "A university in the U.K. has succeeded in producing hamburger from cow stem cells, so there's that to look forward to—less cows killed, less environmental impact. But you can't wait till that's available. Just eat some beans. Please?"

Sunny scooped a spoonful of chili into her mouth, chewed a couple of times, and swallowed. "There. Just for you." She took a drink of water. "I take vitamins with iron and I eat cheese."

Rita asked if Sunny got her period.

"I'm not pregnant."

"I didn't mean that."

"The less I need tampons, the better."

Rita was afraid to start another confrontation. If the girl wasn't anorexic, she was hovering close. She must be chronically constipated and probably found that convenient as well. Something had to be done. Psychotropic medication might be required.

Chapter 29: Sunny Lytle

The temperature felt like low fifties and she was paddling against the wind. A gator lay on the bank near the restaurant, the sun turning his reptilian armor to silver. Poor guy, a gatorsicle trying to thaw.

The thick scent of bacon captured her. It was part of the personality of the restaurant and she connected it to Sunday breakfasts of her childhood more than to pigs. Her mother holding the spatula, spattering the frying eggs with grease.

Ground fog hovered between the trees, and frost spangled the grass. The two eighty-year-old ladies who swam every day, no matter the temperature, disappeared into a mist of condensation as they rounded the end of the spring.

All morning, customers wore their coats and warmed their hands over the griddles. The Sugar Mill was draughty with no heat, except for the fireplace in the far room, but regardless, holiday spirits brought in the crowds, including busloads of tourists. There were rows of smiles when she brought the fresh orange juice, dishes of condiments, and pitchers of batter.

On her break, she went outside and hung her arms and shoulders over the wood fence surrounding antique mill parts, trying to take some weight off her sore feet. This was where the other servers came to smoke, and she could see why. It was on the side opposite the entrance and away from the crowds. Protected from the wind, it was warmer out there in the sun than inside the restaurant.

Worries seeped like water into her spare moments. Tips were good with the tourist buses and lines of people on the weekends, but needs were increasing. Brindle's puppies were now eating kibble, and Ginger had just given birth. Spot looked to be with kittens. They were all going to need shots. Although Rita seemed a good friend, she had to be kept from seeing the babies and pregnancies. People couldn't be trusted when they thought they were right.

She leaned against the warm wood rails and chuckled, remembering how pink Jason's cheeks had turned when he ran into her with two pitchers of batter that morning.

Just then, strong arms went around her shoulders. "Jason! You scared me." It was like she had called him up with her thoughts.

His head pressed against her ear and she smelled ivory soap. "Sorry, you looked like you needed a backwards hug."

She squirmed and faced him. "I don't think—"

He grabbed her in a bear hug and she pressed against him. He whispered in her ear, "See how good that feels. You always liked my hugs."

It took a few seconds for her to pull away. "There were lots of things I liked . . ."

"Liked? In the past?" He tugged her braid, then dropped his arms.

She stepped back, away from temptation. "I don't think about what I like anymore. I work and take care of my family." She put her finger to her lips.

"Tell me more about your fur family."

She had already told him the names of all the dogs, but it was a lot to remember. She recited them down the line and inside the bus, then named the cats, ferrets, and rabbits.

His grin got wider. "You haven't changed a bit, have you?"

She asked if he had any suggestions for puppy names, keeping the conversation light to enjoy him without guilt.

"I'd need to see them. When can I stop by?"

She could never trust herself alone with him. "Soon. I'll let you know."

He took a pack of cigarettes out of his shirt pocket and lit one. "My wife's a lot older than me, you know. She doesn't like to camp out or hike."

She hung her arms back over the fence and turned to the lake. "Camping isn't exactly my choice either."

"It used to be. I miss it—and the swimming and fishing . . . canoeing. Deb and me don't have a lot of activities in common."

"None of my business."

"She's kind of a workaholic—which is helpful, considering my take-home doesn't . . ."

"It's a good job."

He talked along the edges of what was appropriate, pretending to lay out facts, but it was all a con, a sweet con. His warmth crept around her, making her want to tilt her mouth to his, and keep on going.

"Yeah, I enjoy it, but it's not a career, no possibilities for promotion."

It was the highlight of her day, but she couldn't let it go further. She craned her neck to look far down the lake, as if something had caught her attention. There was nothing, but they were off in that direction, the fur family, hoping, waiting, always waiting for her, waiting, waiting . . .

Chapter 30: Pancho

Pancho awoke cold, his two-legger gone again, the bus surrounded by exotic scents. He scratched at the double doors, reeling a whine from his throat into the woods, hesitating, slashing it out again. He pawed, attempting to widen the crack between doors enough to squeeze through, despite cold air that chilled his bare back and made him shiver. His legs were jittery, needing a run. He craved clean air, sniffing space not thick as mud, freedom to explore.

He scratched for a long time, gave up without a change of attitude. He made the rounds, sniffing empty bowls, every part of him irritated, legs, stomach, skin. He craved a skin touch from the two-legger, a scratch behind the ears and down the back, the hard kind that he could lean into.

The other dogs inside were restless, too, making him nervous, their bodies full of energy, some licking and chewing on themselves, digging for ticks and fleas. Dissatisfaction and discomfort, feelings of rebellion.

He clicked across the hard floor of the bus, long nails pushing his pads into unnatural angles. When he slunk into the bed against Angel, she jumped to her feet and nipped his ear. He cowed in front of her trying to nestle, but she growled, unhappy with being disturbed. She had problems of her own, tangles and mats creating dens for fleas, spiny burrs caught in the scruff of her neck where she couldn't reach. He could rip them out with his teeth, but she stood tense, neck fur rising to give final warning that he should vacate the round cushion, even though it would fit them both. He yielded to her posture and crossed the bus, past the two crates of ferrets and rabbits. A round bean had rolled through the grate from the rabbits and he licked it up, crunching with his back teeth and swallowing in bliss.

He needed the mountain of muscle and fur, Rufus. Lying against Rufus' underbelly, how comfortable it would be, but the mountain was outside. He turned two circles and dropped to the floor. He slurped at his front legs, tasting rain and greens from the morning walk and the mingled molecules of strange scent. A rear leg, felt movement and itch under the patch of fur on his ankle. He licked it moist, curled back his lips to mine the spot, the edge of his teeth ñen-ñenning in silent vibration hard against the bone. He dug again, uncovered treasure, three black tidbits. They burst and released tangy juice on his tongue. Movement had stopped. He sat back and licked his testicles.

Chapter 31: Jason Cox

The kitchen was warm and smelled spicy sweet from cooking the apple filling. Jason used his fingers to work the brown sugar, flour, cinnamon and nuts into a topping. Massaged them in lovingly. Took his time. He'd spent most of the morning peeling apples and making homemade crusts, so he would have one pie to take for the Sugar Mill party and one to keep. His bottom crust was legendary, flaky and crisp, just like his mother's. Later he might get Deb to relax for five minutes with warm pie and ice cream.

Sunny had no idea that he'd become an excellent baker over the years. She was invited to help serve and clean up for the big party, and that included time to eat. He would make sure she tasted his pie.

Deb would meet Sunny for the first time. They had a lot in common when it came to animals, but he was nervous. Deb had mentioned how his mood had improved in the mornings getting ready for work. He got her implication. She had asked more than once how Sunny was doing as a waitress and noticed how distracted he seemed. He'd been thinking about the baby, his boy.

Sunny had made it clear that there would be nothing between them, and he didn't want anything like that, not really. He fantasized the impossible, to have both lives without any shame, to confide in Sunny, like in the old days before everything went wrong. Even that was crossing a line, since he had never been as close to Deb. He wasn't capable of making her understand most of the problems in his life, or his feelings.

He put the pie into the oven and walked back to her office where she was clicking away at the keyboard. Weenie dogs were spread out on dog beds and under the desk. He squatted to stroke the nearest smooth brown head, Buddy. "Pie's baking." Buddy lifted his nose and licked Jason's chin. Jason watched Deb type. "You going to finish that report in time to go?" His voice didn't sound as hopeful as he wanted.

She flipped the screen to a medical journal article on high blood pressure, copied a phrase, and clicked back to her report. "I'll be up half the night tonight, but I wouldn't miss the party."

"Good. I mean, sorry you'll be up late, but you gotta eat, right? We don't have to stay long. I'm not on clean-up."

She typed and paused. "No extra money this year?"

He had made the wrong choice, as usual. "I thought you'd like me to sit with you, instead of running back and forth to the kitchen. It's not like we're starv—"

She held up her hand. "I don't have time." She flipped the screen back to the article. "If the drug companies are forced to cut profits, there won't be any new drugs developed for me to research. I have to make the money while I can. We could never live on—"

"I know, I know. I'm going to finish school . . ." She was typing briskly. He patted Buddy's butt, gave Grouper and Wootsie a pet, and went back to the kitchen to check his pies.

Chapter 32: Sunny Lytle

The restaurant was closed for Patty's traditional Thanksgiving party of a hundred or more good friends and important people. Being asked to work the afternoon was considered special, but Sunny figured that most people would rather stay home with their families. Fine with her. Just for loading the dishwasher, wrapping up leftovers and sweeping, she would get hourly pay, anything she wanted to eat, and maybe some scraps to take home.

She walked into the dining room unprepared for the quantity of foods. Tables were pushed end to end forming two long buffets, loaded down with vegetable casseroles, salads, dressing, trays of turkey, pots of mashed potatoes and bowls of gravy. Oval table by the window was covered with apple, pumpkin, pecan, and key lime pies, brownies, and orange crème brûleé in dark chocolate cups. She'd been told that Patty made the cups by dipping balloons in melted chocolate and popping them after the chocolate hardened. So much attention to food.

She was setting out paper plates and silverware when Jason came in, holding the door for his wife. She was at least ten years older. He took her hand as they approached. "Debbie, this is Sunny, the new waitress I told you about, my high school friend."

Debbie was thin and pretty, with short, stylish hair and gold dachshund earrings. She wore a holiday sweater with dachshunds sporting bows. "Nice to meet you, Sunny."

"You too." She thought about her messy braid and the stain on her blue thrift-shop sweater. Normally, she didn't care. Debbie seemed a little cool, but it might only have been Sunny's expectation. The fact that Debbie knew nothing about the past made her feel secretive, yet she couldn't stand there and admit that they had spent many nights in a tent going crazy or, for god's sake, that she had given birth to his baby.

"Deb fosters dachshunds," Jason said. "She feeds them, trains them, and gets them healthy, then finds them a good home.

Sometimes we have five or six dogs around the house—a regular Weenieville."

Sunny tried to speak through her tight throat. "You give the dogs away? How can you stand it?"

Jason nodded. "It's sad, especially when we've made them happy for the first time in their lives."

Debbie shot him a look, and Sunny wondered if she had touched off an old argument.

Debbie's voice was soft. "It's hard, but we know from the start that our job is to prepare them for their real home." She was looking straight into Sunny's eyes, trying to win her over, but it was hard to listen. "They're advertised on the Internet, and when a good spot comes along, we let them go—for their own benefit."

"There are never enough people to adopt though," Jason said.

"I limit myself to the weenies," Deb told her, "but there are so many other breeds, and cats, available online. Especially cats."

Sunny said that she could probably take a few.

"Really?" Debbie pulled a card from her purse, wrote on it, and handed it over.

Sunny looked at the Internet address on the back, petfinder.com, and turned it over, reading Debbie Cox, Medical Writer, with the home phone number and email. Debbie had a high-powered career, for sure. Not the kind of lady she'd pictured for Jason. She put the card into her jeans pocket, saying she would go to the library and check out the site. "Can I call you here?" Debbie said.

"Sure." It flew through Sunny's mind that she already had many cats cramped in with the small dogs and new puppies, but the visions of more furry faces with round bright eyes replaced worry. They needed her. She could always squeeze in a few more, especially in cold weather.

Debbie said something to Jason that Sunny missed. He blushed.

Sunny stepped away. "Thanks. I'd better go. Barbara probably needs me to bring out utensils."

She was breathing hard when she got to the kitchen. It wasn't right. She had to get over him if she planned to stay in DeLeon.

Patty's boyfriend was carving another turkey. Sunny turned back to the sink area so she wouldn't see the seared, headless bodies and naked triangular tails. The goose-bumped tails really got to her, so vulnerable. She reached into the sink for a blackened roaster pan, concentrated on the scrubbing.

When she went back to the dining room, many people were lined up and others already eating. She caught a glimpse of the far room through the glass partition, Jason laughing with his wife.

She joined the line at the vegetable end of one table and made herself a plate with small spoonfuls of mashed potatoes, stuffing, corn pudding, and sweet potato casserole. The crunchy brown sugar crust had her mouth watering. When she came to the meat platters, her eyes riveted to the piles of steaming, glistening flesh. Her throat tightened. She looked around for empty space to sit by herself.

A tap on her shoulder . . . Barbara was behind her in line. "See the girls at right-corner-main?" One of the teenagers smiled and waved as Barbara pointed them out. "Those are my daughters, Rachel and Katie. Come and join us."

She carried her plate to the table and Barbara introduced her. Sunny listened to their cheerful talk of food, their beagle, and the upcoming holiday party. She tried to stop dwelling on slaughter. She mentioned having two huge shepherds, Rufus and Schmeisser, and Barbara said she would round up some turkey skin and scraps.

It was so confusing. She couldn't blame the fur family for wanting meat, or even Barbara and the girls. They didn't mean harm to anyone or anything, loved their crazy beagle and all the wildlife in the park, yet socked away turkey with pleasure.

Chapter 33: Buckaroo

Buck was forced to lie on his back for cloud duty half the day. The thick purple slabs with a low defined edge were the kind that spawned tornadoes, but he didn't spot any funnel tails. Nevertheless, he had enough trouble. The Magnetoids could hole up under the thick cold cover, sleeping like babes, yet pop him in an instant if he let his guard down.

He spent a lot of the time thinking about Sunny. On his last visit, she seemed to enjoy his company. He had carved her a bear cub, brought it to the restaurant, and after he swore the wood was dead long before he took a knife to it, she had accepted his gift. She allowed him to follow her to the camp to place the bear in an honorary spot on the orange crate. They'd eaten and talked until dark, before she sent him back to his place. He probably could have gotten farther if she didn't have all those animals to take care of, but he liked her enough to bide his time. So not to spook her, he'd held off visiting for a few days, but he planned a trip to her camp in the afternoon if he could ever get out from under the threat.

The ice held up longer in the cool weather, but there wasn't much left, and he needed beer. He'd been getting supplies from the Mini-Mart, but it was time to borrow the truck to do a full-scale shopping. He'd pick up some sacks of dog and cat food and some cream and cheese to take to Sunny. She was looking a little healthier the last time he saw her, and even ate some Campbell's vegetable soup, but he knew she liked dairy products best, and they were hard to keep.

Before noon, the clouds passed on, headed south, and he was able to put away his Sugar Mill pan, get the last beer from the cooler, and boil a couple of dogs. He wondered if those guys up there were smart enough to starve him to death or make him die of thirst.

Geordie agreed to let him take the truck and keep it till morning, and Buck's plans became more elaborate. He shopped and dropped his groceries off first. He packed two coolers with beer, ice, and water, and sorted through the bags to put Sunny's stuff together. He'd picked up vitamins and honey, as well as the dairy goods and the angel hair, and the green can of "shake cheese" she'd requested. He piled some of his stash of dry firewood in the back of the truck. Sunny's would be damp if she had any, and this night would require a fire. The air was cold, even with the bright sun.

He rolled his sleeping bag and put it on the floor of the passenger side. If he could convince her to rub skin with him, he couldn't do it in the bus. He'd never get an erection amidst the steaming dog breath and cat pee. He tried to think of a reason why he could say he brought the sleeping bag, but there was nothing she would believe. He'd just wait till he had her hot enough not to ask questions, just get next to her and pull the shorts off her slim hips. A partial woody nosed the seam of his jeans.

He arrived at the gravel road by mid-afternoon as planned, while Sunny was gone, and got to work, to surprise her by having all the chores done. He pulled the truck off the path into the stand of feathery pines, so it would be hidden if he was still there after dark.

He started off with a heavy armload of wood, hoping to find the camp without a misstep. After a few feet into the trees, barking and growling indicated exactly what direction to go. He guessed they wanted to gnaw off his arms and legs, but as he came out of the bushes, most of them wagged and strained at their leashes. Their memories were better than his. He couldn't remember any names and didn't recognize five of the young ones. Since they looked related, he figured they were the puppies that had graduated out of the bus. The Chihuahua with big balls tried to stare him down from the bus window, a growl running through his stiff pinkish body. Buck made a barking sound and stamped his foot, but the little rat didn't react. "Gator bait. That's you," he told him, but he admired the little squirt's psychological *cojones* that matched the size of his real ones. He took the dogs on short walks, three or four at a time, saving the little guy for the last group. The dog was smart enough to go along without a fuss.

Buck had watched Sunny give fresh water and a bowl of dry food to each, and he followed the routine, amazed how fast they gulped, barely chewing. The bus was full of puppies, cats, and kittens. He fed and watered them, wondering if ammonia could make you high, like ether or glue. Wishful thinking.

He drank half a beer, then got the shovel and dug a hole for the crap. There was barely any ground that hadn't been turned recently. He wondered how Sunny could keep up, and work all day besides. He finished the beer and made more trips to the truck for armloads of wood, built a fire and piled the extra wood nearby. After being on her feet all day, Sunny would appreciate a good foot rub by the fire, and that was only for starters.

He sat down to work on his carving, keeping his backpack close by, so he could hide his work fast. He was about half-finished with Sunny's Christmas present, a nativity set with all the farm animals and camels.

When he tired of carving and picked some white blossoms and ferns, and put them in the beer bottle with water to set next to the bear cub. As soon as he set the bottle down, he remembered Sunny's feelings about hurting plants and tossed them into the weeds. The dogs heard her coming just then, and he sat down on the lounge chair enduring the frantic barking, eager to see her smile. Judging by the dogs' postures, she was headed in from the road.

She waved the last palm frond aside and moved into the clearing. "Buck! Hi!"

A muscular young guy stepped out from behind her.

Buck grinned at Sunny, but his stomach went hollow.

"Buckaroo, this is Jason Cox, a co-worker." She explained that she knew him from high school.

The guy looked familiar. Buck stuck out his hand. *Jason Cocksucker*. "Hey, there, Jason. Buccaneer's the name."

Sunny wrinkled her lip. "Buccaneer?"

Buck's hand was filthy, but Jason gave a firm shake, although he didn't look happy.

The dogs tied near the bus whined and wiggled to get Sunny's attention, and she went to them and started stroking heads and rubbing behind ears. "You already fed the furs? And scooped poop? That's so nice, Buck."

Buck nodded. "And built a fire and watered."

She moved down the line of dogs, naming them for Jason, as he followed, giving each dog a quick back scratch.

"Jeez, Buck. You brought wood, too." She pointed at the brown bags he'd set on her cooler. "And groceries!"

"Yeah, I had the truck all day. I knew you'd need some humungous bags of chow and stuff."

Sunny opened the bus door and went inside where he'd put the sacks. "Buck, you're the best!"

Jason had followed Sunny around the side of the bus, and Buck wondered how he liked the smell of cats. He hoped not well. "I thought I'd boil up some angel hair. I got the cheese you like."

Sunny came around the bus, her lips clamped.

Buck had no choice. "There's enough for Jason too. Want a beer, Jason?" He pointed to the cooler next to his chair.

Jason refused the beer, but handed a water to Sunny.

"Sorry, Buck," she said. "I can't stay." She told him about a plan for Jason to drive her to Rita's for a hot shower and a night on the couch. "You know, the vet? I just stopped by to take care of the animals." She beamed. "But you already did everything. And even made a fire." She moved close and gave him a hug and a kiss on the cheek. "That was so sweet of you."

Buck unclenched his teeth. "I can give you a ride to Rita's. Jason won't have to go out of his way."

Jason came to life, waving his hand. "No. No. I don't mind. Sunny and I have plenty to catch up on."

Exactly what Buck was worried about.

Sunny looked at Jason and back at Buck. "That's a good idea." She turned to Jason. "Then you won't be late for dinner."

Buck glanced at Jason's ring finger and broke into a grin, then a low chuckle.

Jason was pleading. "I told you, it'll be fine. Don't worry."

"No, really. I might want to ask you for a ride again sometime. No sense overdoing it."

"Any time." Jason moved in fast and gave her a hug. It was friendly, but smooth, like he knew exactly where his parts fit over her skinny bones—*Papa Bear mauling Goldilocks.* Buck sensed that Sunny was uncomfortable. Was it because she didn't want the hug or because she didn't like him watching?

When Jason left, Sunny pulled a wad of bills out of her pocket and stuck it in Buck's hand. "I know it's not anywhere enough, but I can start paying you back. Tips are good."

He argued for her to keep the money, getting a little feel of her right butt cheek when he missed trying to slide it into her back pocket.

"I owe you too much," she kept saying.

He knew better than to suggest the other way to pay him back. "All right, but you have to sit down and talk to me for a few minutes while I drink my beer."

She had no problem with that, and he found out that she and Jason had been sweethearts in high school. At least now there wasn't any real competition—he hoped.

Chapter 34: Rita McKenna

She was relieved when she heard Sunny's knock. She couldn't help worrying about the girl. She was still torn about what she should do. She had decided to let it go until after Christmas. As they became closer friends and Sunny got tired of living in the woods, surely something could be worked out. She led Sunny to the kitchen to meet John, explaining that they were going out for dinner, but there was plenty of food in the refrigerator, and the kittens would love company.

"John lives in Orlando. He supplies cars for films, so he knows movie stars." Rita wondered if Sunny had been to a movie theater in her adult life, considering her self-imposed deprivation.

John put out his hand, dwarfing Sunny's thin pale fingers. "I'm here for the car show this weekend."

"What do you do at the show?"

"Admire cars, sometimes buy them for my job—or myself," John said. He explained that he was building a race car from a 1908 La France fire car that he bought in Daytona. "It's in pieces in my garage, and I need some accessories for it."

"Fire car?" Sunny was more interested than Rita would have expected.

"Made for the fire chief with a 900 cubic inch, four-cylinder engine, so it would run like hell. Of course, it didn't run at all when I got it."

"Did they have fire dogs back then?"

Rita laughed.

"Don't know. We could Google it."

Rita explained to John that Sunny would be spending the night, then brought out a plate of cheese. "Hors d'oeuvres?"

"I hope I'm not in the way," Sunny said.

Rita opened a box of crackers. "It's a party."

John cut a chunk of blue. "I know Patty, your boss. Great place, the Sugar Mill. That's where I met Rita. My lucky day."

"Not much to do with luck," Rita said.

"Magic?" He gave her a wink and turned to Sunny. "Patty is a car aficionado, too. She has a Citroen 2 CV and just finished restoring a 1961 Panhard Tigre. Just saw it at the McDonald's, Friday night."

"People with their fancy cars eat at McDonald's?" Rita asked.

"Antiques. It's kind of a hangout."

"A Tigre?" asked Sunny.

"Yeah. It has original animal print sections of leather in the interior." He finished off a last swig of wine. "Daytona is the place to be if you like cars and motorcycles."

Rita checked her watch. She finished her wine and pointed Sunny toward the refrigerator. "Help yourself. Everything in there is safe to eat. Promise."

Sunny was looking out at the pool.

"It's too windy and cold for beetle rescue."

"Maybe I could scoop them from the side."

Rita shook her head. "You can't save the world, Sunny. Stay healthy and maybe you can save a little bit of it." She knew the feeling, always trying to make a difference. Acceptance should come with maturity, but she hadn't yet reached that level herself.

Rita sat next to John in a candle-lit corner booth with a lace tablecloth and embroidered linen napkins. He had insisted on ordering two wines, sauvignon blanc for the stone crab appetizers and her lobster, and pinot noir for his prime rib. She swallowed another mouthful of wine from the expensive bottle and felt the glow seep through her chest. It was her second glass of white, on top of the Shiraz at her apartment. This was far better stuff than she could afford, and even tipsy she could tell the difference. He was trying to spoil her, and she was uncomfortable with the prices, but hadn't been able to talk him into anything cheaper. It was their first date after several hours on the phone, and days before, he had already sent her a huge tropical arrangement of fuscia and yellow bromeliads, an orange helliconia, and palm fronds that fanned out higher than her head when she placed it on the kitchen table.

He had suggested a four-star steakhouse in Orlando, but she had declined, saying she didn't eat beef and would rather go to

Karling's, if he wanted fine dining. Choosing the steakhouse would have involved making the decision before dinner as to whether or not to sleep with him, since his place was in Orlando, a fifty-minute trip, and she would have had to drive her own car. Now, she wondered why she had hesitated to let him pick her up. She should have let him sweep her away for the night. It was perfect with Sunny there to feed the kittens and a day off tomorrow. Her head continued the argument with her body, but she knew that the heat between her legs would win.

John seemed older than she, had the ruddy coloring of high blood pressure and carried extra weight around the middle, but he was sturdy and strong, warm and huggable. His decisiveness had attracted her, and his energy and humor kept her intrigued.

He pulled a tender white chunk of crab from the shell, dipped its edge in the light mustard sauce and raised it to her lips. It was nutty and buttery with a soft tang. She chewed slowly, feeling the texture on her tongue, enjoying the luxury. She chased the bite with a sip of sauvignon blanc. Pleasure intensified physical feelings, increasing emotion, and the oxytocin produced by one's own brain. Attraction was a chemical reaction, no matter what started it. The trick was to keep it even on both sides.

John served her the rest of the white and turned the bottle over in the bucket. "Is Sunny your niece?" he asked.

She told him that she was an only child and explained how she met Sunny.

"Tell me if this is none of my business—does she normally sleep on your couch?"

"It's because of the cold. She's a strong girl, much more so than you would think. She lives in a school bus in the woods south of the Sugar Mill with . . . I don't know how many animals—a busload.

John's eyebrows went up, and she wished she hadn't given details. She explained that Sunny wanted to start a shelter, but putting the idea into words made it sound ridiculous.

John chewed a bite of prime rib and swallowed. "A hoarder, huh? Pretty young."

She nodded. "You don't often hear about the young ones. They're able to hide it."

"My mother was a mild case." He paused. "Twenty cats or so—and a fleet of ducks most of the time."

She loved that, *a fleet*, but the numbers sounded unmanageable.

"Dad left eventually—too many animals."

She dipped a flake of lobster meat into the dish of melted butter. She wanted to be romanced, yet was on the verge of giving a lecture about the millions of euthanized animals. "Let's try a more cheerful subject."

John went back to his food, chuckling to himself.

"What? Tell me."

"Twice our house flooded—once from a hurricane, when Mom and I spent the night with friends. We locked the cats in the kitchen because it was the safest place, and when we got home, every cat was packed sardine-style on the counter, the table, the appliances. Like a multi-colored fur coat spread out over the stove and counter top. And they were pissed. They looked at me like 'What the hell is this?—leaving us without a dry path to the food and litter?'"

Rita was laughing. "They know how to get their point across."

"Another time the sink was clogged with dishes—probably my chore left undone. One of the cats must have bumped the arm of the tap and turned the water on—an inch of water on the floor when I came home from school. They were spread out in the living room, mostly on the couch, but had that same irritated look on their faces." "I thought it was hilarious. Mom didn't."

"I can imagine."

"It took a day to wet-vac. Some cats jumped down after a few hours and headed to the food, water, litter. Others stuck it out, afraid to get their feet wet."

She smiled. He was an animal-lover, too—or an amazing ad-libber.

"You know the expression, 'like herding cats'? One night I heard weird rumbling—they were all in the living room circling, nose to tail. Herding! In step, as if they could hear a beat. Kept it up for fifteen minutes."

"Seriously?"

"Exercising. Like old people walking in the malls."

She was laughing again. "You're a hoot." She put down her fork and crossed her arms. "I have to stop eating or I'll burst. Tell me more stories."

He took a long drink of wine. "You should see my garage."

"Cats?"

"Fire Engine parts. You need to see it."

"Oh, I get it. Tonight."

He winked.

It was time for truth, before he found out by accident that she wasn't licensed as a vet at the shelter. She told it all, about her the drugs she sold, her prison sentence, and her past involvement with a younger man who used her and betrayed her.

He teased out the last bits of prime rib from between the fat as she spoke, the longest he had been silent since they met. She stopped talking, waited for a verdict.

He lifted his glass. "To the challenge."

"What?"

"To redeem mankind and put your trust issues to rest."

She hadn't realized that her "issues" were so obvious.

His hand dropped to her thigh and his lips touched her ear, warm breath on her neck tingling into lines of pleasure down her back.

At the apartment, she turned the key, and they stumbled through the living room to the bedroom, trying to be quiet past Sunny on the couch, but dizzy in the swirl of wine and heat. Fingers fumbling as clothes came off, lips seeking skin, all blended into a roar that drowned reality, like the sound inside a seashell. They fell on the bed, rubbing, sucking, gasping, locked in primitive sensations. There was no going back to the safety of being alone.

Chapter 35: Sunny Lytle

She had heard John and Rita come through the living room, moving past the couch into the bedroom, clutched together, hushing each other. She felt comfortable with them there. She wished they were her parents. Rita was smart and understanding and John seemed tough and worldly, able to remedy any situation.

The fighting had been frightening when Sunny was little, and from early adolescence, she was mostly left on her own, with food, laundry, and cleaning as her responsibilities, Lytle gone trucking.

Sometimes he'd bring a woman to the house for the night, and they'd spend hours in the kitchen or on the couch drinking and smoking. It was hard for Sunny to keep out of the way. She remembered once, when she first began to develop, Lytle dragging her over, pulling up her T-shirt, rubbing across her nipples with his rough finger, telling a redheaded woman, "Look at these skeeter bites. Barely nothing there." He stuck Sunny's hand down the woman's low-cut blouse between her breasts. "You'll be lucky if you get nice titties like them."

She had flown to her room, and Lytle and the redhead started to argue and fight, knocking over chairs and breaking glass. When things quieted, she heard the grunting, then snoring. In the morning the bathroom was tied up for hours, while somebody puked their guts out.

She opened her eyes to the bright light from Rita's living room window. She'd been calling for help in a dream, croaking the word deep in her throat, not able to yell. Rita's pool had been carpeted with a roiling layer of beetles and Sunny was saving them by the handful, using both hands, but there were millions. She couldn't tread water and slipped down where sharks and gators cruised between her legs.

John's laughter and the sound of silverware on plates reminded her that she was warm and comfortable. This was the first time she had slept through the night since Louisville. She stood and stretched, full of energy. The fur people would be hungry and nervous without her, but feeling good almost overpowered the guilt.

Rita, in a fluffy robe, looked through the kitchen doorway. "Do you want breakfast? I have cereal."

"Sounds great, but I'll take a shower." She thought they might want some more time alone, and then maybe someone would be ready to drive her back to her camp.

When she came out to the kitchen Rita and John were sipping coffee and reading the newspaper. She found a bowl and the cereal and milk and sat at the end of the table. It was like a TV sitcom, everyone being nice to each other in a clean, bright room with cute curtains.

Rita asked if she would like to go to the Antique Car Show.

Sunny explained that she had a lot of chores and needed to spend some time with the fur family.

"Bring 'em along," John said.

Rita looked at him and laughed. "She's talking about her dogs and cats. Lots of them."

"And a couple of ferrets and a rabbit," Sunny told him.

"We can take a few," he said.

Sunny watched Rita roll her eyes and John smile back. There was something good between them.

She wasn't sure if the offer was real, but she begged off anyway, just wanting to get home. Home, she was actually calling the camp *home*.

They dropped her off on the road. John wanted to walk back to visit the dogs, but Rita suggested some other time. *Thank god.* Rita had no idea of the number of newborns since she last visited.

The dogs heard Sunny and put up their fuss. As she stepped out from the palmetto scrub, she saw a skinny, light-furred male shepherd-mix run behind the bus. "It's okay." She made smooching noises and called to him in a soothing voice, but the others drowned her out. She went to the front of the bus and peeked around the side. The shepherd was already moving quickly through the trees. She hated it when animals were afraid of her. She wondered if he or she had been hanging around while she was at work. She hoped the dog would come back so she could give it something to eat.

Chapter 36: Bear Hansen

Bear woke up in the cold, damp room, feeling lonely, with nobody to talk to. His last guilt-steeped phone calls to Marci had been filled with details about what he was supposed to be doing. She had sounded snippy as soon as she heard his voice, so he told her that he was getting paid to help rebuild an antique engine, and since he hadn't been able to find gaskets to fit, he was making them himself. His lying had improved, and he wasn't completely happy about that.

The whole Florida ordeal was discouraging. Thanksgiving had been lonely. He'd stayed in bed dozing and watching the Macy's parade all morning and then driven to Denny's for early lunch. Every bite of hot turkey with institutional gravy reminded him how much better the fare was at home, as well as the conversation. He missed the Thanksgiving morning smell of onions and celery frying up for dressing that would sink down to his basement workroom, making him hungry for dinner already at breakfast time. Marci always cooked the liver separately as a nibble to hold him off. Probably boiled it and cut it up for the dog this year. He missed the dog too, sweet Kelly, his fluffy black lab. He always told her she looked more like a bear than he did. Kelly would be wondering why he didn't come home.

He must be obsessed. He'd been gone for ten days and driven past acres of shaggy, vermin-infested jungle, with plants and roots clogging everything, thick undergrowth where nobody could possibly walk, much less live. There were palms and scrawny pines sticking through meshes of vine, and trees with low horizontal branches covered by moss and ferns, a conglomeration with no symmetry. He didn't recognize the tropical beauty he'd heard so much about or understand why Sunny would want to live in a place suited only to spiders, reptiles, and plant parasites.

He'd bought a beer in every bar in DeLeon Springs and several bars in Deland, besides checking out some shops and restaurants. He had recently begun asking everybody if they'd seen the bus. Nobody had.

His stomach motivated him for Denny's again, eggs and bacon. Lots of hot coffee. Denny's was cheap and anonymous. In the friendly little places he would start to need explanations if he didn't want to stand out as some kind of loser. People often remembered him for his cap that said *Bear. He* thought about leaving it in the car, but he couldn't. It covered his bald spot.

The Denny's décor started him thinking again of how much he missed his cheery kitchen, the steamy windows overlooking a snow-covered field and the bird feeder where Blackie the squirrel performed acrobatics to get to the feeder. She was looking pregnant when he left. He picked up a newspaper from the next table. The Daytona Car Show was still running and he hadn't been there yet. He might see some interesting automotive work and buy an accessory for the Bel Air he'd been restoring back home—make his trip more purposeful.

He had driven all this way, spent all this time for what? Love? Pussy? He had never seen an indication from Sunny that she felt anything for him beyond friendly affection. Her neediness had drawn him in until his attachment had overwhelmed every bit of sense, and he had risked his marriage. It was all pretty clear. He was an idiot.

Chapter 37: Rita McKenna

She walked with John through rows of vehicles shined to a glare under the clear skies. They passed a car the color of bubble gum or Pepto Bismol. "I've never seen anything like that," she said. "I'd rather not see it again."

John said that he had bought multiple Toyotas and had them all painted a similar color, each with a Barbie face on the hood, for use in *Fast and Furious II.* "There was a crash in almost every scene, and then the same car had to return later unscathed. Big budget." He took her arm and turned her. "Let's look at the older cars."

He strolled through more rows of shining paint and chrome. Rita pointed out the car her father had driven. "I don't know if it was exactly the same, but I remember turquoise with the white stripe."

"Fifty-seven Bel Air," John told her, "a classic from my youth."

"It was an old clunker as I remember it."

"You're a young chick."

Rita made a face.

He gave her a kiss on the forehead as if it sealed his case. "I have to head back to California soon. I'll be working on a fifties period film, and I need a few Chevys. I might be able to get some leads today." He paused to look into her eyes.

Her stomach contracted. It was his first mention of leaving. "You would bring cars all the way from here to California?"

"Depends on the price. We ship from all over the country. Aren't you going to ask me how long I'll be gone?"

She wondered if he had seen disappointment in her face. "None of my business."

"I would like it to be. I'll be there for months, starting right after Christmas—but back for some weekends. I'm hoping you'll come out for a visit. I'll get you a flight and a room. Your own room, if you want."

She told him it would be nice, but she wasn't sure. She had work. Something crumbled inside her chest.

"Give it some thought—so many beautiful places I'd like to take you."

She nodded, not letting anything show. "Maybe."

He squeezed her hand and kept it until he stopped to speak to a seller and she pulled free. She walked several steps and gazed blankly at bright red car. She couldn't stop the questions. Why hadn't he mentioned this earlier? Did she really want to risk starting a serious relationship with somebody across the country? Was she confusing love with the need to change her situation? She couldn't let her life become reliant on a man. Was she analyzing too much?

An old hippie guy bumped her as he stepped backwards, and grazed her toe with his boot. "Sorry. You okay?" He pointed at the car. "I was stunned by this beautiful Chevy. Working on one like her at home. Your foot all right?"

Rita nodded. "No problem."

John was beside her. "You have a '57 like this?

"Rebuilt and ready for paint. Needs some interior work. A Bel Air four-door, V8 with fender skirts."

John asked him if it was a fuelie, and Rita zoned back into wondering if she really had anything in common with him.

"Four-barrel carburetor."

"For sale?"

She saw two Jack Russells on leashes. One was skidding on three legs across the blacktop, being pulled along by the owner. The dog tried to reach his back leg with his mouth, but the leash prevented him. She couldn't believe the woman didn't feel the drag as the dog twisted and slid along the pavement. The little guy was in pain. Rita stepped in front of the woman. "Excuse me. I'm a veterinarian. Would your dog let me take a look at his paw?"

The woman stared at her, then looked down at the terrier. He was standing on three legs, the tight leash preventing him from reaching the left rear leg with his mouth. "Sure. He won't bite."

Rita moved toward him, and despite the problem paw, he ran around his owner's legs and tangled with the other dog. They popped up and down within the few inches of slack.

"Pure Jack Russell energy," Rita said. She held the dog by his collar and lifted the paw. There was a large burr stuck between the pads. She was able to pull it from his skin. It stuck in her fingertip. "Ouch! I can see why he wanted this out." She left it on her finger, looking around for a trash can, letting him lick her other hand.

"Thanks. He must have picked it up in the parking lot," the woman said. She walked off, the Jack Russells following, nearly bouncing.

John came walking over. "Finding customers?"

"Just a burr in the paw." She held her finger.

"I wouldn't call that delicate hand a paw," he said. "Here's a paw for you." He held up his large hand and pretended to paw her shoulder. When she giggled he slid his hand down her arm to take hers again. "Time for lunch. Let's split."

She asked if he had found a car for the film, trying to be interested and think of something besides his keeping her in the dark about leaving when she had already revealed her soul.

He held up a piece of paper. Bernard Hansen, it said, with a phone number. "He's headed back home to Louisville in a day or two, so I'll have a contact up there check it out."

He picked the burr out of her finger, getting it stuck in his own before managing to fling it off into the trash can. "He asked me if I'd seen a girl living in a camo-painted school bus. Sunny?"

She nodded and said that it must be. "You didn't say anything?"

"No. He said if I saw her to tell her to call."

Rita wondered if it might have been Sunny's father. She couldn't remember if the girl ever mentioned family. "Maybe I should call him."

John said that he didn't have the feeling that the guy was related.

She agreed that it was best to let Sunny make the decision. The girl was an adult, as difficult as it was to think of her in that way, but an older friend or relative might have influence. She was grasping for anything besides calling in the rescue team.

Chapter 38: Bear Hansen

Bear didn't expect to hear back from John Wonder about the Bel Air, but he hoped to. He had been working on that vehicle for so long that he'd lost interest. He dreaded interior work. Engines were his specialty, and he would be happy to let somebody else finish the rest.

Anyway, Wonder's card might be key to saving his marriage, as evidence of time well-spent. Luck had dropped into his lap on this one. He decided to pack up and git outta Dodge while the gittin was good.

He went back to the motel, took a piss, and got his stuff from the bathroom, slamming toiletries into the suitcase, making a racket. The trick was to keep moving. Damn that girl. Where had she taken the fucking bus? It was frustrating after all this time to leave with nothing but questions.

He tore out onto SR17, planning to drive straight through to Louisville and stop for coffee when he got tired. He could pull off the highway for a few hours' snooze, if need be. He took out his cell phone and called Marci. She wasn't home, so he left a message with his E.T.A., pretending that everything was rosy. He was excited to get back to normal life, and he knew she could hear it in his tone. Still, he wasn't sure how much trouble he was in, and he couldn't stop his idiotic mind from wandering back to the skinny-bones blonde.

Chapter 39: Rufus

Thunderous barks powered deep in Rufus' lungs exploded rapid-fire. His body lurched against the leash. Scent filled his nostrils and took shape, size, and movement into his brain: a two-legger, unknown by eyes or tongue. Large and male with acrid fumes and rotted organs.

All dogs inside and outside the bus inhaled molecules, erupted in alerts of aggression and fear. The nipper's screech cut ears.

A sharp scent brought the juice of desire to Rufus' mouth. Familiar, heavy aroma of concentrated meatness, salt.

Large rotting two-leg male approached, arm forward.

Rufus yanked to break free, teeth bared, could not.

Meatness offered.

Rufus' brain-focus snapped. *Bite* changed to *eat*. A shining red bag gushed scent, and saliva-welling strips appeared at eye level. Instinct roused against them, but hunger overwhelmed. He sat, took food from hot fingers. It was not meat, but something like it. He mouthed up another.

"Good boy, good boy." A hard hand pounded his shoulders and the two-legger moved to Schmeisser. Unmeat aroma rose, then faded into breath. Leads taut, others woofed and whined, reached and nudged against the two legs and the pounding arm.

"Good boy, good boy."

Ears and heads flashed at the bus windows, a shrieking dance to draw attention. Those standing on the table pressed noses against glass. Tongues flickered between huffs. Paws scraped. Nipper's squeal penetrated Rufus' ears.

No unmeat went into the bus. The two-legger walked backward, rumpled the red bag into memory. All stared and whimpered, still hopeful, as the male shape got smaller and rot-scent became trail then trace.

Chapter 40: Buckaroo

Buckaroo leaned on the metal rail and watched the water twist a swath of long jade grass in the little waterfall. He'd told Sunny to meet him by the waterfall to get a ride home. No more doing chores while somebody else made the moves. She had seemed happy to see him.

The sky was holding out, a sizzling blue, blue enough to hurt if you stared. Happiness was supposed to be attached to a sky like that. He'd forgotten what joy felt like, except for the kind when he jacked off. Or was that pleasure? Joy in the mind, pleasure in the body. What was that saying—a dirty mind is a joy forever? Anyway, the open blue would let him concentrate on getting the young lady to her campsite for a little romance.

He never arrived empty-handed. In the truck was a fifty pounder of Purina, half a dozen cans of Kennel-Ration and a twelve-pack of Fancy Feast. It was only a week since he'd brought supplies, but those dogs gobbled. He had also bought a tent and a brand new sleeping bag so he could spend the night. He planned to leave the stuff for her, and she wouldn't have to sleep in bus anymore. Money was running low, and he hoped not to run through the month without ever getting laid.

She was worth it though, super sweet, and he worried about her and where it would all lead, the animals multiplying and him getting caught up in it. Didn't seem much chance for a happy-ever-after ending, but then, most times, there was no ending. One thing just turned into something else.

When he led her to the truck, Sunny seemed less enthusiastic to see him than earlier. He mentioned the food he'd brought, and she said thanks, but didn't get excited. Maybe she was wrestling with the idea of letting him jump her bones.

They walked under the sprawling branches and wisps of Spanish moss. She took off her flip-flops and wiggled her toes on the smooth wood walk.

Sore feet, he could imagine. He pointed to some low hanging moss. "Remember not to touch that." He didn't think she was listening. "Don't touch the moss."

"I know, I know! Chiggers! I'm from here, remember."

"Big day? Tired?" He might as well find out what his chances were. "Dollar for your thoughts." He fumbled in his pocket and pulled out a single.

She didn't look at it. "I feel terrible. I was supposed to call somebody. He drove all the way down here from Kentucky."

"Who?"

She got into the truck without answering, so he kept quiet for the short drive. He parked near the gravel road by her camp.

She stepped out of the truck and started through the woods.

"Sunny, I can't carry all this stuff by myself."

"Sorry! Sorry, Buck—Buccaneer." She came running back. "Buckaroo."

She squinted at him.

What was the matter with her? Was this new guy another long lost boyfriend? Maybe she had them all over the place. He handed her a bag to carry.

They doled out rations together. Then he suggested cleaning up. He dug and she scooped. He hauled water from the lake, carried the cooler from the truck, stacked wood for the fire. He needed a nap more than sex, but after he had built the fire and cracked a beer, he sat down and got horny again. She was out with the last group for walks. He would put on the spaghetti pot while she was watering and petting, and then finally . . .

She'd eaten her pasta with half a can of shake cheese and set her plate on a rock. "So what's this about a guy after you?"

She shook her head, went to the bus, and brought out a white puppy with brown spots. She sat back in her chair, cuddling and kissing it, staring into the fire.

"Who's this guy?"

"Bear. He's not after me." She pointed at the bus. "I borrowed his camper."

"I don't much like bears." Buck glanced at the bus. He'd wondered where she got that monstrosity. "He wants it back?"

"Not yet. He was bringing me money. He . . . I . . ."

"Boyfriend?"

"No. He's married. We were good friends and, you know, we messed around."

A groan came out that he couldn't stop. "I see." In a way, it was a minor relief that she'd actually had sex.

"I feel bad. Bear's nice. I never met his wife, Marci, but she's probably nice too."

"Bear. Figures." Another animal in her collection. She didn't seem to have any deep feelings for him. "How did he find you?"

She explained that her veterinarian friend had met him at a car show.

Buck took a slug of beer and got up to put wood on the fire. "Is Bear a nicer guy than me?"

She looked at him, as if she was trying to decide, or maybe she was thinking about Bear.

"You're supposed to say that I'm the nicest guy you ever met."

"You're pretty nice."

He moved his plastic chair next to her lounge chair. She was holding the squirming puppy across her chest and he reached out to pet it, thinking that it would be easy to slip his fingers across its back and onto the sweatshirt covering her braless little titties. She wouldn't suspect, probably wouldn't even notice, busy as she was kissing all over the pup.

He kept petting, got close once, but didn't do it. He was proud of himself. He reached behind her awkwardly and massaged her neck. She melted down a little, resting her cheek on the puppy's head. He got up and stood behind her, using his thumbs under her braid to rub the base of her skull and work next to her spine, careful to be gentle. Her shoulders finally relaxed, and he knew he was on the right track. He continued massaging and she leaned forward to give him more space. He pulled up the back of her sweatshirt to work the bare skin above her jeans. Hers was the first flesh he'd touched, beside his own, in maybe a year. He slowly lifted the back of the shirt higher, gathering it to pull it all over her head, giving her time to stop him if she wanted, or time to put down the dog, but she raised her arms one at a time, shifting the squirming fur bundle side to side on her lap, letting the shirt come off and her tits pucker in the breeze.

He dropped his head and kissed the back of her neck as his fingers went around front to slide between her and the puppy, stroking her nipples and making her giggle. He took in the smell of her hair—a little smoky, not a molecule of bus odor he'd feared.

She stood and turned to him and he yanked off his shirt. It was both of them or nothing so he wrapped himself around her and the dog. He nibbled her lips and covered her mouth for a long tongue kiss. He slid his hand to her waist and farther, slowly, expecting that she'd stop him, but she unzipped her jeans and pushed them down past her hips and straight thighs, showing a fine blond thatch, all innocent and nearly childlike. Thank god, she wasn't a child. He dropped to his knees, feeling the eyes of those who had tongue power and stamina he could never manage. He looked up to see what effect he was having. Her face was buried in fur.

Chapter 41: Sunny Lytle

She slipped into the tingling universe of Buck's fingers and mouth, snuggling the warm puppy like a pillow. If she had been saving herself for Jason, it was wrong. Buck was good to her.

She invited him into the bus on her mattress.

He sat back on his heels, wiping at his beard. "Wait a second. I brought you something."

She tried not to laugh as he ran into the woods, hunching and trying to arrange himself in his pants. She hoped he would come back fast. She was freezing, standing naked, even holding the puppy, who was getting antsy. She wondered if Buck had gone for a blanket. There were plenty in the bus. She put the pup back with his mother and wrapped herself up.

Buck was back with a big box and two sleeping bags. He dropped everything on the ground, spread one sleeping bag, and lowered her to it like a precious lamb. He whipped her blanket away, covered her with the new-smelling sleeping bag, and crawled next to her. She flattened against his warm skin and lost her thoughts in his hungry kissing.

Sometime in the night she heard him banging around, but went back to sleep. Kisses woke her and he pulled her up to walk, one arm supporting her sleepy body, the other dragging the sleeping bags. She could see a tent in the moonlight that crept through branches. He shook out a sleeping bag and arranged it on top of the other. By that time she realized he had set up everything while she slept.

He got inside and patted her spot, then zipped the door behind her. "Sleep in the middle where it's safe."

She felt a shiver, not knowing what he would be afraid of. "What is it?" she whispered.

"Bears."

It was crazy. "Buck, they're rare—and scared of people. I don't think there's ever been a bear attack in Florida."

"Not reported."

She moved closer to him under the warm, thick cover of the fresh sleeping bag. Her nose filled with the smell of newness.

He turned on his side toward her and whispered. "I was there. Two guys sharing a tent next to me—one guy on a cot, sleeping with his foot against the tent. A bear bit right through the nylon and his ankle. His buddy had to play tug-of-war with the bear to save the guy and some of his leg."

"Ate his foot?"

"Chewed right off and swallowed in one chunk."

"You sure you didn't dream it?"

"I heard the screams, but it was too late by the time I got my gun. We put on a tourniquet. I saw him carted off in the ambulance. I think he got a new foot from the V.A.—a prosthesis."

She didn't quite believe it. She'd never seen a Florida bear except one poor little dead one on the side of the highway. She tried to clear the image from her mind. She was more worried about Buck having a gun, shooting at bears, than getting eaten. "Okay, I'll keep my feet inside."

"The guy had stinking feet, and bears just love that ripe odor. Draws them into camp."

She explained they were usually attracted by food, especially meat.

"Not when nice pungent feet are available." He gave her a kiss on the ear. "Mine are fresh."

"You always smell good, Buck, head to toe." She was glad he had clean feet for whatever reason. She curled on her side, tucked into his warmth, ready to drift easily into sleep. She heard her name.

"Hmm."

"If you're ever here and a bear turns up, just let him have the food. And if he shuffles his feet, huffs, or pops his teeth, run."

"I will." She snuggled closer and pulled her legs up. If he was trying to make himself needed, it was working.

Chapter 42: Sunny Lytle

She didn't open her eyes until she heard the dogs stirring at half-light. Buck was already up. She could hear the undertone— *meat, meat, meat*. The usual wake-up call. They could wait a few minutes.

She noticed her foot sticking out from under the blanket. The bear story seemed silly, but it was nice to be protected from mosquitoes and dew, and the air inside the tent was warm from body heat.

Buck had a fire going and coffee. She wondered if he would feed and walk the furs if she pretended to be sleeping, but her conscience wouldn't let her. She wrapped up in the blanket and dragged herself out.

He was toasting bread in a skillet and looked up, nearly tipping it into the fire. "Morning, sweetheart," he said, and poured her a cup of coffee.

She was already his sweetheart. She sipped the coffee. It was good. She had trusted him with her body, but could she trust him with her secret? He was practical, would make a good business partner. "I was thinking . . ."

"You think as much as you want. I just burnt the toast." He held it up, scorched in the center.

She put out her hand. "I like mine crunchy." He dropped it on a plate and passed it to her. She took a bite. "I was thinking that I could make some money, Buck. I mean *real* money to get my shelter started."

He buttered another piece of bread and placed it into the pan. "Hell, I'm all for that. These guys need a bigger place."

She hesitated. The idea would sound crazy.

"Don't worry. I've heard it all."

She took a breath and let her enthusiasm carry her through. Told him how she was telepathic and felt processes inside the dog's bodies, how she diagnosed a Pomeranian, a greyhound, and a Doberman, although nobody had given her credit. Buck nodded and smiled as she gave details about the nighttime fatherhood conflict in the bus. "I wasn't dreaming. The puppies were there in the morning."

Buck opened his arms. "Stranger things have happened." He took the empty plate from her lap and kissed her and held her cheek against his. "It's because you're so close to them. If any dawgs can talk, then yours can."

"Thank you, Buck."

He sat back. "You thinking of hiring out to a circus?"

She wrinkled her nose. "Nothing like that. She explained her plan to be the middle man between the animal and the veterinarian. "If I get business cards and make appointments, people might take me more seriously."

"You should rent an office down in Cassadaga. That's where all the palm readers and crystal ball gazers work. People flock there. The kind of people you want."

He wasn't getting it. She remembered the Tarot card prediction when she had visited Cassadaga with her high school friends. According to the reader, she was supposed to marry Jason. She didn't believe in the Cassadaga crowd. "I thought I'd go to the clients' houses."

He offered to drive when possible.

"The problem is how to get the word out."

"Signs on the bulletin boards in Winn-Dixie and Publix. We can make those little tear-off tabs with a phone number on each one."

She reminded him that she couldn't afford a phone, but he suggested using the Sugar Mill number, briefly, and she could soon buy a reload-able cell phone cheap. "Charge fifty bucks a visit. People expect to get what they pay for. If you're too cheap, they'll think you're no good."

She gave him a hug. "Buck, you're almost as fun as a Christmas pony!"

He tickled her ribs and she burst out in a giggle that caused a barkfest. The furs didn't like missing the fun.

She got a pen and paper and wrote out the words for the sign so Buck could take it to Office Depot for a professional look. She handed him a twenty, and he promised to have the signs posted that afternoon. He believed in her. The first human ever.

She put on a sweatshirt and jeans and started the chores. The dogs picked up on the excitement of the new plan. The big guys strained at the leashes for a good-morning rub, but she didn't have time to deal with the itching and stepped inside the bus to get dressed. The droning for meat was deafening.

When she came out, Buck put down his coffee and swallowed his last bite of toast, ready to help with the feeding. A true sweetheart. She handed him a stack of bowls, but they fell from his hands. He stepped back and stared at the sky.

She looked up to see what had startled him. The sun, breaking the horizon with a pretty red hue, was disappearing behind a dark patch of clouds.

"What's wrong?"

Buck looked left and right, his body jerking, as if he wanted to run in both directions at once.

"You okay? What can I do?"

He dashed to get his backpack and ran with it to the opening of the tent.

"Buck? What's the matter?" She eased toward him. "Buccaneer?"

"Don't come any closer."

She walked slowly, rounding the tent in a wide curve until she could peek through the side window. Buck had unzipped the front screen and was lying on his back with his head out the door, staring straight above him, holding a foil-covered pie plate on his chest. She walked to the opening and looked down at him.

He jerked. "Move. Back up. I can't see!"

She took a step backward. "What are you doing?"

"Get away, quick! They'll zap us. I still can't see!" His hand swung out grazing the side of her knee. She stepped farther away.

"What are you doing?"

He was breathing hard. "You don't want to know. Go to work."

"Maybe I can help."

"Help by leaving me alone."

She scanned the sky from east to west, north to south. Clouds.

Buck groaned. "If you go over to the big tree and stay there, I'll tell you."

Walking the few yards to the nearest trunk, Sunny heard the dogs whimpering. She thought one aimed an obscenity her way—or she was thinking *fuck* to herself. It was hard to sort out, but they were hungry and needed to be walked. She still had to water them and clean up poop. But Buck wasn't joking, and she didn't know how to help him.

She waited for him to speak. She waited and waited. "What's going on?"

He was still flat on the ground, staring into space, tilting the plate. His words came fast between tilts. "Magnetoids . . . demons from outer space . . . Zap you dead . . . Hiding . . . in that cumulous."

She tried to keep an open mind. "Really?"

"You're in danger near me. I don't want anything to happen to you."

It clicked. Clouds were the reason he'd run off the first time they'd met, and why he lived alone in the woods. Some kind of phobia. The bear thing and now this. "Are you talking about lightning? Lots of people are afraid of it. I don't think that plate will help though."

"No, not lightning. It might feel like being struck by lightning, but it's a different . . . energy . . . a certain frequency of light rays, radiation . . . magnetism to hit the target. Brains gone in a flash—the whole body!" His arm jerked sideways. "Close one!"

"How do you know all this?"

"Army . . . electro magnetic pulse and nuclear magnetic resonance. Set up the right resonance to vibrate cells and disintegrate them, like cancer radiation—but as a weapon. I'll be turned to ash if I don't deflect it."

"Wouldn't you be better off inside?"

He angled the plate and his arm muscles tensed. "Ooh!"

Sunny looked up. Nothing. She chewed her lip.

"They see me through windows. . . I get glancing hits . . . Painful . . . lose memory. I need open sky."

It didn't sound rational, but she wasn't one to judge. She asked why they were after him.

He wiped his forehead, still staring upward. "Here's a break. A reload." He set the plate on his chest. "Why me? I keep trying to figure it out. Maybe because I know about them. Or blond hair might be a target. There's a rivalry—up in the heavens—angels with blond hair operating the machines, thinking I might try to take over their territory."

"You lost me."

His eyes darted her way, no doubt checking to see if she was making fun of him. She looked at her watch. She was going to be late for work by the time she finished everything. The dogs caught her eye and started barking their loudest, triggering yapping from the bus, the undercurrent of *meat, meat, meat* rolling over her.

"Look!" She yelled over the uproar to Buck and held up a chunk of hair. "I have blond hair, and nobody zaps me!"

"Shit! Fuck!"

"What?" She turned to quiet the dogs. "I'm coming!" She started toward them and they became attentive. She looked back at Buck. "You okay?"

"Shit, Sunny. Now that I've told you . . . you're in danger. Do you feel anything? Prickliness in your head? Tingling?"

She thought about it for a second, felt her scalp. Nothing but some itchy no-see-um bites. "I'm fine." She hoped not to start imagining something.

"You might be okay. Most of this is theory."

The dogs started again, frantic. "Listen." She told him she had to hurry. He could stay there and keep the dogs company.

He nodded. "I'd help you, but I can't." He glanced her way. "Be careful, Sunny. I hope I haven't set you up . . ."

Chapter 43: Sunny Lytle

She was over an hour late to the restaurant, missing her part of the prep. Customers were already being seated. She went behind the counter where Patty took her place, filling little dishes with frozen blueberries. All she needed to do was lose this job and that would truly be the end of the world.

"I'm so sorry, Patty. My friend had an emergency this morning, and I had to help him."

Patty set a dish on the tray and stopped. "I know it's your first time being late, but it would help if you called in."

"I'm sorry. I don't have a phone."

She handed Sunny the bag of blueberries. "Are you living in the woods?"

Her face and neck got hot. She looked down, filling the little dishes. "I'm saving up for an apartment. How could you tell?"

"You're not the first. It's a look I recognize, an . . . outdoor style."

"Is it a problem? I really like working here. I'll be able to get a place soon."

"You're always clean. I'm worried though. I see you dozing on your breaks."

"There's a lot of work to do, camping." She looked hard at Patty, trying to show her deepest sincerity. "I'll have a place soon."

"Okay." Patty squeezed her shoulder and went to the cash register, but it was a first strike.

The morning was chaotic, and she became energized, making the rounds with coffee every spare second. She enjoyed delivering big bowls of bacon strips and didn't mind wiping down the crusty griddle. Egg yolk and syrup, dribbles of pancake mix dried to concrete, sometimes even on the seats, no problem. It was easy, compared to taking care of the camp.

In the afternoon when the rush was over, she sat down at the front table with an iced tea, knowing she had earned a break. Jason passed by with a tub of dirty dishes and winked. She controlled her smile.

He came back and sat down. "Have you seen that meerkat show?"

"Meerkat?"

"*Meerkat Mansion*. They're slinky little guys, even cuter than ferrets, and they stand straight up on their back legs and point their noses into the wind. There's somebody telling their stories."

"Stories?"

"Like one of the females gets in trouble for mating and having too many babies.

I thought maybe you'd seen it with your vet friend." He invited her to his house on Friday night. "We can make popcorn. Bet it's been a long time since you've had popcorn."

She took a slurp of her tea. She couldn't think of anything she'd rather do than watch meerkats, or anything, with Jason, but she didn't know how to act in front of his wife.

He poked her side. "I saw you eating corn pudding on Thanksgiving."

Knowing that he'd been paying attention stopped her in mid-breath. "I've gotten bad—or better, depending on who you talk to."

"So, come over and have popcorn."

She would love to see his house, find out more about his life. All fodder for guilty fantasies.

"Wife's out of town. Gone a lot lately."

Her face was blazing, giving her away. "I can't leave my family alone at night."

"I can pick you up. You'd love Christian the Lion . . ."

She was barely listening, trying to convince herself that she could be his friend and everything would be perfectly all right.

"A year later, the lion still remembered those guys. He nearly knocked them down, rubbing his face all over theirs, putting his arms—legs—around them."

"He was hugging?"

"Yeah. I guess hugging comes naturally."

She wanted so badly to say yes to his offer that she could barely speak. "Can't make it."

He looked at the floor. "Well, you're welcome anytime. Deb wouldn't mind."

She didn't know whether that was true or not, but it didn't matter. Bear's wife didn't care what he did either, supposedly. She stabbed at the lemon slice with her straw, sinking it to the bottom of the murky tea. She remembered watching—and not-watching—TV at his parents' house on the big green corduroy couch when nobody was home. She didn't look at him, fearing what showed in her eyes.

"I thought Debbie would call me at the restaurant—about adopting cats. But maybe she doesn't like me."

"She likes you fine." He blew out a breath. "I might have mentioned that you were full up."

"What?" It jolted her.

"I thought you must be having trouble feeding all the animals you've got. I'm sorry." He scooted out of his chair. "Gotta finish cleaning off my last table."

His attitude surprised her, but she let him off easy, not wanting to start an argument. "I should have called Debbie."

He still stood there. "What about Christmas? Want to join us for dinner? We have some really cute doggies that would love to be fed scraps under the table."

Now he was luring her with the weenie dogs. He knew what buttons to push. "I can't. I have my own Christmas." In fact, planning something for the holiday hadn't crossed her mind.

"I understand." He walked toward the kitchen with the same long strides she remembered. He filled out his jeans even better now. He turned and caught her looking.

"Don't you have a table to clear?" she asked.

He walked back. "Remember the time we drove over to the fish camp in New Smyrna to see the beer-drinking pig with two snouts?"

"Sure. The black pig. We fed him a Bud Light so he'd keep his trim figure." She held back tears brought by the sweetness of the memory.

He bent close to her face. "One night, after you left town, I went back there. The pig had been stolen."

Her stomach clenched. "I wish you hadn't told me."

Jason's face clouded. "Maybe he got a better home. Why would somebody steal a two-snouted pig if not for love?"

She didn't want to say *bacon*, but it was as obvious as the aroma saturating the room. "Our thinking is different from other people's, Jason. You know that. I never should have left you." She grabbed her cup and went into the kitchen before he could say anything. The seething inside her was like scalded milk, always just a few degrees from heaving over the sides of the pan.

Chapter 44: Sunny Lytle

It took only two days for the Winn-Dixie sign to pay off, and Sunny made her first appointment that evening with a woman who had a listless golden retriever. Buck had promised a five o'clock ride, but his promises were conditional on the weather and he often lost track of time, even though she had bought a battery-powered alarm clock for the tent.

She hadn't noticed if the sky had been cloudy earlier, but only wisps drifted by as she sat on the picnic bench facing the water. There was a breeze blowing toward her off the lake, and glinting ripples rolled her way, broadening and multiplying, lapping the shore near her feet, like a silver lining—a change in her luck. If only Buck would get there.

The sun slid below the trees, turning cool air into chilly gloom. Everybody was gone. The water darkened. It was nearly time for the park to close. She wasn't sure whether to walk up to the entrance gate and wait outside or paddle back to camp and forget the whole deal.

She had started up the wooden path toward the exit, when she saw the truck round the curve from behind the trees. She ran back down to the gravel path and climbed in. "Magnetoids?"

"Sorry."

"They make you dysfunctional."

"That's a harsh word for *late*."

She huffed. He didn't understand how important this was. "I'm never sure if you'll show up. How can I expect to run a business this way?"

He turned to her. "Consider yourself lucky. How could you get anywhere without me?"

She had done him wrong. She scooted over and gave him a kiss on the cheek. "I'm just nervous about getting off to a good start. Please, forgive me."

He kissed her hard.

The address was in Deland, and it was dark by the time they arrived. The small concrete block house, enclosed by chain link fence, stood in a yard of weeds and sand with one sickly palm.

The only light came from a TV screen in the front room. These were not the rich people with wealthy friends that Sunny had hoped for.

Buck pulled into the driveway and cut off the lights. "You better go in by yourself. People don't always like the looks of me. Yell if there's a problem."

She was spooked by the dark house, but there was a sad retriever inside waiting for her. She knocked on the door.

"Sunny?" A woman yelled.

"Yes!"

"Come in! I'm in the living room with Lucky."

She turned the knob. The door was unlocked. She walked through the pitch black hall toward the flickering glow. Around the corner an older woman was visible on the couch, a cast on her ankle and a beautiful golden with his head resting on her foot. "I'm sorry, Sunny. It's hard for me to get around."

"Oh, no problem." Lucky sat up. "Would you like me to turn on the lamp? Nell, right?"

"Yes. Sure. Please turn off the TV too."

Sunny did as Nell asked and sat on the floor next to the dog. He seemed frightened by her closeness, but didn't growl. He looked alert. "Is it all right to pet him?"

"Of course. Thank you for coming. My son thinks it's a psychological problem. He should be here any minute. He's bringing the money."

She stroked Lucky's head and blackness swam across her eyes. It was a frightening sensation. She held his head, making sure. "Nell, I'm sorry. Lucky's losing his sight. He only has a little vision left, shadows."

The woman let out a painful groan. "I should have known."

"I'm so sorry." Sunny dropped her hands to her sides and waited for the darkness to clear.

Nell sat crying. She reached for Lucky and put both hands on his head.

Sunny tried to stay cheerful. "He's getting old. He's a smart dog, but he's afraid."

"I know how he feels." She lowered her head to rest it on his. "This is terrible."

Sunny told her not to worry, that Lucky would adapt. She advised Nell to keep him inside or in the yard until he got over his fear.

Nell sobbed. "That won't work. You don't understand."

"I do. He's upset, but he's strong. He'll learn how to get around."

"I'm blind," Nell said. "He's my service dog."

Sunny's energy drained. She was so stupid when it came to sensing human problems. She had given away Lucky's secret.

Nell asked for a tissue and Sunny found the box on the end table and pressed one into Nell's hand. She clutched Sunny's fingers. "I should have known. Lucky led me across a hole and I stepped in it and broke my ankle. He never did anything like that before."

A white cane was leaning in the corner. She hadn't realized that a blind person would watch television. She sat back down next to Lucky. "If you get a second dog, he can help both of you."

"Lucky's my man." Her voice cracked. "Can't afford two dogs. If I get another dog, I'll have to put Lucky down." She covered her face with her hands and sat rigid, her chest convulsing.

It was too much. Sunny ran to the window. "Buck, Buck!"

The truck door opened and he stepped out, shaking his head to wake up. "Sunny?"

She waved him inside and went to Lucky.

"What are you doing?" Nell asked.

She was frantic. "Can I take your dog? I'll give him a good home and he'll make lots of friends."

"I don't know. I can't think. If he's scared and miserable, it might be better to . . ."

"Kill him? I'm taking him right now, while I have a ride and—" Buck stepped into the room. "—a friend to help me."

"No. I don't think so."

"Buck, can you carry him? He's blind and afraid to walk."

"What's going on?"

Sunny petted Lucky, and held his head as Buck grunted and eased the dog up off the floor and stood holding him.

Nell waved her arm and grabbed on to Lucky's tail. "Put him down!"

"Good boy, Lucky," Sunny said. She tried to calm him, but he stayed rigid.

"Let me think about this," Nell said. She reached out.

Buck moved closer, so she could stroke the dog's side.

"He wants to go," Sunny said. It was a lie, but the best thing she could do for him. "You get your new dog and Lucky will be happy with us for the rest of his life." She turned to Buck. "Go on, take him."

"You can't have him!" Nell grabbed her cane.

Buck backed up. "Can't. I just ate an orange."

"What?"

"I mean I just can't do it."

"Buck, don't get crazy on me. Let's go before her son shows up and gives us trouble."

"You're stealing my dog?" Nell waved the cane in Buck's direction, and tried to rise from the couch, but Sunny held her down, pressing her shoulder.

"Nell, Dogs don't belong to people. Lucky has a right to life, and he wants to be with us. He's telling me that." He wasn't. He still seemed to want down, to stay, but he didn't know what was likely to happen.

Buck whispered to Sunny, "Steal a blind woman's dawg?"

Sunny put her finger to her lip, motioning him quiet. "Nell, please. I don't want to take a chance that some well-meaning, but unfeeling, veterinarian will talk you into putting Lucky to sleep. I bet your son will see it my way."

"Get your hand off me! You should be ashamed."

Still holding Lucky, Buck hooked Sunny by the finger and pulled her into the hall. "We already have so many dawgs. Besides, she's got your work number. She could send the police in there."

"She'll have him put to sleep! I just know it."

"What the hell are you going to do with a blind dawg? I hope you're not expecting me to lead him to each tree and lift his leg."

She cut her eyes at him, but he was right about the police. If they arrested her at the Sugar Mill, all the fur people would suffer for it.

"I can't do this to a blind woman with a broken leg, Sunny."
She slumped and nodded.

They stepped back into the room, Nell clutched a portable phone near her chest. "Leave right now, or I'll call 911."

Sunny asked Nell to please call her before having Lucky put down, but she knew the woman was spooked and wanted nothing to do with her.

On the drive back to camp, she felt the rock inside her chest and clawing pain in her stomach that always came with losing an animal. It was murder, pure and simple.

Buck reached over and patted her thigh. "I don't suppose she paid for your services?"

"Doubt she has any money. I bet her son wouldn't have shown up either—if she has a son." She shook her head. "You'd better take down the signs."

Chapter 45: Bear Hansen

Bear was on the outskirts of Louisville, feeling good to be home, admiring wide clean pastures neatly squared and fenced along the highway. "Freebird" started to play. Relieved, he fumbled the phone out of his jacket pocket. He'd been trying to reach Marci all day on her cell and at home since six, and left messages in both places. "Hi, sweetie."

"Hi, Bear."

"Sunny? Where are you?" He couldn't believe it.

"In DeLeon. Got your message. I would've called if I'd known you were in town. I'm so sorry."

His feelings ranged somewhere between angry and hurt. "Jesus! I looked everywhere for you!"

She apologized again and explained that she'd gotten a job at the pancake restaurant and thought it would be better not to bother him.

He wanted to bang his forehead on the steering wheel, but there was too much traffic.

"I've been so busy with work and the four-leggers that I didn't think about you waiting to hear from me."

He could turn right around and head back down to Florida. It might be too late to save his marriage anyway. But he wanted to go home and try.

"Hang on a minute. I'm getting off the road." He turned off on the exit and headed for a gas station. "Are you doing okay, Sunny?"

"Tips are good, but so far I haven't been able to get ahead. I thought I had something big going, but it didn't work out." She explained how the pups were growing and eating more, and there were new litters on the way.

He detected hopelessness.

"It's like you said, unrealistic. Gonna take much longer than I thought." Her voice cracked a little at the end.

He wanted her to succeed. His heart was invested in it. He was an animal softie, but more than that, it would be a shame to see her innocent ambition die. There needed to be more Sunnys in the world, not less, even if she was a little crazy. He couldn't let her give up her dream. "Listen. I can't drive right back down there, but I'll come after Christmas. I'll help you with money to get into an apartment."

"Bear! I'll pay you back! Promise. You're wonderful. It'll be great to see you."

He smiled at her enthusiasm, but he knew he'd gone insane. "You sure I'll be able to find you next time?"

"Positive. The Sugar Mill Pancake Restaurant. I don't think I'll get fired."

"Just in case, where are you camped?" He found a receipt for tires in the glove compartment and put the directions on the back. It occurred to him that he would feel better if he mailed a check in advance. He asked for an address where he could send a Christmas present.

"I have a friend Rita, a vet, but I don't know her address. Oh, wait. I have a card in my bag."

He took down the address.

"Send it in care of Jason Cox."

He was stung by the name he had heard more than once. "Isn't he your old boyfriend?"

"Yeah, but he's married. We work together. You're my only married man."

She was still bringing that up, ironically, when it might not be true much longer. He started to feel more doubtful about the visit, but he'd already gotten her excited. "You're sure it's a good idea? I don't want to get into the middle of something."

"Promise. No more married men. You tricked me, remember?"

"I guess."

"Just come on down. I'm taking good care of your bus."

"I'm sure you are." He didn't want to think about that. The bus he'd lovingly converted to the perfect camper, now likely to be carpeted in clumps of hair and reeking of cat piss. He pictured barking heads out every window. But it was all for a good cause.

He pocketed the directions and got out to fill up on gas. Only a few miles from home. He started thinking about Marci again, wondering if she hated him and how he was going to explain. He made a promise to God that he wouldn't have sex with Sunny ever again if he could have Marci back. He would be a father to the girl.

He turned onto a familiar country road. On either side, the fields were striped with icy rivulets and snow. Winter days with Marci came back to him, sitting by the fire sipping wine or playing Monopoly and smoking dope, listening to Crosby, Stills, and Nash. How long had it been since they did Bike Week? Ten years? Trailered the Harley down to Daytona, or way out to Sturgis, paraded around town with Marci on the back looking like hot shit in her leathers—the low-cut vest that laced up the front. She would fill it even better now.

They were too old for that. But there were other things. The Sunday drives looking for yard sales or tracking down car parts, stopping for a beer, having dinner in a small town cafe. It was a damn fine life that he ruined.

He couldn't remember when everything turned to crap. They'd still managed time to be together when he was working an eight-hour day for the electric company, even with overtime for snow and ice storms. After retirement he'd filled up every minute of his days studying investments and working on vehicles, withdrawn into his own world. He'd wanted to take to the road. His pension, stocks, and rentals were enough for a leisurely life for both of them, but Marci wasn't ready—as if the sick people couldn't do without her . . . That was the kind of thinking that corroded their relationship. He'd been so sure of himself.

Now all he wanted was to be home with her, doing dishes, anything. How many years had passed since he'd stood beside her at the sink and peeled potatoes and carrots?

It was dark when he turned into the long driveway and drove toward the house. A light was on in the living room, but sometimes she left it on, especially if she planned to get home late. He'd made record time driving fast and straight through. Now he was so tired that the thought of a confrontation was almost enough to make him cry. He hoped she would be asleep. He pulled around the side of the house and opened the garage door. No car.

Kelly came to the side door wiggling and whining. At least somebody was glad to see him. He scratched her ears and let her run loose on the grass for a few minutes. He fed her and went upstairs. Kelly stayed in the kitchen waiting for Marci. He put on the new flannel pajamas that Marci had given him for his birthday. He hated pajamas, but sleeping naked seemed a little forward. He fell into bed, hoping that whatever made her love him for forty years would kick in, and she would crawl under the covers beside him. He turned on his side and exhaustion took over.

Chapter 46: Rufus

He listened to bird-screech. Watched crowns of feathers bounce, and flat-eyed tail feathers trailing ground. They never came close or saw him, their heads down pecking.

He gave up watching, dropped rear first and lowered himself against cool ground. He jerked to chew his hind for roving fleas under the coarse black hair, then fell into deep calm.

Breeze brought new scent and his nostrils flared. Female. Rufus-like. His ears twitched and turned toward the crack of twig and brush of stems.

She cowed, toeing along an edge of bush, riveting on bowls.

Rufus stood. Others stirred. Schmeisser, Angel, Wookie, Willie, Pancho, Brindle. They raised their heads, stood, flicked tails, held silent.

Rufus wagged, arched, flattened his front legs on the ground, offering play.

The female stepped close, slow, sidling, back-tracking.

Rufus whined and met her eyes, cocked his head, sat.

She rushed his bowl, empty but for smears, and licked. Her hind waited near his nose, and he pushed into the spicy bud. No fertile juice of welcome, but savory promise. He tongued her fold until she moved on, presented the hind to Schmeisser, to others, as she licked bowl after bowl, found nothing, slunk back into the woods.

Chapter 47: Bear Hansen

"Oow!" A rock or something had hit his head. He sat up. He was in bed. A paperback was sunk in the pillow. Marci stood above him, her face a dark shadow under the brightness of the ceiling light.

"You have your nerve!" she yelled.

He rubbed his forehead, looked for blood on his fingers.

"I barely whacked you. Nothing like what you deserve!"

"I know." He handed her the book. "Hit me some more."

She took the novel and flung it back before he could get his hands up. The spine hit his eyebrow. He rubbed it. Her face was red and seething, mascara running. She aimed again, but he blocked. Kelly jumped up on the bed and barked. Marci's throwing arm froze in place.

He petted Kelly's head. "Quiet, girl, quiet. Go on, Marci, get the Bible and smack me with it. Get the gun—"

She stopped and took Kelly's collar, calming her. "Enough dramatics. Get out of bed and pack your stuff."

Adrenalin started to flow with the realization of what she was saying. "Good god, sweetie. Please! I know I'm an asshole. I've been acting like a damned idiot. Please, give me a chance. Just let me explain. Please." For some reason, the Far Side cartoon of a dog hearing people talk—blah, blah, blah, blah—came into his head.

Marci stepped back and sat down stiffly on the chair next to the bed, leaving the overhead light to glare in his eyes for the interrogation. "Start explaining then, asshole. I don't think it will do you a bit of good, but I'm curious. I know you've been lying to me. I found out about the woman. Your buddies at the saloon aren't all that smart."

He stopped cringing and pushed himself up straight, his back against the headboard. "Who?"

"I want to hear about the woman. Your affair."

"Not a woman, exactly." He tried to think, but his thoughts were jumbled with the shock. He hadn't expected her to know anything for certain.

She looked at her watch and curled her lip. "I'm putting a time limit on this, Barry, so get your jaw in gear."

"She's a poor sick girl. Mentally . . . . I tried to help." He didn't like the look in Marci's eyes. "Okay, I admit I—"

"A mentally ill teenager? –that's what you're telling me?"

"No, no! She's almost thirty." It was an exaggeration. He was all over the place. "Not mentally ill! Please, give me a chance, Marci," He wiped sweat off his forehead, still expecting blood. "She just seems like a girl because she's so scrawny and shy, and she's normal, except she collects strays." The contradictions made him sound like he was making it all up. Marci's teeth were clamped on her lip. He lifted the corners of his mouth into a shy smile, and cast his face down, knowing his lashes were dark and thick against his cheeks, and she'd always found that innocent face irresistible.

A half laugh burst from her open mouth. "That explains it. I bet most of her strays have even more hair than you."

He nodded, thinking Pancho was the exception. "This sounds stale, but we were friends. I met her at the saloon and helped her out with a few extra bucks for dog food. She was always struggling. Then she had an electrical problem—some dog chewed through a wall and almost electrocuted itself. She was upset, and I volunteered to fix the wiring and put up new drywall so the landlord wouldn't find out. I got caught up. There were lots of crises—"

"Why did you follow her to Florida?"

He'd never figure out the answer to that one, or why he promised to do it again. "Mid-life crisis? Brain tumor?"

She tossed her head, scoffing at him.

He wasn't making any ground. "Idiocy, stupidity? All of the above. I don't know, Marci. I don't know."

He went on to admit his lie about the bus and explain Sunny's desperate need for it and her promise to bring it back. "I thought you didn't care what I did. You never said anything when I stayed out late, never asked any questions. You don't need me for anything."

Her face seemed to be softening. "I thought you had more sense. I never dreamed—"

He hadn't dreamed it either, just did it.

She revved up again. "Are you that stupid? You drove all the way down there trying to bring her back?"

All he had left was the truth. "She's so young and she likes me." He knew he was whining. "I just wanted to give her a little cash. She was starving." He looked into Marci's eyes. "I ran around to every crappy bar in town, like a damn fool, and never found her."

"So you don't know where your camper is?"

"Well . . ." He tried to finish it. "Well, I . . . She . . ."

Marci stood up. "I'm not going to wait for you to make up a lie."

"She called me on my cell, on the way home. I just kept driving. I only wanted to get back to you. I think she's got some other guy to buy her dog food."

Marci shook her head. She sat down. "I'm second choice to some pathetic user."

He slid off the bed and knelt on the floor to put his arms around Marci's waist. "Never. Please don't think that." He hugged her as hard as he could and his tears fell on her arm. "You're the best. You're my true love. I lost my mind. I was some needy old fart looking for the Fountain of Youth. Now I'm done. Please, forgive me. Please? Let's go back to how we used to be, take walks and work puzzles, go for drives—"

He looked up hoping for a kind face. It was stern. She wouldn't meet his eyes. "Go down on the couch."

He hid his face against her side, holding tight to hide any relief on his face, conscious of her slim hips and how he'd like to pull them down next to him on the bed. He'd made some ground. He'd never seen her so upset, but the anger was gone, and there was a glimmer. She had a soft heart. He stood and kissed her forehead. "I'll sleep on the couch as long as you let me."

He got a blanket and pillow from the closet. He knew he didn't deserve her, but thank God, the world wasn't fair very often.

Chapter 48: Sunny Lytle

With work from dawn till dark and very little sleep, Sunny had no enthusiasm for the holidays. The Sugar Mill closed early for Christmas Eve, so she took her tips into the little gift shop and bought Buck a T-shirt with an alligator and a walking stick. He liked to have plenty of socks, and there wasn't any selection for men, so she picked out a large brown pair with bears, a joke or charm, depending on how he reacted.

She hadn't gotten any presents for the fur family. She always bought some cans of human-style tuna for the cats and burger to cook up for the dogs to celebrate the holidays. So busy all the time now, she couldn't think. She paddled back to camp, feeling cold and tired.

She revived when she heard the joyous family greeting. There was a healthy fire lighting up an open patch in the night, and something that looked like soup cooking. Buck had decorated a nearby scrub palm with candy canes and half a dozen Coors Light cans twinkled. She heard him rummaging in the cooler and went to give him a kiss.

Beer was heavy on his breath and beard, but she ignored it, making the kiss last and putting her arms around him.

"Need a few more of these," he said, holding up a can. "Still some bare spots."

"Good choice. Much more Christmasy than Budweiser."

He took one hand, put her other arm around his shoulder, and danced her across the clearing. He was chanting or singing, or something in between.

"Had a little monkey. . . brought him from the country . . . fed him on gingerbread. Ankle Spankle bit him on the ankle . . . Now my monkey's dead."

Buck stopped and gave her a big smile. She didn't ask if he'd really owned a monkey.

"Wait till you see what else." He took her to the tree and pointed out several small packages wrapped in newspaper. "Forgot the gift wrap."

She couldn't believe he'd gotten her so many presents. He told her to go ahead and open them. The animals were already fed and walked.

She squatted in front of the tree and picked up the smallest gift. "I have presents for you, but not so many."

"Just open it." He sat down on a log close to her and watched.

She caught his excitement and ripped open the paper and let out a squeal. It was a carved lamb, grinning at her, painted white with a black spot. "I love lambs!"

"I never would have guessed. Keep opening."

She tore open the next one and the next, finding another lamb, two donkeys, a cow and calf, and three camels. They were all happy fur people with big brown eyes. She was giddy. "They're beautiful! It's a nativity set, isn't it? Buck, you're a true artist. You could make a lot of money on these."

"There's more."

She reached farther under the tree, pulled out the last two, and unwrapped figures of German shepherds, one wearing blue and white robes and the other in brown. She giggled. "Canine Mary and Joseph! I'm so glad you didn't ruin it with statues of humans."

"I know what you like."

Nobody knew her better. She leaned over him on the log and hugged his head into her stomach.

He sat up and pointed out one more. "But you have to wait until Christmas morning."

"The infant?"

He kissed her and tucked her hair behind her ears. "You'll see in the morning."

She handed him the bag of gifts, knowing they weren't enough. He gushed over them, and slipped on the alligator shirt. She thought how Jason would fill it out with his broad shoulders and wondered what Debbie was giving him for Christmas. "How about these socks?" she asked Buck, holding them up.

"Bear repellent. Is that what you were thinking?"

"Exactly!"

He gave her a serious look, but maybe he was teasing. "I keep my feet inside, but extra protection never hurts."

He hung them on his ears, made a goofy face, and leaned on the walking stick. "I'm nearly old enough to need this cane." He grinned and his eyes were shining.

The pot held a light cheese soup with chunks of potato and macaroni. It was warm and tangy and she had learned to like potatoes. Buck said that he had invented it for her, Sunny soup. She wondered if he was falling in love with her and whether that was a good thing.

As they ate, she told him about the Christmas Eve when she rescued a stunned squirrel from the side of the road and hid it in her room. "I was little, but I snuck him bread and peanuts. One day my mother saw that the tops of the curtains were chewed off. The next day Mom dropped a blanket over him while he was eating, and out he went. Lytle never found out. Mom bought me a hamster—Miss Poodle, a tan long-hair. It was really a boy."

He told her about his hamsters, Therm and Rafferty. "Me and my brother saved up for them when we were nine and ten."

"You have a brother?"

"Yeah. An astronaut." Buck chuckled. "Anyway, Rafferty turned out to be female. We'd squeeze her poontang and a little juice would come out. We stuck Therm's face in it, and he would lick like mad."

She hit him on the thigh. "Why'd you do that?"

Buck puffed out his cheeks and released the air. "We were boys."

He started into the details of the babies and how they had to get rid of them, but Sunny cut him off. "I had a friend in Indiana with a super-smart rat named Claudine Longet, a white one. My friend moved in with her boyfriend and Claudine ran loose and mated with wild rats—right away there were over fifty. Some pretty color mixtures."

"Whew."

"Her boyfriend couldn't handle it. He gave her a choice—the rats or him."

"I can guess who went."

"Yep. Happy ending." Although, she hadn't heard the final ending. There was a sad ending to every animal story.

Buck supervised as she set up the nativity in the corner of the tent, in case of rain. They settled into the sleeping bag, and she flopped her arm across his chest and nibbled his ear. He had drunk too much beer to get inside her and fell asleep in the middle of trying.

He was up first in the morning, making coffee at the fire. She stretched and noticed that he had added the crib, a carved piece filled with dry weeds. She leaned over and picked it up. Nestled inside was a Pancho in swaddling clothes. Sweet, delicate. She put it to her cheek. Buck had propped the other animals in sexual positions, sheep humping sheep, the two donkeys together, two camels, and the last camel on the cow, since neither had mates. Sunny burst out in a laugh. "Pervert!" she yelled.

"Merry Christmas to you, too."

Hearing her voice, the dogs had started a racket, their needs assaulting her on all levels. She wiped her eyes and dragged herself out, carrying the infant Pancho. Through a hole in the trees a swath of filmy light slanted over Buck as he rooted in a cooler, reminding her of holy card pictures of Jesus. Buck was her savior. She made him stop whatever he was doing and hung her arms around his neck. "You're the sweetest."

"I thought of putting a little figure of myself in there, but I knew you'd like Panchy better."

"You know what, Buck? I always wanted a crib set, since I was a kid.

"Took a chance on it."

She kissed his ear. It didn't matter if he was crazy.

"What else have you always wanted? Old Buck might be able to arrange it."

"Nothing. It's all perfect." She tucked the straw in neatly around Pancho. "I do want a miniature horse, but he's in Louisville."

"Some dreams are best let go."

She knew that, and she was trying, but on the word *dream* her head spun away to Jason opening presents under a sparkling Christmas tree, and weenie dogs racing between wads of gift wrap, dragging red satin ribbons through a big country house.

Chapter 49: Sunny Lytle

The morning after Christmas, the Sugar Mill was hectic with large tables of families that included visiting relatives. Sunny enjoyed the chatter, rather than listening to the drone for walks and meat. She felt less and less like staying at camp. If Rita saw it, she would say the number of animals was the problem, but to Sunny, more fur meant more love. It always had.

In the afternoon business slowed, and she took a tray of syrup pitchers to the kitchen to refill them. She finished the molasses and honey and was headed out from behind the counter when she glimpsed a profile she recognized. Goose bumps stood out on her neck like fur on a dog. Lytle was leering at Ellen. Sunny backed up behind the wall and set the tray on the counter by the refrigerator. He would never go to a family place for breakfast, so he must have heard that she was working there. She looked toward the rear exit, anything but go back out on the floor. She hadn't noticed if he was eating or had just sat down. He could make a scene and get her fired.

Ellen opened the refrigerator. "Sunny, the old guy at left-corner-porch is asking for you."

"I think I'm getting sick."

Ellen touched her forehead with the back of her hand. "You're feverish. I'll finish the syrups. Just tell Patty."

"What does he want?"

"Just to say hi. I was going to give you his table, if you wanted it."

It had to be more than that. He wouldn't go out of his way. She pictured him yanking out a molar and whopping it down on the pancake grill. "Could you do me a favor and tell him I quit?"

"Huh?" Ellen frowned. "He saw you."

"Please, Ellen. It's my father. I'm afraid he'll keep coming back, looking for me."

"I guess I can say this was your last day and you just left."

"Thanks, thanks! I appreciate it." She went to the corner for her backpack.

"I doubt he'll believe me." Ellen took bacon from the refrigerator. "I'm worried about you, Sunny. Can I do anything?"

"Split up my tables, please." She looked around. "Where's Patty?"

"Outside, talking to a vendor."

Jason caught up as Sunny headed through the kitchen. "Your old man. Left-corner-porch."

"I know. I'm out of here."

"Okay." He shoved an envelope into her hand. "Here. I've been meaning to catch you."

She looked at the return address. It was from Bear.

"My wife was a little confused by your mail coming to our house. I didn't know what to say."

"So sorry! I forgot to warn you!" Now she'd started trouble. It was a thoughtless thing to do. "Tell her I'm living in the woods."

"It's okay." He glanced toward the dining area.

She stuffed the envelope into her pack. "I'm afraid he'll follow me to the camp. I don't want him snooping."

He promised to keep an eye out and try to slow Lytle down if he decided to leave in a hurry.

She ran out the back door and around the side of the building. Patty was sitting at the picnic table with a young woman. Items for the gift shop, furry animals, bears, gators, manatees, otters were spread out in front of her. Sunny tried to calm herself, pausing a few steps away, but she was afraid Lytle might come around the corner any second.

Patty looked up. "Is there a problem?"

"No. I mean, everything's fine inside, clearing out. I'm feeling sick." She didn't have time to explain the truth.

"Are you walking home? Sit down. I can take you in a few minutes."

"No. Thanks. I'll be okay." She started off in a run and called back, "Count me out on the tips. I didn't work enough. I'll be in tomorrow. On time." She ran behind the building and up the hill. Breathing hard and sweating, she cut through the live oaks, to stay away from the road until she was out of the park, just in case Lytle drove by looking for her. She stepped into the woods outside the gate. It was a long walk to the camp around the perimeter of the park, but he might have seen her from the window if she went for the kayak.

There were a few clouds. She hoped Buck would still be lying on his back in the tent so she could fill him in. He didn't like Lytle either. She felt better when she plunged out of sight into the thick cover of her woods. When she was surrounded by nature, her mean old man seemed less real—or less important.

Some dogs barked their greeting as she got close, but their cheerfulness was a thin veneer over a painful whine. Something serious was going on. Angel lay on her side panting.

She had tied Pancho at the head of the line and he was hidden. Peering under the bus, she found long streaks of fresh diarrhea with a sulfur odor. He didn't stand up to move toward her or wag his tail. His eyes were dull, not even focused on her.

The sand near the fire pit was swept and wood piled neatly, the tent zipped with both sleeping bags inside. That meant Buck would be coming back later to eat and spend the night.

She drank some water. She would have to get Rita, regardless of the new litters. The dogs might have eaten some poisonous plant. If Buck came back soon with the truck, she could get him to give her a ride. Otherwise, she would have to bike.

The pack went wild. She looked toward the path, expecting to see Buck pushing through the branches. A whiff of cigarette smoke drifted into her nose. The palmetto scrub parted and Lytle stepped into the clearing. "Why the hell are you living back here?"

She swallowed hard. "Who told you?"

He laughed, walking toward the plastic lawn chair, and sat. "Nobody. Got any beer?"

Jason would never have told him. "How'd you find me?"

He nodded toward the bus and the pack standing quiet, at attention. "I guess you got all the dogs you always wanted."

She wondered why they weren't barking their heads off. A few tails wagged. "How'd you find me?"

"I seen your little camp years ago. Always knew where you hung out." He tapped a cigarette out of a pack and lit it. "Didn't want to cook any pancakes for your old pop?"

It brought back memories from the farmhouse, his hung-over breakfast demands. "I already did enough of that."

"Your attitude hasn't improved." He pointed to his cheek, speaking softly. "Come on. Gimme a peck. With you living this close, we should be friends."

Anger turned to fear as she realized how alone they were. She felt like a kid again, not knowing what he would do. "I'm expecting company."

"Jason's at work." He started a wheezy laugh that turned into a deep cough.

"Not Jason."

"Get lots of visitors back here, huh?" He took a drag from his cigarette, threw it down and ground it into the sand.

"Little Sunny. Your cheek bones are still sharp as hatchets." His eyes wandered down her slowly. "And your hips. Goddamn. Those look painful for anybody that might bang into 'em." He chuckled. "But you always have boyfriends. Ain't it handy you and Jason work at the same place? I seen that Rainbow guy hanging around too—Buck. Nut case. He don't scare me."

She wondered if Buck had found him at The Outpost. She walked over to the pack and stood between Rufus and Brindle. She put a hand on each one's head, hoping their aggression was boiling up inside, in response to her fear, but all she felt were stomach cramps. She crossed her arms. "Leave now or I'll let these dogs loose."

"Oh, yeah? I been here with treats." He limped toward her.

She knew he was going to plant a stinking kiss on her cheek, or even her mouth, to show he had control. Bile burned in her throat, black spots appeared, hovering in front of her eyes. Her legs went loose. She steadied herself on Brindle and let Rufus off the leash.

"Get him, Rufus! Get him!"

Rufus looked up at her. He knew the command. He chuffed, soft air bursts inside his closed mouth, but didn't move. "Get him!"

Lytle pulled something from his pocket. "Here, doggie. Sit." Rufus moved toward him, sat, and took a Beggin Strip from his hand, chewing and swallowing in two chomps.

The dogs looked at Lytle, ears up and heads tilted, eager for their turn. How could they take his side for a few treats? Weren't they the least bit grateful to her?

The old man stepped close and grabbed her arm. "See. They like me. Now how bout a kiss for your pop?" He pressed hard against her, one hand holding her arm behind her and the other catching her wrist. His eyes were like old marble, yellow with rusty cracks, and his face was bloated, but he was strong enough to hold her. As he came close, alcohol sweat, rotted teeth, and cigarettes swept over her, the odor of terrible memories. "Give us a kiss, darlin'."

She tried to wrench her wrist from his hand.

"Sunny, I'm not gonna hurt you. I came to say sorry for not being a better daddy. If you'd be nice for once, we could talk."

Having her wrists held inflamed her. She turned her head to the side, as far from him as she could, and tried to twist her arms away.

"Oh, C'mon. Let's see a smile. I don't want to call you Little Gloomy. Remember?"

She remembered and wedged her elbow into his stomach, but it was a weak jab.

He laughed it off. "You're all alone out here. Anything could happen." He grinned. "You better come stay with me."

She wrestled against his hands. "Let me go!"

Pancho responded with a snarl, pulling his sick body up on frail legs, stiff and shaking, lips curled back. He lunged forward at Lytle, but was yanked back by the leash.

"Oow! Fuck!" Lytle let go of Sunny and stepped back. Rufus was connected to his right calf, canine teeth clenched through denim into flesh. Lytle swore, pulled another treat from his jacket, and waved it near Rufus' nose. The dog didn't blink. A growl vibrated in his throat.

Sunny stepped between Schmeisser and Brindle, both now baring their teeth. "Get out of here!" she yelled, "Git! While you can still walk!"

Rufus growled again. A trickle of blood ran down Lytle's exposed ankle.

"I *can't* walk. Get this dog off me!"

She wasn't sure what to do. The dogs were in control. "When Rufus lets loose, you head straight out of here."

"I will. Get him the fuck off."

She hadn't taught him a particular command, but she called his name and told him to sit. Rufus opened his jaws, drew back, and sat, focusing on Lytle's face.

Lytle backed away and inspected the holes in his jeans. "Got the fucked up leg. Didn't need that." He rubbed at the bloody rip and stared at Sunny. "I brought you something, but now I'm not going to give it to you."

"I don't want it. The best thing you can do is go away."

"Sunny—"

"Don't you ever come back here. Don't come to the restaurant. I'll have you arrested."

"For what?" He limped a few steps.

"Just keep moving."

He shuffled a few more steps. "Don't worry. I won't come back here."

"You're drunk. You won't even remember this."

"Not drunk enough." He looked down at his calf and shook his head. "Well, you're my girl. Whether you like it or not. Whether either of us likes it." He turned to walk. "You know, I'm not gonna be around much longer."

He'd been saying that as long as she remembered.

He bent and rubbed at his leg, grimacing, then went into his shirt pocket and dropped some bills on the lounge chair.

She waved it away.

"I should have given it to you when you asked. It's not much. You need it, living in this pigsty." He shook his head. "The house is paid off. I got plenty of room, but you can't bring these filthy animals."

Sunny stared past him, keeping her face blank, as he limped away into the scrub. She put Rufus on his leash and hugged him. A wrenching bowel cramp bowed her in half. She hadn't realized how sick he felt. She started to cry. Pancho lay panting on his side, and she knelt and touched his head lightly, trying to let him know he was her savior. His pain sliced her guts. He had no strength to respond and moved his head away from her hand. She wiped her eyes. *God!*

She went to the table. There were five twenties and two fifties. She got the envelope from Bear and tore it open. A check for two-hundred dollars. It was more money than she'd seen in one place for months. She might need it for medicine.

She went back to Pancho. There was fresh diarrhea on his back legs. He started to cough. Rufus was sitting up, and she massaged him behind the ears, enduring the pain. He dropped down flat, panting.

She slunk onto the lawn chair. Lytle would be back when he got drunk enough. He hadn't done anything she could report to the police, but for her part she had plenty to hide. She put her hands on her head and looked skyward. "Buck, where are you?"

Chapter 50: Sunny Lytle

She took a deep breath when Buck strolled into the clearing. Some of the dogs gave a weak whimper in greeting.

"Sorry, I couldn't get the—" He stopped and looked around.

She ran to him, tears starting to flow. "Buck, Buck!"

"Sunny! What's the matter?"

Her throat was almost too tight to squeeze out the words. "Lytle was here and everybody is sick."

"He poisoned them? Jesus!" He tilted her chin and looked into her eyes. "He didn't hurt you, did he?"

"No." She shook her head and wiped her nose on her shirt. "Rufus bit him."

"Smart dog." Buck called toward the bus, "Good boy, Rufus. I'm not surprised it made him sick."

"They were already sick. Pancho's the worst. He used his last bit of energy to tell Rufus to bite."

"The little stud bosses the German shepherd around?"

She nodded. "I can't handle this by myself. They're all in pain. Could you stay here a while? In case Lytle comes back."

"I'd love to see him come around on my watch."

She remembered the money, stepped back, and pulled the envelope out of her pocket. "Take some of this. He left it."

Buck gave her a hug. "No way. Put it somewhere safe."

She could see it wasn't worth arguing, and she needed the money. The sooner she could get an apartment the better. A small place with big locks.

Eating was a good indicator of their health, so she fed them. Rufus and some others wouldn't touch it. Pancho ate a bite. She left Buck fixing dinner and rode to the Mini-Mart to call Rita.

The recording answered. There wasn't going to be any help that night. "Hi, Rita. It's Sunny. I need you to look at Pancho and some of the others. I'll call you early tomorrow." If they improved overnight, she'd cancel so Rita wouldn't see all the new litters.

Sunny hadn't been this miserable since she lost her fur family in Indianapolis. The night was pitch black with no moon, the universe in motion against her.

Chapter 51: Buckaroo

"Buck, Buck, Buckarooo!" The rays were driving hot and heavy, and the chant helped him to ricochet them in Magnetoid rhythm. Each time he yelled Buckaroo, he tilted the plate and sent a Toid into the earth to die.

At last it was slowing down. His wrists were tired. He hadn't been able to move from the sleeping bag all day. He'd heard the vet for a long time in the morning, checking them, talking to them. He'd kept quiet inside the tent, and she never looked around.

He stretched his legs toward the top of the tent and wiggled his toes. Ooh! Fast one. "Buck." He shifted the plate. "Aroo."

It would be dark soon, finally. He wondered, did they sleep or were they night-blind? They never struck at night, even if he sat by a fire or walked under street lights. He wished he knew more. All trial and error, with the sting of close calls when he erred. He could tell he'd lost some brain capacity.

Finally, the sky cleared and he was able to put down the pie pan. Sunny was late, and he hadn't even fed the dogs, as promised.

Yappy Pancho was missing. The runt was like a rat on bad acid, but Sunny was crazy about him—now supposedly he saved her from her mean father. Two big shepherds were gone, Rufus and Brindle, maybe more dogs. He groaned.

Four of the worn spots under the bus were empty, just shit streaks in the sand. If those dogs died, Sunny would go right over the edge.

He threw dirt over the diarrhea and smoothed the areas where dogs were missing. He was measuring kibble into the bowls when a racket started up. Finally.

Male voices came through the trees from the road. There were two, at least, moving fast. They talked loud, not trying to sneak up, but they could be teenagers, a local gang looking for trouble. He'd need to scare them off.

He darted into the bus, automatically holding his breath as he made his way through the obstacle course of boxes, animals, and cages. Sunny hated guns because they were used to kill animals, so he'd hidden his .38 Police Special inside a plastic tub under a pile of blankets. He dug down and found the box, watching out the window at the same time. A man in uniform broke through the bushes, followed by a man and a woman dressed alike. Fuck! They stopped short in the clearing and he ducked, holding his hand over his mouth to stifle a cough. Not a good time to bring out an unlicensed firearm. He tossed the blankets back into the tub, hoping there was no search warrant. His next thought was drugs. Any roaches left on the rocks near the fire? No. He hadn't had pot in years. Just a conditioned response.

The dogs went wild, barking, growling, and screeching. Puppies yapped in their high pitch from the back of the bus. Buck straightened himself and yelled through the window. "Can I help you?"

They looked up, startled. The first man was from the county sheriff's department. The man and woman were dressed in uniforms he didn't recognize, green shirts and black pants and caps, with badges, but no guns that he could see. The man in green carried a zippered bag.

The cop stepped close to the bus in the gap where Rufus and Brindle were usually tied, and yelled through an open window. "Yes, sir. How are you today? Can you come out here for a moment? Quiet these guys down."

Buck was already headed for the door. He took the bowls of kibble, trying to seem natural. "Good dawgs, good boys." As he passed out the food, they gave up barking, but barely licked at the kibble. "What can I do for you?"

"These people are field investigators. There was a report of abused animals living here in the woods inside a bus. Is this your bus?"

"No, sir. The lady of the—bus—isn't in."

"Would that be Miss Sunny Lytle?"

He wondered where they got their information. "I believe so."

"Mind if we take a look?"

"How about—come back tomorrow?"

The woman spoke. "We need to determine immediately if there are suffering animals inside the bus."

"No, there sure aren't. I can tell you that. We had a vet here earlier today." He pointed to the food bowls. "That's why dinner is late."

They woman nodded to the cop and spoke. "We need to see for ourselves."

"Got a search warrant?" Buck asked.

The cop stepped up. "The animals' welfare is at stake. We don't need a warrant."

The woman walked up to Buck. "Sir, our goal is to educate people. We want you to spend your money keeping these animals healthy, rather than paying for fines and court cases."

"I'm just helping out."

The cop folded his arms. "You're lucky this bus is parked on private property. A little farther north on county land and I would have to move you. As it is, you can take care of this with Animal Control, but if you don't cooperate, I'll have to bring out the property owner."

Buck's shoulders drooped.

"Please, have a seat, sir, while they take a look."

His head felt ready to implode, like a Toid had got him. Dogs carted off. Animal Control. The vet must have reported them. He wondered how many more they'd take. Sunny would go ballistic. He dropped into the plastic chair.

The two stood at the front of the bus to put on gas masks, goggles and gloves. They walked slowly through the inside, stopping to pet cats on the table and seats. When they got to the back, they leaned over the wall of cardboard boxes, looking into the puppy corral. The gun was close enough to bite. His heart thudded against his lungs.

They came out ripping off their gear. The woman walked over to Buck, her face dripping. "The sanitation is unacceptable, but there don't seem to be any starving animals. Fleas are severe and the space is insufficient, especially for when those puppies get bigger. There's a serious need for neutering and spaying." She turned to the man. "What do you think of this set up with dogs tied outside?"

The man shook his head. "They're exposed to wild animals and diseases they carry."

"My thoughts exactly. No rabies tags." She turned back to Buck. "We need to speak to the owner of the bus to make a plan for these animals' welfare."

He wasn't about to give out any information he didn't have to. "The owner is probably with the veterinarian."

The woman went into the bag and brought out an official looking sheet of paper. She wrote something on it and handed it to Buck. "This is a legal notice. She needs to let us know when she'll be here."

"She's really busy at work. I'm not sure—"

"We'll be back out in forty-eight hours if we haven't heard from her."

He was amazed that they were leaving empty-handed. He promised to have everything taken care of. It was what they wanted to hear. "I think she has some people who want to adopt puppies."

"That would be great."

The sheriff gestured toward the bus, the sheets, the surroundings. "It'll be better for everybody if you let these people help."

Buck nodded, in sincere agreement, but he knew Sunny would rather die than allow strangers to take away members of her family.

Chapter 52: Sunny Lytle

Rita had promised to bring medicine to the camp on her mid-morning break and pick up Sunny after work. She sat at the picnic table near the screen door and watched for Rita's car. The restaurant calico was nearby in the grass flickering her whiskers and eyes, trying to charm a bird from the wooden fence around the antique mill stones. The bird was tiny and tan with some bright yellow under the tail, and it kept twitching its hind feathers as if nervous. Sunny had seen cats use hypnosis to lure birds, but never with a successful capture. It was another kind of communication between species that people knew nothing about. She shooed the bird away then put her head down on the wood table. What was holding Rita up? Sunny should have taken off work to be there. If Rita thought the situation was bad enough . . . She closed her eyes.

She felt a tap on her shoulder.

It was Rita. "I'm so sorry. I had to take in four of them."

"What?" She felt dizzy as she stood up, still half-asleep. "In where?"

"To the facility. No choice. It's parvovirus. I could smell it before I even got to the camp. The Chihuahua and the Westie are critical. I've been working on them all afternoon.

"Pancho and Angel? At the shelter?"

"Yes. They were badly dehydrated and needed IV's. Electrolytes, dextrose, potassium chloride, and vitamin B, as well as a round of antibiotics for secondary infection. Two of the big shepherds too. Pancho is the worst, maybe because he's so small. Some others had milder cases, and I treated them with Kaopectate and antibiotics. There is no cure. The disease has to run its course. You'll have to watch them and keep up on their medications."

Sunny held herself stiff to keep from breaking down. "Is Pancho going to be okay?"

"I can't say for sure—if only you'd called sooner—this is a dangerous disease."

"I just saw that they were sick yesterday."

"That's because you're not around to give them proper attention."

She could hear anger in Rita's voice, and it was true. Sunny was gone most of the day and barely touched them when she was there, trying to avoid all their burning itches.

"I'm upset about the way you're keeping them, Sunny. Not only the disease, but the unchecked breeding, crowded quarters, filth. I know you're trying your best, but it's too much for anyone. These animals are highly stressed. Have you brought in another dog lately?"

"No. Nobody."

Rita looked doubtful.

"I saw a stray, maybe a week ago, but I couldn't catch her."

"That's it then. She visited while you were gone and left Parvo. If we searched the woods, we would probably find her body. It moves fast untreated. The bowels slough off. Blood in the stool creates the terrible smell."

Sunny covered her face with her hands. She had caused all of it.

"I'm sorry, Sunny, but you need to listen to the facts. These animals are exposed to everything out there. I bet their shots aren't current either."

She couldn't speak.

"I should have said something about vaccines earlier. I should never have let this go on for months. It's a wonder they haven't contracted rabies."

"I know you're right. I planned on getting their shots soon."

"Besides that, what about the bus? I didn't even look in there. It's only a matter of time until the cats and rabbits get sick from something. Do you understand what I'm saying?"

At least, Rita hadn't seen the new puppies. "I know, I know." She wiped her face, and tried to stop tears. "I thought I could handle it."

"How long has Pancho's coat been sparse like that?"

"Forever. I got him from a lady who moved into a nursing home. She said he had mange when he was a pup and the hair would never grow back."

"Okay. He isn't contagious anymore or they'd all have that too."

Sunny took Rita's hand. "Please, don't be mad at me. I just want to die."

Rita sat close and tucked a stray piece of hair behind Sunny's ear. "I'm not mad. I'm upset. I know exactly what you're trying to do, but it's never going to work. Not like this."

She took Rita's hand. "I have Buck. Buck is with me now. Really. In a few weeks I'll have enough saved up for an apartment, and they can be indoors. I've done it before. I can handle it. I swear, Rita."

"I didn't see Buck. Are you telling me the truth?"

"Yes. I have four hundred dollars."

Rita looked unconvinced. "We're going to have to work out something. I'm upset with myself because I should have seen this coming." Rita pulled her up from the bench. "Come on, I'll take you for a visit."

Sunny knew what would be worked out, and she couldn't let it happen, but she had to go along with Rita until the dogs were healthy. Then she'd move on to another county or state. But she liked her job and the people she worked with—and being near Jason. She liked Rita too—and Buck—not a chance he would go with her.

Chapter 53: Rita McKenna

Her anger condensed into tears and she pulled off the road to wipe her eyes, ignoring Sunny's discomfort in the passenger seat. *How could she have let this happen?* It was a classic case. Still she didn't know what to do, short of turning the girl over to the county—complete betrayal. She blew her nose and looked at Sunny. She was calm and distant, staring into the darkening woods, probably already planning to run. Rita couldn't let it happen. Anti-depressants and behavioral therapy had been prescribed with some effectiveness for hoarders. But how would she ever get Sunny started? "You only told me about the outside animals. Do you have more dogs in the bus?"

"Just Ginger and her babies. No diarrhea. I separated the older ones a couple weeks ago."

"How many puppies?"

"A few."

"You're going to have to take them all out in a clean place and mop down the floor with a Clorox solution. Virus could have gotten tracked in. You'll need to dowse the whole area outside, wherever the sick ones have been tied or walked."

She explained how she had them blocked off in back. "I'm worried about the others, their pain."

"Having your intestines slough off is a bit uncomfortable."

Sunny started to cry. Rita felt harsh for being facetious, but she had to get her message through. She handed the girl a tissue.

When they got to the shelter, she took Sunny to see Angel first. The little dog wagged her tail, but didn't get up. Rita looked at Angel's eyes, palpated her abdomen, and checked the IV. She asked Sunny to hold her so she could get a temp. "It's come down some."

"I can take her home then?"

"Sunny. No . . . she's still sick. I have to leave in the IV until she starts to eat and drink." Rita turned to go down the hall. "Let's see the others." She couldn't tell the girl that animals being treated at the shelter wouldn't be allowed to return to their owners and had to be put up for adoption.

The two big shepherds, Rufus and Brindle, were standing in their pens wagging and woofing. There was no diarrhea on the floor. Sunny held each one around the neck as Rita took the temps. "They'll be on boiled chicken and rice for a few days now, no grease."

Sunny petted them and rubbed behind their ears. She asked to see Pancho.

Rita led her to the isolated cage in a treatment room, hoping to God he was still alive. Pancho was curled on a blanket. He managed a weak tail-wag when Sunny reached inside the cage. "Poor sweetie, poor baby."

The Chihuahua was too lethargic to move even during his rectal temperature. "Still spiking a fever." She might lose him yet. She changed the IV, added some Vitamin B and Ampicillin to the Lactated Ringers. She tried to start into the risky topic. "If you had only one or two dogs you could treat them special."

"I treat them all special."

The girl was exasperating. "What about the puppies? You've let these animals multiply."

"They deserve to have families."

She wanted to say that they didn't deserve short, miserable lives. "Every big-eyed, furry-faced pup and rambunctious kitten breaks your heart—my heart too—but there have to be limits. It's selfish to let them breed so you can enjoy them."

Sunny's face was grim and frozen. "You wouldn't say that about humans. Fur people have the same biological rights."

She was getting nowhere. She gave the girl a hug and invited her to stay at the apartment for the night after they checked the camp dogs. Sunny refused, saying Buck would be waiting. She offered a ride to the shelter for the next day, but Sunny said she didn't need one.

She dropped the girl at the woods, relieved to be finished with the questions. She considered taking a risk to spring Pancho so Sunny could keep him—if he made it. Nobody else would take him. She wasn't sure what to wish for.

Instead of wishing, she let her mind bathe in warm thoughts of pleasure. She would be visiting John for the weekend, and could let all her worries go.

Chapter 54: Buckaroo

He was sitting by the fire with a beer, heating some beans, when she came crashing through the scrub. He had walked, fed, and watered everyone. Anything to help her mood.

She sounded worn-out. "Buck, you're the best. I was over at the shelter. Paunchy's so sick. They're all sick." She told him about the disease and what Rita had said. "The best thing to do is move the bus. Clean it and move closer to the water. It'll make the chores easier and we'll be away from the germs."

Too much for him to think about. "Sit down." She stayed standing, but he took out the paper from Animal Control and handed it over.

She scanned it and looked around, frantic. "Who did they take?"

"Nobody. I used my old-fashioned charm." He explained the two-day time limit and tried to convince her that they were nice people who wanted to help.

"How did they find us?"

"Somebody reported you to the sheriff's office."

"Shit! Every time I trust . . ."

"The vet?"

"She's the only one who knows where we are, except Jason."

"There you go!"

"Buck! Jason would never set the police on me."

"What about Lytle?"

"No way. He steers clear of cops. It must've been Rita."

"These county people seem to care." He put his hand on Sunny's shoulder. "We could use some help, you know?"

She jerked away and walked down the line of dogs, kissing and rubbing ears frantically. "Been there, done that. Tell you how this works, Buck. They think we're sick. They'll pretend to be helpful the whole time they're carting away every single fur person, mostly to kill them. Then they'll leave us with a big fine, or maybe toss us into the local jail, depending on the laws."

He realized that he had become part of the "us." There could be bad sides to it as well as the good. He followed her one dog to the next, patting butts like he'd seen Jason do. "I'm not a guy who trusts uniforms, but they didn't seem like that to me."

"We've got to move far enough away so they can't find us, maybe farther south. Make it look like we're long gone. Will you help me?"

He gave her a kiss. "Sure." He disagreed, but she was the expert, and he had a hard time refusing her when she asked so sweetly.

She said they would need to start in the morning. Another advantage was that Lytle wouldn't be able to find them.

"Does that mean you won't need me to sit here?" He was thinking of his clean, quiet camp.

She settled down on the lounge and cracked open a water. "Do you mind being here?" She explained that she didn't mean to depend on him so much.

"Don't worry. It's just that sometimes I'm pretty busy."

"Yeah, I know. Magnetoids."

He admitted it had been a bad day.

She gave him a look, gnawing her lip. "Buck, think about it. Nobody else has this problem."

"They're out for me, what can I tell you?" He knew she was going to suggest seeing a shrink. "How about you? You've got some—"

"Listen, I wish I was imagining all of it, Buck."

"I feel exactly the same way." He opened a bag of chips, got two bowls, and dished up some beans. She sat down by the fire, but refused the food.

He set the bowl of beans on her lap so she had to hold it, thinking of how he could cheer her up. "Listen, I know you think animals are all innocent and everything, but they're not. When I was a kid we got two birds from a pet store, one named—"

"You and your brother—the astronaut?"

He didn't know what she was talking about. "No. The film star."

She frowned. "Do you ever see him?"

"Naw. He's a big shot in Hollywood—California. We were teenagers when we got the two birds."

"What kind of birds?"

"I don't know, but the clerk said we had to get a pair because one all by itself would die of loneliness. Petey and Sweetie. But Sweetie wasn't sweet." He paused. "One morning I found Petey's plucked carcass on the floor of the cage."

"She killed him? Why are you telling me this?"

"Yeah. And a few days later she died of loneliness."

Sunny bit her lip, but the corners of her mouth pulled upward. "Did you just make that up?"

"Pretty clever, huh?" He burst out laughing and she laughed with him. Better not to admit that the story was true. He put his arm around her.

"You're so bad," she told him. She laughed and chuckled until the tears came, and he held her and let her cry away as many sick dogs as she could. He wiped her eyes with his bandana and told her to make a list so he could shop while she was at work. He let money she shoved into his pocket stay. She needed a lot of leashes.

The bus would be disinfected and moved the next day, before the law came back. He knew it was a mistake.

Chapter 55: Rita McKenna

Pancho's high-pitched yowl greeted Rita the next afternoon as she walked into the treatment room. He bounced against the front bars and yapped.

"Hungry, little fellow?" She opened the cage and set his portion of boiled chicken and rice on the metal rack, and he gobbled the meat in seconds. He wagged and wiggled as she petted him. Using a stiff brush, she scrubbed feces off the grate, then washed the tray underneath.

His temp was gone and he was much stronger. All four dogs were doing well, and she knew that Sunny would be stopping by or calling to ask when she could take them home. Angel, Rufus, and Brindle were already plugged into the system, the word being sent out online that they were available for adoption. Angel was borderline for getting a home because of her age, but she was still fluffy and cute. Rita knew she should do the paperwork for Pancho, but she couldn't. There were so many healthy dogs, nobody would take a yappy pink doglet with dandruff.

She was likely to get fired if Jackie caught her returning Pancho to Sunny. She finished the checkups and went to the office. She filled out an adoption form for Pancho with John's name and address in Orlando. He'd gladly help her out if Jackie made a follow-up call.

Rita planned to return Pancho to the camp in the evening, after Jackie left. It was going to be bad enough breaking the news to Sunny that the other three had to stay, but the situation would be somewhat alleviated with a few less animals.

At five, Rita was straightening up at the front desk, just ready to grab the little dog and leave when the door opened.

"Denise—hi—I didn't know you were coming in this afternoon."

She explained that she was there on a whim to take a look at the male shepherd and the shepherd-lab female that were ready for adoption.

Rita followed Denise back to the kennels, feeling like a traitor, but excited about the possibility.

"I'm ready to replace my last shepherd, Munchen, not that he could actually be replaced."

Rita opened the pen. "They're fully recovered from the parvovirus. Luckily, they all made it."

"Not luck—good treatment, I would guess."

Rita smiled and ruffled Brindle behind the ears while giving both of them her highest recommendations for temperament and intelligence. "They belonged to a girl who loves them, but couldn't provide basic care. Sunny—she's been here a few times."

Rita realized that Sunny could appear at any moment and went to lock up the front. She looked out the window in the office. If Sunny could meet Denise and say goodbye to Rufus or Brindle, Rita would feel better, but it would mean a major battle.

When she got back, the dogs were butting against Denise's legs, slapping their long tongues on her arms, and wagging themselves almost in half. Denise probably weighed a hundred pounds, and either of them could easily knock her down, but she didn't seem stressed.

Rita stepped out of the pen for Denise to test them. Both dogs responded to basic commands. There was no question that Denise was boss.

Denise said she'd bought several acres nearby with a house and a barn, in order to have horses and start riding again and, eventually, open a refuge, The Haven, where unadoptable animals could live out their lives. She'd been working on grant proposals and had a few prospective donors. "It's always been my dream. Of course, I need a lot more money—a partner probably."

This was the first personal information that Denise had shared. They hadn't had much contact, mainly because of Denise's short hours, but Rita had avoided the "real" vet in the break room on a few occasions. Jackie had led her to believe that Denise felt herself too sophisticated for friendly interaction.

Denise checked the dogs' teeth and gums and looked into their eyes. "I'd hate to split these guys up." Brindle cocked her head. Her long-lashed chocolate eyes poured emotion, the raw need that no dog-lover can refuse. "They know how to turn on the charm."

Rita suggested that if Denise wanted to take either or both of the dogs, she could come back and meet Sunny the next evening. *Traitor* pounded in her head. Denise agreed to come back, giving herself time to sleep on her decision.

On the way out, Rita pointed out Angel as another dog from the same group.

Denise put her hand over her mouth. "She's so much like my old dog, Hershel."

Rita walked her to the front. "I'm glad we had a chance to talk. You know I had my own practice until—"

"I've seen enough of your work to know that you're a fine doctor. It doesn't seem fair that you don't get a second chance."

Rita felt her face reddening. How could she have mistaken Denise for a snob?

She waited for Denise to drive off before she took Pancho from the cage. She was positive that Denise would keep the secret, but there was no sense in involving her.

Chapter 56: Rita McKenna

She approached the camp, Pancho in the lead. At a hundred yards he went crazy, yipping and hopping, choking himself with his collar. Up ahead it was already an insane asylum for dogs, high-pitched yelps and thundering barks in chaotic bursts. She parted the last clump of palmettos and Pancho took a turn toward the bus. A hippie guy walked up, carrying a five gallon bucket of water. "Are you the vet?"

Rita tied Pancho to the empty rope where she'd found him. She put out her hand. "You're Buck?" It seemed that Sunny adopted any needy individual, man or beast.

The girl came out of the tent. "Rita, you brought Panchy!" She ran to him and crouched down, cuddling him to her chest. Rita watched, waiting for questions about the others. Sunny kissed Pancho and stroked his back. Finally, she looked up. She was somber. "Thank you for saving his life."

"I'm glad I could do it." She handed over the chicken and rice.

Sunny stood there, holding the tiny pooch and his food, swallowing hard. Rita could sense an outburst building and she hadn't even let out the bad news. "Sunny, I'm doing what's best for you and your family, but there are problems."

Sunny's face blazed and her chin went up. "Don't you think I know? You called the police!"

"The police?"

"They brought Animal Control over here," Buck said.

Somebody else had taken the lead. "Sunny, I had nothing to do with it."

"You're the only person who could have told them."

Rita's mind raced. She had only mentioned Sunny to Denise, not even an hour ago.

"If you didn't do it, then prove it by calling them off."

She let out a long breath. "Where are they from? I'm not sure I have the authority."

"I want to believe you, but I can't."

"Look. I've wrestled with the idea for weeks because I didn't want to hurt you. It was irresponsible, but I didn't tell anyone." She pushed the hair back from her face. Someone else taking the initiative made her feel even worse.

"So call them off."

"These people are all animal lovers or they wouldn't be in the business. They want to work with you, help the fur family—you need to let them."

"That's what they said," Buck told Sunny.

Rita knew the girl's heart was broken, and another stroke added against the human race. She said that she was leaving town for a long weekend and would try to find out who was in charge and talk them into waiting until she got back before doing anything.

Sunny nuzzled Pancho, not seeming to hear. "How are Angel, Rufus, and Brindle? My friend Jason can bring me to pick them up tomorrow."

"I can drive you," Buck said. He glanced at the sky. "Probably."

Rita took a breath and told her the bad news.

Sunny looked up, pale.

"I had to sneak Pancho out, risk my job." She explained that the facility wasn't a veterinary office, and she was only able to treat rescued dogs there. "Tomorrow the other veterinarian is coming back to adopt one or maybe both of the big dogs. I'm sure she'll let you visit them."

"No!" She dropped to a sitting position in the sand, holding Pancho to her chest, putting her face into his neck, her shoulders shaking.

Rita touched her hair. "I know Pancho is your favorite, so I took a big chance."

Sunny wiped at her eyes and asked about Angel.

"I'm hoping she'll get a home, too."

The girl held out her hands, pleading. "Why didn't you tell me? I could have taken them somewhere else."

She wanted to shake her by her boney shoulders. "Pancho would be dead." Reminding herself that the girl had an illness did little to cool her down.

Buck put his arm around Sunny. "She's right. You must know it. There are too many dogs to take care of."

Sunny jerked herself away. "They love me. They won't know why I sent them away."

"Just tell 'em," Buck said. "Anyway, all they do is complain, right?"

Sunny shot him a look and he shut his mouth as if on orders. Rita wondered what that was about. She wanted to bring up the need for spaying and neutering, but she held back. "Let me take a look at the puppies, to make sure they're okay? They need distemper shots."

Sunny dug her toes into the sand and wiped her eyes. "Not today. I need to clean up. They're fine."

She agreed to bring the vaccine after work the next day and drive Sunny back to meet Denise.

Buck motioned to the bus. "We're getting ready to move—"

"Oh, yeah," Sunny said. "We're going to move the bus to the other side of the clearing where it's fresh."

"I'm going to douse the ground good over there with Clorox solution," Buck said.

"Perfect." Rita turned to go. There was no means of repairing any trust. She walked through the brush into the woods, shuffling to warn snakes and keeping a sharp eye out for spiders. The terrible news was out of the way. Still, major hysteria was likely when Animal Control came to remove the pups. It couldn't go any other way.

Chapter 57: Sunny Lytle

She sat down next to Buck and stared into the fire, trying to calm herself until she knew Rita would be out of ear shot, but she was drained and shaky. She touched Buck's knee. "We've got a lot to do if we're going to move before she comes back tomorrow."

"What? I thought everything was copacetic."

Somehow, he had believed the lie. "You kidding? She'll be back with those guys to take all the pups."

"I trust her. She snuck Pancho back and she's doing everything she can for the dawgs. My money's on Lytle as the snitch."

She considered the possibility. "No way. He hates police— and he wouldn't want me chased away." She chewed her lip. Rita had sounded sincere, but it wasn't the first time for being caught off-guard. "Buck, you don't know these people like I do. In her mind she's doing good—the end justifies the means. She believes in the system. But it'll be terrible for us."

Sunny woke before dawn, blood tingling through her body. Buck was snoring beside her. She unzipped the tent and stuck her head out. The sky above was starry, fuzzy clouds crossing the moon like a herd kicking up dust—a stampede. A sign that she was doing the right thing by moving the camp where Rita couldn't find it. She gave Buck a kiss on his beer-and-cigarette morning mouth and told him to sleep a little more while she took the first group on a walk through the woods to find a well-hidden site that would keep them safe, at least temporarily. It was going to be a long hard day of disinfecting and moving with no time to waste.

She watched the sturdy steps of furry hind legs over branches and dips, the bounce of cute butts, and the naked pink butt with over-sized testicles that was Pancho's. There was no patting or stroking any of her family anymore. No burying her nose in the luscious pleasure of fur since she had become sensitive to all their discomforts. It was a hard reality. She tied them to trees and walked back to the old camp, thinking about rescuing Angel by giving a false name and address to a volunteer who wouldn't know her.

She picked a spot a twenty-minute-walk away with low weeds and a nice canopy, forty or fifty feet from the water, bushes and a few trees in between. She didn't want to be spotted by boaters, but there seemed to be enough cover since the bus blended in with the foliage.

It was after four by the time everything was clean and ready to move. Buck was at the new site, on his back, dodging Magnatoid shots. Sunny turned the key to start the bus, in panic that Rita might be there any minute. She pushed in the clutch, gunned the motor, and lurched into motion. She had planned to drive slowly, creeping between bushes and plants and staying on bare sand as much as possible, but now she was forced to plow through ruts, mow down some scrub, and scrape through outer branches. Cages holding cats, rabbits, and ferrets banged into each other, and pups bounced loose, unable to walk, tumbling and yapping. Cats yowled, worse than mating cries. She had put old Wookie in a wooden orange crate wedged between seats, knowing he couldn't walk all the way to the new site, and he gargled a weird cry. The right side of the bus smashed into a branch and a window broke. Glass fell inside.

Finally she glimpsed the tent tossed on the ground with Buck on top of it, and the dogs she had tied to the trees waiting and wagging. She slowed down and took a breath. Buck waved, still facing the sky, and she drove past him to park between the camp space and the water. The bus was in chaos.

She righted one of the crates stuffed with cats that had tumbled on its side, the cats packed too close together to upright themselves. She checked Wookie, then ran to the back, seeing a blood trail from a puppy. It was the apricot and white cockapoo she called Peaches. Sunny screamed as she picked up the fluffy pup and saw the gash in his paw, felt his stinging pain.

"What happened?" Buck yelled. "You okay?"

She threw a jacket over the glass, and ran toward him with the pup. The paw was dripping. "You've got to help me, Buck. Either bandage this little guy or run back and camouflage the path I left."

"Hand me the puppy and my handkerchief. I'll fix a tourniquet between strikes. He tilted the plate. "Ouch! A close one. You, mother-fuckers!"

"Buck, there's nothing there!"

He wouldn't look at her. She put the bloody pup on his chest and ran to get a clean T-shirt from a box in the bus. She brought it back and flung it at him. "Wrap him up. I'll be back."

She tore off through the weeds, cutting the shortest path under branches and over shrubs, tripping and falling to one knee, pulling herself up, continuing to run. She prayed she could camouflage the tracks before Rita got there with her crew.

She was out of breath and dripping sweat as she reached the edge of the camp, but she was alone. She picked up dry palmetto fronds and held them together like a broom to whisk at the tracks on the thin layer of sand and leaves. Bent over and sweeping, she ran ahead on one track, then doubled back on the second, until she had camouflaged the first twenty yards or so of bus tread. Still, it wasn't enough. Rita was smart.

Sunny kept up until she had set the ground right and bent back the undergrowth for at least fifty yards. She bent bushes back into place. It would have to do while there was a bleeding puppy on Buck's chest and fur people freaking out in the bus. For once, a bit of luck with timing, but she knew it wouldn't last. She'd made too many wrong choices, trusted too many people.

Chapter 58: Rita McKenna

She learned that Dave and Maria from the South Shelter Animal Control were in charge of the Sunny Lytle case, and they promised not to proceed until Rita returned from California. Someone out of state, apparently a visitor to the area, had made the call to the sheriff's department, not knowing the animal rescue number. A stranger had taken the first step. Rita began to wonder if she ever deserved a veterinary license. Maybe she should get out of the animal protection business altogether.

Still, she was eager to get back to Sunny with news of the reprieve and to administer the vaccinations. After hydrating two dogs that had been left without water or shelter for days, she was finally on her way, an hour late. Denise had decided to take Rufus and Brindle and was waiting to meet Sunny.

Rita rushed to the camp, hoping to finish quickly. She would be flying out early in the morning to visit John. Besides Sunny, the trip was all she could think about, feeling both excited and hesitant. She and John had been together on most evenings in DeLeon, but she wasn't sure what it would be like in LA without her own transportation and no private time. She suspected that her anxiety was baggage from the last mistake, but they hadn't spent many waking hours together beyond fun times with plenty of alcohol.

She pulled off the road and grabbed the plastic bags of needles and vaccine vials from the front seat and stuffed them into her shoulder bag for the trek into the woods. She hoped she had enough and that Jackie wouldn't notice how much vaccine was used before the new order came in. It was a risk she had to take.

She drifted into memories of fun with John and visions of being spoiled by lavish dinners and good wines. He spent too much money on her, but for a fault, she couldn't think of a better one. She was lucky to be able to take the trip, with Denise filling in for her, one person she could count on.

She walked among the scrub without thinking, until she noticed that she was in an unfamiliar spot. Had she gotten off the path? She was pretty sure that she had gone too far. She turned back and walked slowly, peering into the woods on all sides. It was already dusk and there was mist in the air that shortened her range of vision. Still, how could she have missed the bus and hanging sheets? She smelled bleach, like a heavily-dosed swimming pool. Sunny must have followed her instructions for cleaning.

Maybe she hadn't walked far enough. She turned around again, walked farther, became totally confused. The smell was unmistakable, but no camp. The mosquitoes were vicious.

It was now dark enough that she could see the glow from street lights out on Ponce DeLeon, so she followed the light toward the car, giving up on finding the path, moving fast and trying to dodge foliage, slapping at bugs and feeling like she had lost her mind. Then she saw something large and light in color between the trees. It looked like an elephant—a spooky trick of light. The bleach was stronger. As she walked closer she identified a sodden mound of bedding and clothes, carpeting and wood, all kinds of junk. Sunny had run. Damn it. Where could she have gone so quickly?

She could only see a few feet around her so there was no sense in searching. They could be anywhere. At least Buck would be some protection. He seemed to have some sense. She pictured Sunny's innocent eyes, taking in the world and transforming vision to fantasy. They gave her a look of being touched somehow, a little crazy, yet endearing, sad, and mostly vulnerable.

Selfishness had allowed this to happen. With all her own plans and infatuation, Rita hadn't been paying enough attention. Now it was too late to do anything until morning, and if she did find Sunny, there would be no time to vaccinate before she went to the airport. She toyed with the idea of staying home. As a vet, it felt like her duty to stay. Yet, she wasn't a vet, didn't get paid like a vet, wasn't respected as a vet. John had paid her airfare and Denise planned her week around filling in at the shelter. Would one long weekend make a difference to the animals? John would never forgive her.

On the way to the airport, fingers crossed, she stopped at the Sugar Mill. Sunny was behind the counter filling bowls with blueberries. Rita stepped in beside her and gave her a hug. "Thank god, you're here."

Sunny pulled away. "I love this job, Rita. Please don't make me find a new one somewhere else."

Waiters and waitresses were piling up, staring, unable to pass behind them into the kitchen. She took Sunny's hand and led her out to the floor. "I'm going out of town for several days, and nobody will be looking for you. When I come back, I'll help you make a plan. Please, please, wait for me. Just give me a chance to straighten things out. I promise, I'll help you." She explained the details she'd been given about the rescue call. "I swear, Sunny. I didn't know anything about it."

A family of six walked behind them up the path. Sunny looked inside as the door swung open. "I have to go."

Rita caught her by the arm and told her about Denise and her plan, the no-kill facility, room for the whole fur family, a place for Sunny. They were false hopes, basically lies, but she had to make sure Sunny stayed in town. She stared steadily into the girl's eyes, still seeing no promises. "She plans to take in horses."

Sunny paused, chewing her lip. She gave Rita a hug, her ribs cutting into Rita's. When Sunny pulled back, her eyes were huge, watery, and earnest. Rita grinned, letting all her hopes shine in her face. Enthusiasm was easy at the moment. She had five days in California.

Chapter 59: Bear Hansen

Bear managed to reap enough forgiveness to stay in the house, but was still waiting for an invitation back into Marci's bed. He helped with cooking and cleaning, and repaired the gutters and downspouts that he'd let go while in his Sunny coma. He worked hard at being amusing and set up a winter scene jigsaw puzzle on a card table near the fireplace. Marci gave up one of her volunteer jobs, and they spent time together after dinner, but he wasn't sure if it was for the pleasure of his company or to keep an eye on him.

Christmas was one of the most enjoyable he could remember, with the whole family around. There were just a few off times when they were alone that Marci mentioned her future and didn't seem to include him. She said how nice it would be to spend time in California after her retirement. Bear noticed that the joint account wasn't increasing at the usual rate, and she admitted opening up a personal savings account.

Still, even on such shaky ground, he couldn't forget his promise to drive back to Florida with emergency cash for Sunny. Her skinny bones haunted him, the innocence of her misguided ways. He felt partly responsible since he had made the whole mess possible by loaning the camper. He also wanted it back. Marci had agreed to travel as part of their trial reconciliation, and it would be silly to spend money renting an expensive vehicle when he had designed the perfect set up.

His emotions were a tangled mess, but he could collect his property with no fooling around, and then head straight back home, provided he could convince Marci to let him make the trip. It didn't matter how much he lost on the Chevy. He'd been tired of looking at it taking up space in the barn, had gotten it painted the original Matador red and white, and proclaimed it done. John hadn't called back, but it was car country down there, so somebody else must be looking for a gorgeous, fine-tuned vehicle. He could kill two birds—sell the car and collect the camper. It made sense . . . to him.

Marci loved nice jewelry so he bought her a new ring, a ruby-crusted diamond set in white gold, as a concrete vow that he would only be going to Florida to sell the Bel Air and bring his camper back. He thought of inviting her to go along—major stress—but he doubted she could take vacation days anyway if she was going to save up for camping in the summer.

He took her to her favorite steakhouse and brought out the ring.

She cut her eyes at him as he slipped it on her finger. "It's beautiful." Clearly, she was suspicious, as expected.

"This is my promise. I'm completely done with all my stupid shenanigans—the happiest man I can be." He gave her time to admire the flickering facets in the candle light and go back to eating. "I think I've got a buyer for the Bel Air—down in Florida."

"What?" Her eyes were slits.

He pulled out John's card. "When I sell the car, I can get the bus and drive it home so we can use it this summer."

She looked at it. "Run down to Florida?"

"Yeah. Quick trip. Drive the car, come back in the bus."

"I can't believe you have the nerve . . ."

He didn't have any nerve at all. Whining came naturally. "Marci, listen. I don't want to see the girl. I just want to sell the car, get the camper, and be done with all this forever. She used me! She was in a tough spot, but I was an idiot. She's like a daughter to me. I'm more disgusted with myself than you are." He let out a breath of exasperation. It wasn't that simple, but he couldn't communicate his feelings any better.

He was losing track. "I told you, I thought you didn't care what I did."

She made a noise that sounded like disgust.

He worked at swallowing a small bite of steak. "She has a new boyfriend."

"Sunny? How do you know that?"

"She told me—"

"You were the old boyfriend?"

He swallowed hard. "No. *Friend*. The other stuff only happened a couple times, stupid . . .stupid. I told you the truth."

The discussion seemed to be closed. He looked down at his food. His marriage probably didn't have a chance now, whether he went or not.

"Sign the divorce papers before you go. I'm not waiting while you check out your options."

At a loss, he pulled his last card, inviting her along to see for herself. "We can take turns driving, make it a long weekend. Thaw out on the beach."

Her face showed disbelief. He sweated while she clamped her lips, sighed, and clamped again. "Where's the waiter?"

Bear signaled, wondering if this would be some move to humiliate him in public. Not like Marci, but he deserved it for trying to railroad her in a restaurant.

"A shot of Maker's Mark, please."

The waiter was quick to bring it. Bear's mouth fell open when Marci downed the shot.

Her eyelids flew up and she licked her lips. "Okay, bud. I'm in. I'll take a couple of days off work. It'll be worthwhile just to satisfy my curiosity. When do we go?"

His stomach turned acid. At that point his strategy seemed a losing one. Introducing the two of them was something he couldn't envision.

Marci's grin showed excitement—or anxiety. It was settled. Bear wondered if he should call the restaurant to warn Sunny, but she might have to phone him back. Marci would be paying close attention to his calls, and he didn't want to start new suspicions. He gave it all up to fate.

They left on Saturday. The Bel Air drove like a champ. He figured it would, with the amount of money he'd poured into it. People stared at the shining, smooth-running antique as they cruised into downtown Nashville for lunch. He had the same feelings of pride as he did in the old days when they would ride the bike. Fine car and a good-looking woman. He tried to forget what was to come. They took turns driving in the afternoon and talked about the interests they'd shared in the past, books they'd read, trips they'd taken. Marci seemed amused.

They found a Ramada for the night, and he had hoped the romance of a hotel, maybe some Magic Fingers, would work in his favor, but Marci insisted that he get a room with two doubles.

She chose the bed near the bathroom, suggesting he would be comfortable by the air conditioner. He agreed, face tilted downward, as contrite as he knew how to look, again relying on his thick lashes and soft bottom lip to inspire second thoughts.

She changed into her nightgown in the bathroom and he was naked under the covers on his bed when she came out. "Night, sweetheart," he said.

"Barry—" She turned out the light.

He sat up, hopes rising and a feeling under the covers. "What?"

"I—oh, nothing. Good night."

He whispered, "I love you."

Anxieties took over as he tried to sleep. He thought of asking Marci to cuddle, to help him fall asleep, but she would never go for it, and asking would annoy her. He felt she was holding back something and hoped it wasn't that she'd hired a lawyer.

They crossed the Florida state line in the early afternoon and found a cafe for lunch just off I-95. The waitress brought Old-Florida style placemats decorated with sea shells and pink flamingoes, advertisements of alligator farms and Weeki Wachee mermaids spread across a map. Marci snickered as she read aloud about the old-time tourist traps, and he was glad to see her in a good mood, although her general attitude came across as resolve. He measured the distance to DeLeon Springs on the map, estimating that they would be there in a couple of hours—"too late to go to the pancake restaurant."

She gave him a suspicious look. It had become a habit.

His stomach wanted Sunny to be gone. The closer he got to her territory, the queasier, and the more he worried about giving the girl rent money. He would have to sneak, or else dump her and her family out in the woods. He couldn't do that. He didn't think Marci could either. He stared at his cheeseburger until he realized Marci was watching.

Chapter 60: Sunny Lytle

The restaurant was slow Sunday afternoon, so Sunny took a break and stood under the trees to enjoy the spring. Its natural beauty always made her optimistic, an impossible feeling at her camp. They were all sick of living in the woods and so was she. She went to the edge of the swimming area and squatted to run her hand through the crystal water. Miracles were possible—the continuous flow from prehistoric times, water still pure enough to drink at the source. She would never give up her dream.

A couple had stopped on the bridge to talk. The woman had a beautiful bird on her shoulder, a hyacinth macaw. No scenery could rival its bright painted-yellow smile, brilliant against dense blue feathers.

Sunny's only table had just started to cook when she stepped out, so she strolled over to visit the bird. She pretended to be interested in the waterfall below the woman's feet. The man pointed toward the mill wheel, saying something, and the woman looked in that direction. Sunny smiled at the macaw.

The bird turned expressive eyes on her. She winked, feeling his male spirit. He cocked his head, seeming to like her attention, but his expression was sad, and she sensed disturbance. She didn't want to know his story. It would upset her and she would be unable to help, as always.

The feathers were sparse on his chest and wings. As she walked closer to the older woman and her husband, she was drawn magnetically toward the bird, feeling a rush of fear and hope. "Can I pet him?"

The woman moved closer and dipped her shoulder, still speaking to her husband. As Sunny ruffled the feathers on the macaw's back, distress filled her in the unexplainable way, centering at her throat in a lump that nearly blocked a swallow. His neck pouch was compacted with something so that food and water could barely pass through. He was suffering and weak. The light breeze threatened to blow him down onto the pavement.

Sunny stepped back and the couple resumed their quiet conversation, seeming unaware of the macaw's suffering or

Sunny. After having her heart broken by Lucky, she had vowed not to risk another diagnosis.

The couple turned.

Sunny couldn't let the bird down. "Excuse me. "I work in the restaurant." She pointed to the Sugar Mill logo on her T-shirt. "Um . . . I know this will sound strange, but I have to tell you that your bird is very sick."

They looked at each other, then at Sunny. "I don't think so," the woman said. She reached toward the macaw and it nibbled at her fingernail. "You're okay, right, sweetheart?" She made a kissy mouth in his direction.

Sunny pointed at his partially plucked chest. "He's losing feathers. See."

The man reached to ruffle the chest feathers. "Allergies. He's always been a little scruffy."

"To us he's the most beautiful bird in the world," the woman said. "Aren't you? Pretty bird. So pretty."

Sunny tried to project to the bird, concentrating hard. Tell me your name. Tell me your name, Mr. Macaw. Tell me your name, so they'll listen. She felt a tight connection. Maybe the name began with an S.

Their attention had shifted and she felt them pulling away, trying not to be rude.

"Just check him, please, please. Before it's too late. Make sure he's eating and drinking—and pooping. His neck is clogged and he can't digest. He's weak and won't last much longer."

"We appreciate your concern," said the man, "but he'll be fine. He gets bored."

"That's why we brought him to the park. Have a lovely day." They walked away.

There was nothing she could say to make them listen. She called after them anyway. "Please, just get him checked out."

They were already off the bridge and on the path passing the entrance to the restaurant, getting away as fast as they could from the nutcase. Probably couldn't even hear her. If only they would check his cage . . .

She walked back into the restaurant. Maybe she was crazy after all, as loony as Buck. The insane were the last to know.

Was she paranoid about Rita?—maybe the pups could have gotten their shots.

A tour group was piling in through the door. Once inside, she realized that most of the people had already been seated, and her tables were waiting to order.

She apologized and caught up fast, doing fine until she tossed an empty pitcher into the sink of soapy water and heard a crack. There were seven people waiting to be seated, and her eight-top was open, but she had to let out the water and pick up the shards of ceramic so nobody would get cut reaching for utensils.

She rushed out of the kitchen, her arms loaded with pans, spatulas, placemats, and menus. Patty stopped her at the counter. "Slow down, Sunny. You're a hazard."

"I'm sorry. I broke a pitcher. My table is waiting."

"Hold on." Patty called to Jason to ask him to take Sunny's table.

"No, please. I'm fine."

Jason passed by sending her a questioning look. She didn't have any answers.

Patty put her hand on Sunny's shoulder. "Put down that stuff and step outside with me."

Sunny stiffened. Was she being fired?

Patty led her out to the picnic table.

Sunny sat across from her and gripped the edge of the bench. "Patty, I love this job. I'm sorry. I got caught up with—"

Patty told her that there was a message.

Sunny bit her lip. Police.

"The hospital called. Your father is very sick."

She couldn't think of anything to say.

"He told them they could reach you here." She paused. "I didn't realize you had family in town."

"It's his liver again."

Patty's mouth opened slightly as if with a question. "Sunny, he isn't expected to leave the hospital."

"He's dying?" She had thought she would feel relieved to hear this kind of news, but she was numb.

"Jason can run you over."

"No. Thank you. I'll just stay and do my job."

Patty paused. "Let me know if you change your mind. You only get one father."

She nodded. "Thank god for that."

Patty's mouth opened again, but she turned and walked ahead.

Sunny's legs were rubbery as she made her way back inside. It didn't make sense. She hated Lytle and should be glad he wouldn't bother her any more.

Barbara was seating a couple at right corner main, another of Sunny's tables. Jason came from behind her. "Should I take this one, Sunny?"

"No, got it."

"You okay?"

She told him she was, but he stood frowning at her. "Take a break with me when it slows down."

He met her at the picnic table with a coke for himself and an iced tea for her.

"It's the old man. He's nearly dead. In the hospital."

Jason sat next to her and took her hand and squeezed it. "Liver?"

She looked into his eyes. It was good to have a friend who understood.

He put his hand on her forearm. "You might regret it if you don't visit him on his death bed."

She turned toward the spring.

"I know you hate him for sending you away, but if he's dying . . ."

He didn't have all the facts, but she focused on the concern in his face, not wanting to think about anything else.

"I bet he came in here that day to make up with you."

She looked down and picked at splinter of wood. "I thought he was going to rape me that day."

"What?" He squeezed her arm.

It was the first time she had used the real word, even to herself. She gave him the details.

"You should have called the police."

She didn't remind him that she had no cell phone or address.

He put his arm around her shoulder and pulled her to his chest, holding her head against his shirt. "I'd like to kill the son of a bitch." His finger was partially in her ear, like a lock that shut out the world at the same time as it held her close. For a few seconds she let herself feel rescued.

Chapter 61: Rita McKenna

She couldn't stop smiling as John carried her suitcase down the hall and opened the door into the suite on the beach at Santa Monica. Murano glass chandeliers hung from the cathedral ceiling reflecting a coral sunset. The ocean gleamed through the sliding doors across an expanse of shining Italian tile. She had already guessed that acquiring cars for the movies was more lucrative than veterinary medicine, even in her good years, but she never expected such lavish accommodations. John's home in Orlando was small and sparsely furnished.

He set down the suitcase. "So. Not bad, huh? Belongs to an investment banker. I'm house-sitting."

She was a little disappointed, but also glad that he hadn't spent a fortune to impress her for the weekend.

"Walk this way." He picked up her bag hunching with one shoulder higher than the other.

She giggled and followed him, mimicking his posture. "Nobody can resist that line."

"I've got the video, if you want to watch it."

Somehow he knew exactly what she liked in everything. They were the same age, from the same mid-west schooling. She thought about the unique painting of Noah's Ark he had sent her. Acquiring exactly the right thing was a talent that he had turned into a career.

She followed him into the master bedroom, classic style, in olive green satin and cream, overlooking on the ocean with its own balcony. She put her arms around his shoulders and kissed him hard. The suitcase hit the floor. His hands went for the edge of her blouse and it was over her head and off in seconds, his face nuzzled into her cleavage. She was all over him, pressed into his heft, ruffling his short thick hair and tweaking his ears, feeling his hands down the back of her pants. There was no wine in her system. They were just plain good for each other. The Fountain of Youth had worked its magic.

The days went too quickly, between crawling over each other's body, walking on the beach, eating gourmet foods, watching films. She insisted on seeing his work, despite the genre, and even enjoyed *Fast and Furious III*, punctuated with his funny stories and interesting incidents involving stars and their foibles.

On Sunday she made a huge pot of minestrone soup so he would have something healthy on hand when he got in late during the week. They sipped cognac on the couch and watched the sun flow like gold into the Pacific. "I surely don't want to leave tomorrow," she told him.

"Don't. Stay and enjoy yourself."

She reminded him of her responsibilities and told him about Sunny's worsening situation, the Parvo, and how the puppies needed to be vaccinated. Being with him, she had almost forgotten her guilt. "I don't know where to start with all those animals. And she needs a psychiatrist. Medication is usually the only thing that works."

John said he knew a doctor in Orlando who was highly recommended.

She told him about Denise, her new friend, and how she wanted to start The Haven. "I can't help dreaming." She explained that under Denise's authority, she would be able to practice again and could quit her job with the county.

"Why not move in with me? You'd need less salary without rent to pay."

She wasn't ready for the discussion. "Nothing's happening. It might never."

He snuggled up. "If I had any idea you'd go for it, I'd ask you to marry me. Your work could be all volunteer."

The air went out of her. "That's a little fast."

"That's why I'm not asking."

"Good." She sat up straight. "Let's just figure out when we'll be able to see each other again."

He gave her a kiss and reached into his pocket to pull out a key chain. "When you get home, something will be parked in your guest spot."

She felt her eyes bulging. She couldn't accept a car.

"I buy cars for fun as well as profit. It's a few years old, but in great condition. I couldn't pass it up for the price—nice little

Mini Cooper. It was Patty's—from the Sugar Mill. She bought the new Mini S."

"No! Really, John, I can't—"

"Look, it's no big deal. Your Corolla has close to 200,000 miles on it. I worry about you on those dark country roads. Besides—" He checked his watch. "It's already delivered."

"You're scaring me." She rested her chin on his shoulder. Worrying about the car dying was a major source of stress, but so was diving in that deep. "It's only 170,000 miles. I can't. I just can't. I'll have to pay—"

"You can owe me. Until you decide to marry me."

She pursed her lips. "Quit it."

He patted her hand. "No pressure. I enjoy seeing the look on your face."

"No, really."

"I would feel good knowing you have reliable transportation. You can give Sunny your old car. I bet she could use it."

Certainly true. It would make life easier for both of them, but that wasn't the point. "You're too generous for your own good. Let's see how things go."

He sighed. "Run it once in a while to keep the battery charged until I can pick it up."

She sighed. "No problem."

"So, is Sunny still camping?"

She gave him the story of how Sunny blamed her for the visit from Animal Control and told him about the weird out-of-state call.

"In the long run it's probably the best thing. Poor girl. Have they taken the animals?"

She explained that they were waiting and she hoped to work something out so Sunny could keep her favorites. Rita choked on a sip of her cognac. She remembered telling him where the bus was located on the day of the auto show. "John! You didn't?"

"What?"

"Call Animal Control?"

"Of course not. Why would I do that?"

He had sympathized with the caller. The pieces fit together and it all made sense. Her throat tightened. "Because of your mother . . . Being a hoarder ruined her life."

"My mother? No."

"Maybe you thought you could fix everything—did what you thought was right, and didn't mention it to me?"

"Rita! For Christsakes, I didn't call them."

"I've been trying to build up enough trust to help the girl." She stared into his eyes. He looked sincere. He was good at the look, just like the last man. "Did you think you had to take charge because I was too weak to handle it?"

"Not at all." His hands dropped to his thighs.

"The person called the police instead of the shelter." She watched his eyes, trying to read them, thinking he wouldn't have wanted to risk her answering the phone.

"This is crazy, Rita. Let's not argue on your last night."

Tears were on the way, a humiliation that wouldn't allow her to finish expressing her anger. A controlling personality was natural for a man with his lifestyle. She had been negligent. She was weak in his eyes.

"Rita, we've had a lot to drink. Let's go to bed and forget about this."

Attempting to make light of the issue was more evidence against him. She nodded, unable to speak in a normal voice. She desperately wanted to forget everything, but she couldn't do it.

Chapter 62: Sunny Lytle

She had taken an extra day off for the first time, and she sent Buck to get the truck for grocery shopping. There was good news from Dr. Denise that the little beauty, Angel, was completely recovered. Rita was still gone, and she hoped the rules might be different so she could adopt Angel back.

While she waited, she dumped buckets of water on the dirtiest dogs, easy bathing, being situated close to the lake. She would need money for fees to get Angel, besides the groceries, and she had already dipped into the apartment fund for leashes and bedding.

Buck came thrashing his way through the woods. "I had to stop—almost an hour—big ones."

She looked across the sky.

"Let's go," he said. "I don't know how much time I'll have. Weather report says cloudy, chances of thunderstorms all day."

She bit the inside of her cheek. It would start an argument if she said a word.

He saw her. "Don't make faces at me, Sunny. I drive you all over town for your freaking animals."

She didn't mean to take advantage of him.

"If it clouds up, just let me out, and I'll meet you back here later."

She nodded. "You really are sweet, Buck. I don't know what gets into me."

"Me either. I risk my life for you at least once a week." He stuck his face into hers so she would kiss him.

When they pulled up at the shelter, she told him she'd be right back, hoping it was that simple. Denise had said she'd be at the desk all day, but it was Jackie.

"Is Dr. Denise here?"

Jackie looked up and frowned. "Out back." She pointed to the door.

Sunny went down the hall to the loggias with open air pens. Denise was straddling a Doberman, swabbing inside his ears with long Q-tips, bringing out clumps of dark wax.

"We talked on the phone. I'm Sunny."

Denise looked up and nodded. She was a small woman with black hair, thick and glossy like a horse's mane. Even with bleach and urine in the background Sunny could smell a musky perfume.

"Hi, Sunny. Rita told me about you, how much you love animals."

"You have my Rufus and Brindle."

"Yes, I do. They're great. You can visit them any time you want."

Sunny took the opportunity to ask about the new shelter.

"I need operational money for the first year, at least, and I don't see that coming any time soon."

Sunny huffed. Rita had been exaggerating.

"We can't be taking in animals if we're unable to ensure their care."

"Nope." Sunny figured that Rita had given Denise the details about her.

"I stopped by to pick up my Westie. Angel?"

Denise patted the Doberman's head and moved her leg over its body to stand straight. She frowned. "Angel's in the second last pen on the end, but you have to fill out paperwork up front. I don't handle any of that."

Denise started on the next dog. Sunny wondered whether she could sneak Angel out the back gate, but it was probably padlocked. She was afraid to ask Denise to open it. She decided to go back to the office and try Jackie, rather than get Angel excited.

She stepped up to the desk, hoping she hadn't been recognized. "Is the little Westie up for adoption?"

The woman crossed her arms. "You already got the Chihuahua back, didn't you? Sunny. It's against the rules."

"Oh. I know that. I'm just asking for a friend. He's outside having a smoke."

She turned and walked before Jackie could reply.

Buck's head was leaning on the window. She pounded. "Buck, go in there and get Angel. The old lady won't give her to me."

He yawned and shook himself awake, stepped down and turned a circle, doing a quick weather check. "People don't generally like the looks of me."

"You've gotta, Buck. Somebody else will snatch Angel right up."

He smoothed his hair with his fingers, but it sprang back up. She handed him the adoption fee. "Make up an address and phone number."

After a few minutes he came out the front door and motioned for Sunny to start the truck. He dashed off around the side of the building. Something was up. She turned the key and scooted back to the passenger side.

Buck came running from behind the building with Angel in his arms. He pushed the dog across the seat at Sunny and jumped in, wiping sweat from his forehead. "Let's skedaddle." Money fell between them. He peeled out of the parking lot.

Sunny held Angel on her lap and kissed her nose and rubbed her ears, feeling furry love, and no pain or itching. Buck reached across and stroked the dog's rump. "Good job, eh?"

"You stole her?"

"No stealing. She's your dawg. You shouldn't have to pay."

She nuzzled Angel, her voice softening into baby talk. "Oh, my widdle, widdle girl, my pitty, pitty sing." Angel licked her chin.

"Ack." He stuck a finger in his open mouth pretending to gag. "Is that dawg language?"

"Dog, cat . . . She likes it." She kissed Angel's head, murmuring into her ear, feeling her relax. "You wike it, don't you? You weely weely wike it, sweet widdle sing."

He cupped his hand on his ear. "Is she answering? I don't hear . . ."

Sunny hit him on the forearm, laughing. "Quit it!" She settled back on the seat. "Think they'll call the police?"

"Might."

"Did the woman see the truck?"

"Doubt she's noticed anything yet. I slipped in the back gate and swapped another white dog into Angel's cage. Pretty much the same kind."

She quickly covered the dog's ears. "There's nobody like Angel!"

He reached in his pants pocket and pulled out a Swiss Army knife with several utensils. "Nobody saw me."

"You picked the lock?"

"No." He laughed hard, hee-hawed. "It was open. But I could've."

Sunny tilted the furry white face and looked into Angel's eyes. Her pink tongue flicked out, catching Sunny's nose. "You're the best, Buck."

She thought about Jason, wondering if he would have done the same.

"No time to shop." Buck pulled to the side of the road and hopped out.

She scooted toward the driver's seat, setting Angel beside her. A damn cloud had found them.

Chapter 63: Sunny Lytle

The Sugar Mill was busy with snowbirds that morning, retirees who migrated to New Smyrna or Orlando for the winter. They came by the carload or busload to make pancakes and enjoy the green lawns and romantic trees of the park. The air was cool, but the sun was strong, and a few children played like frisky otters in the water, tossing a ball and diving for it. Sunny kept an eye out, wishing a real otter would swim by to bark and join the game.

Her tables were packed when Patty called her to the phone. Her breath caught. "Who is it?" There was the chance that Lucky's mom might call.

"I don't know" Patty said. "She asked for the thin blonde, and you're the only one we've got "

Sunny moved next to the cash register in front of the jewelry case to take the phone. As she picked it up she brushed her fingers over sparkling silver earrings of birds, turtles, manatees, and alligators on the shelf.

"Are you the young lady who spoke to us about our hyacinth macaw?"

She had no idea. Then she remembered the poor bird. "How is he?"

"Smiley's fine. Wonderful! This is Helen Lake. I called to thank you. He needed emergency surgery, and we got him into the veterinary hospital in time. My husband and I are so grateful. The doctor said Smiley wouldn't have had a chance if we'd waited even a day longer."

She could barely stand still. "People don't usually believe me—or else I cause trouble." She saw Patty pause in ringing up a customer and glance her way. Sunny flashed a grin. "I'm so happy for Smiley."

"I admit, we didn't believe you either, but when we checked the cage, it was exactly as you had described. A full nut dish and no droppings."

"He's the first bird I diagnosed, but I was sure."

"You have a unique gift. If you have a favorite animal-based charity, we would like to make a contribution in your name."

Sunny needed the money more than anyone, but it sounded so selfish to ask.

"You can take your time thinking about it. It's a big decision. We've earmarked thirty thousand of our charity fund to go for animals this year. We want to save the lives of poor neglected creatures."

"Thirty thousand?" –A huge sum of money from the blue.

"That's what we have in mind."

She straightened herself against the counter. "Actually, I'm setting up a shelter of my own for all kinds of animals. My ability will help me make their lives happy. I could really use the money." She made big eyes at Patty staring in her direction.

"Don't you work at the restaurant?"

"I have two jobs, if you count animal care as work."

"Give me your address. We would like to take a tour before we make the donation."

Sunny leaned hard on the jewelry case. "It's not ready for visitors yet. The money would go toward getting started."

"I see. You're not a licensed charity."

Helen's tone struck Sunny with the realization of her ignorance. "No, Ma'am. Not yet." She hadn't known she needed a license.

"I'm sorry. Our contribution needs to be tax deductible."

"But the purpose is to help needy animals, isn't it?"

"Certainly, but if I give to charities that are tax deductible, I can afford to give to more. It's a small benefit that encourages generosity."

She didn't know what to say. She remembered Bear grumbling about tax deductions he deserved. This was her only chance for a start, a miracle, and she would never see a dollar.

Patty had finished with the line of customers and was watching her. Sunny told Helen how to contact Dr. Denise.

"Oh, I don't know. I think they euthanize over there. "

"This is something new. Be sure to talk only to Dr. Denise."

Helen thanked her and said goodbye, and Sunny handed the phone across the counter for Patty to hang up.

"I overheard your call. I'm sorry you didn't get the money."

She couldn't dodge the disappointment, and was near crying, despite the joy of saving Smiley. "I have to learn about finances."

A little while later as she carried plates back to the kitchen, Patty motioned to her with the phone. She wondered if Helen had called back, but Patty's face was grim. Servers weren't supposed to get calls. Sunny looked toward her tables. A man waved and raised his cup for a refill. "Please tell them I'm busy."

Patty nodded and Sunny went for the coffee pot. When she returned it, Patty put a slip of paper into her hand. "You need to call. Your father is in ICU. Jason can drive you."

She looked at the number and stuffed it into her pocket. "Thanks." A table emptied and she hurried to clean it.

Chapter 64: Buckaroo

Scattered cumulous billowed up early and hung around all morning. He lay on his back, tilting the pie pan, feeling groggy. There seemed to be less strength in the Mag rays than usual. He figured they could kill him with a direct hit to his cortex, but the clouds weren't ferocious enough to provide full power. It took longer between strikes, too, but sporadic bursts were too dangerous to ignore. He thought about how happy it would make Sunny if he could wipe them out—nearly as happy as it would make him. He'd been stuck there with nothing to eat for hours and had forgotten to move the cooler where he could reach for a beer. He was thinking of taking a chance after the next long volley.

Some low growls started in the line up by the bus, escalated, and turned into full-out manic barking. "That you, Sunny?"

It was way too early for her to be home. He was used to unexplained outbreaks from the furps. Probably a raccoon.

The barking went wild, with a frightening pitch. A stray nosing around the camp? A person? "Who's there? Anybody there?" The commotion was so loud he knew he couldn't be heard. Maybe it was better that way if somebody was looking for trouble. Lytle? Fuck. He barely deflected a Magnetoid shot. He was helpless. His Police Special was in the plastic tub inside the bus. He had started keeping gun by his side, but got tired of hiding it from Sunny. He fingered the key in his pocket, but decided against making a run for it. From the sounds of the dogs, if there was a looter, he was likely inside the bus already, probably not staying long.

He reached out and felt the handle of the aluminum bat he kept for emergencies. He would be exposed to Magnetoid attack in the time it took to use it, so it was a last resort.

A screech cut through him, turning into a bleating gargling cry, amid ferocious barking and growling.

The hell with them! He yanked himself to his feet, dropped his pan, and stepped away from the tent, looking toward the noise. The dogs strained on their leads toward the end of the bus closest to the water. Schmeisser bared his teeth, crouching to stare underneath. In the shadows among the weeds, there was something resembling a tractor retread. He looked closer. *Gator!* The jaws opened and snapped shut on a bloody mess. Buck froze in shock.

Blood still dripping from its mouth, the alligator aimed a snap toward Schmeisser, barely missing the shepherd's front leg. Buck shrieked. Determined to get at the creature, the dog jerked and twisted, his collar cutting hard into his throat, strangling his growl into a whimper.

There was no time to go for the gun. He grabbed the bat and leapt across the fire pit into range, hoping to scare or stun the bastard. He smashed the bat with all his force into the head. The impact was solid, like pounding a rock, and dented one side of the bat. He struck downward again, expecting the gator to turn and run, but it challenged him, rising on straightened legs. The reptile head slung out toward him, higher than the chassis of the bus, an arm's reach away, black eyes focusing. Buck cracked a blow to the hard snout with all the power of his shoulders. Blood trickled from the teeth onto the sand, but there was no sign of pain. If only he had an ax.

The alligator hissed and launched at the bat and Buck whacked again and again at the arc of long yellow teeth. The bright pink throat and bloody tongue were shocking inside the dark prehistoric skull. Buck cracked hard and the bat was nearly jarred from his hands. Teeth snapped shut close to his leg. He jumped back, thinking to jab the bat straight down the fleshy throat, but the slashing movement of the jaws was too swift. It was like fencing jaws of steel.

As the gator turned, the tail whipped, a live wire, catching Schmeisser in the legs, taking him down. The beast shot under the bus and thrashed its way through bushes toward the water. In seconds there was a splash. Buck had scared it, but his feeble blows wouldn't keep it from coming back, or others from finding their way. He shook his head at the full menu laid out for them, appetizers to dessert, a dozen square meals tied down in a row. He hadn't expected a gator to come that far through human territory, but the lure of fresh dog must be strong.

He stood there breathing hard, not eager to inspect the damage under the bus. The barking settled, except for a few whimpers and whines and Pancho still yapping his fiercest. Buck stepped closer, peered under the chassis, and spotted the remains. It resembled a gray chunk of shag rug with an edge dipped in red paint, possibly a paw or a tail. He didn't recognize it. There was a collar still attached to a rope.

Pancho stopped barking, and they all stood mesmerized, straining toward the far end of the bus. Sitting ducks. They were rattled. He couldn't remember which one had been tied in the end slot, but the collar was medium to small. Somehow the head had slipped out, or . . . It must have been fast and painless. Then the worst hit him. Telling Sunny.

Suddenly he remembered the sky, jerked his head up, and ran from under the tree to get a good view. The clouds had mostly thinned and scattered, but there was a mound in the west where he would have expected action. He remembered that it had been coming in from the east when he was on duty, so it must have blown completely over him. He'd been an easy target, all the while, yet here he was. They were weaker than he'd realized. His perseverance had paid off.

He took a warm beer from the dry cooler, cracked the top and drank half. He walked down the line, scratching ears and patting butts. "Good dawg . . . good dawg . . . Everything's okay . . . Good girl . . . good boy." They were far from settling down, growling and whining off and on, a few shivering. He still couldn't remember who was missing, but Sunny would know.

He squatted down when he reached Pancho at the far end of the line and gave the rough pink back a good rub with his knuckles. The little guy seemed angrier and less shaken than the rest, still stiff and focused toward the lake, thinking he could take that gator, given a chance. "Don't get too cocky, Señor Villa. You're one lucky appetizer." Now *he* was imagining dog feelings. Didn't need to start that.

He sat down and pondered the situation. It had been an accident waiting to happen. Fifty feet was too close to the lake. He had gotten careless sharing the lakes and rivers with gators over the years. Now what? The camp would have to be moved again. It wasn't safe, even for one more night. A headache throbbed behind his ears. Those fuckers might have zapped him after all.

He went into the bus to find the aspirin, and the pups went wild, jumping on him, yapping and whimpering, scratching his legs with their claws. Instinct told them all something deadly had happened. Cats were clumped together in the corner like a multi-colored fur cushion. He figured gators were like birds. One gets fed and a flock shows up. He set the plastic tub on the table and dug under the blankets, took out the box and unlocked it. A secure feeling came over him as he felt the weight of the .38. He'd kept it clean and dry for twenty years, but never had to use it.

He had one partial box of rounds and he loaded up. He wasn't much of a shot, but he could get close enough to unload six rounds into the next mother-fucker. He wondered if the .38 would penetrate the skull. He'd seen skulls an inch thick. He remembered somebody saying to shoot for the base. With all that mouth jerking and head slinging, aiming would be tricky.

He'd have to sit guard duty until Sunny got there and they could figure out what to do. A long night of packing was in store. At least the shit and piss and hairball puke was still in control so there wouldn't be much cleaning.

He held back the pups and slipped out the door, got himself another warm beer, and sat down in the plastic chair with the gun beside him. He was starting to feel better until he remembered the bloody collar and clump of fur still under the bus. He got the shovel and dug a hole near the site of the disaster. The rope leash was bloody too, so he untied it and tossed it in with the collar, then kicked the unidentified chunk next to them. He covered it and spread a few shovels of sand over the dark splashes nearby. Wookie. That's who it was, the old schnauzer. He wasn't in the bus, and he wasn't tied outside, not anymore.

He got another beer and sipped it, shifting the gun now and then to be sure it was in the handiest position on the crate. If one had to go, Wookie was the best choice. Over twenty, he remembered Sunny saying, half blind and deaf. An old fart, but still a nice dog.

What if he said Wookie passed away in peace and was already buried? But he had to tell her about the gator to convince her to move the bus again.

There was a hollow drumming bellow from the lake. Mating sounds. No wonder they were active. Christ, he never thought they'd come right into the camp. If he hadn't been caught up with the fucking Magnetoids, he might have been in time. Sunny would know that, whether or not she said so. He wasn't up to the job. Animal watch was too much responsibility. He missed his quiet camp. Damn. He needed a six-pack and some ice. A couple of six-packs.

Chapter 65: Pancho

Pancho could not settle. He sorted layers of scent, caught the tang of raccoon, smelled leathery hands digging for snails. He scuffed up dirt, turned around, dropped. He licked his paw, twisted to nibble a prickle on his side. He pulled himself up, stood straight, cocked his head to hear movement of water, his neck straining toward the strong odor of hard-mouthed lurkers. Nothing moved between the leaves. Blood scent glazed the sand where the old one had been torn. To smell is to know. The old one, Wookie, gone.

His gaze fell into shadows under the bus. Schmeisser was still, open eyes shining. Pancho pulled toward the curl of his black furred haunches, digging in, straining to rub against softness. He pulled on the leash till he choked.

Far from him, inside, Angel made sounds in sleep, squeals, like the old one. Pancho whined, pulled hard. He tensed and shivered. He squatted, dug. His front legs clawed and scooped, and back legs kicked dirt aside. He locked into the process, not hearing, not seeing. Blood dirt went up his nose. No stopping the digging. He was going deep, deep. Where nothing could get him.

Chapter 66: Sunny Lytle

When the crowd slowed, Sunny called the hospital and learned that Lytle was asking for her, unlikely to make it through another day.

She walked with Jason to his car. "Lytle had one of his legs amputated and then his liver shut down."

"The leg the dog bit?" Jason asked.

"Don't know." She'd been afraid to ask.

"You know it's not your fault, right?"

"Yes . . . No . . . Not sure."

"Sounded like he deserved it."

At the hospital Jason walked with her to the entrance. She took a deep breath, trying to get up her nerve. "Will you come in with me?"

He held her hand at the reception desk. Lytle had been taken out of ICU and put into a room. Sunny felt woozy as they stepped off the elevator into a strong chemical smell. The AC was freezing cold. She stopped at the door of the room. The first bed was empty, and curtains were drawn around the second one.

Jason stood aside. "I'll wait here."

Her legs wanted to give way, but she reminded herself that Lytle was helpless. Otherwise, he would be out somewhere guzzling. She peered through the crack of the curtain. His eyes were closed. He had an IV taped to his hand, a plastic tube in his nose, and was connected to a monitor. His face was sallow, and his stomach swelled like a beach ball under the blanket. She could see the indentation where his lower leg should have been. It was the leg that Rufus bit.

She couldn't face him. She turned to leave, but Jason was watching from the hall.

She looked back at Lytle. Spider veins stood out on his nose and cheeks, but he looked younger than when she'd last seen him, clean-shaven. His thin gray hair was dry instead of plastered to his skull with sweat.

She pulled the curtain a short distance. He opened his eyes at the tinny sliding of the rings. The whites were yellower than before. He seemed dazed.

She swallowed and moved closer. "I'm here. Jason brought me. I can't stay long."

"Jason?"

"Yeah." She stepped out from the bed and motioned. "You remember him."

Jason came to the curtain. He put his arm around Sunny's back. "Hello, Mr. Lytle."

"Yeah, Jason." She expected some nasty remark, but Lytle just nodded.

"Sunny—" It triggered a gasp that turned into a cough. He lay there choking and wheezing, trying to get a breath. Bright blood splattered the front of the light blue hospital gown.

"I'll call the nurse," Jason said.

"No." Lytle coughed. "Get a towel."

Jason went into the bathroom and brought back a white towel and covered the blood. Lytle coughed out some more.

"Help me sit up, Sunny. For christsakes." He reached toward the bed controls.

She touched the controls and the head of the bed rose, but Lytle slumped down.

Jason went around to the other side of the bed so they could hoist him together. They pulled him upwards a few inches by his shoulders and she felt his thinness. His hands pushed feebly at the mattress. Jason pressed the control until Lytle was sitting up. He pointed to a styrofoam cup with a bendable straw.

Sunny put the straw inside his mouth, holding it while he drank. He pointed to his leg and swallowed. "Look what your dog did. Animals been coming between us all our lives."

She gave him more water. "You scared me holding my wrists, breathing in my face—"

He waved her words away. "Don't need no leg. Not going to be standing up any more."

His kind attitude was unexpected. "I'm sorry. I didn't want—"

He coughed some more and she waited. "No matter." He took water. "They asked me about the dog. I said stray . . . at my place. Otherwise, you'd a been in trouble. It was a nice thing I did for you."

She realized he was talking about rabies. They would have confined Rufus for weeks. "Appreciate it."

He motioned toward the drawer in the bedside stand. "Take the envelope." He laid his head back on the pillow and closed his eyes. A trickle of blood ran from his nose, and Sunny lifted the towel to catch it before it ran into his mouth.

Lytle kept his eyes closed.

Jason opened the drawer and picked out a dirty yellowed envelope. He handed it to Sunny. It was addressed to her in care of Lytle. No name or return address, but postmarked Commerce, Georgia.

"It's from Pam," Lytle said.

"My mother?" The postmark was from six years earlier. "Why didn't you give me this?"

"Didn't know where you was till lately. There were more, but I lost em." His voice faded to a whisper. "Done my duty."

Sunny frowned at the jagged paper where the envelope had been ripped open. She put two fingers inside. There was a check on top from Lytle, $2,000.

He kept his eyes closed. "Pay for the cremation. If some's left, adopt a cat." He snickered, then coughed into the towel, making blood spots bloom on the outside. "Can't laugh no more."

Sunny put the letter on her lap and rested the cup on Lytle's chest, holding it until he turned his head.

"I was gonna you that letter at the restaurant, but you ducked out on me. Then your dog tried to finish me off."

She held up the envelope. "It's too old to matter." She was desperate to read, but not with him watching. She put it into her backpack.

Lytle's head lolled, but he lifted it again slowly. "My liver's done. Your dog didn't have anything to do with that."

He looked down at his fingers and picked at a thick dark thumbnail. "You used to love your pop, remember? When you were little we'd go for walks in the woods and I'd teach you about the plants and critters. Bet that's why you like nature so much."

She mainly remembered him drunk, slapping her mother around in the kitchen.

"You were a real smart little girl. I'm sorry everything went bad between us."

She had nothing to say.

Lytle rested his head back on the pillow and closed his eyes. Whatever he had been, now he was a vulnerable wounded animal. An ancient iguana, ready to molt. The dry roughness of his sagging yellow jaws and triple chin looked like thick, dead skin. She followed the sheet down to the where it dropped flat from his knee. Intentionally or not, she'd taken his leg, and maybe that made them even. She put her arm around his chest and gave him half of a hug, as much as she could manage. His hand tapped her back like patting a baby. She held until he sat back. He coughed more blood into the towel.

A nurse walked in with a full IV bag and asked if Sunny was the daughter.

She nodded. "Can't you stop the bleeding?"

"It's the varices—swelled veins in his throat, breaking open. He's only on pain killers now." She hung the bag and stripped the air out of the tube. "He's been in and out of coma all day. You might want to stay."

Sunny nodded. "Jason, go. I'll get a cab."

"I can't leave you like this."

"What about your wife?"

He waved off any problem.

The nurse put her hand on Sunny's shoulder, staring into her eyes. "Are you okay?"

"Fine." She wondered how she was supposed to look. She was freezing and her stomach was grinding, but she probably didn't look sad.

The nurse left, and Sunny took Jason's hand and led him into the hall. "Are you sure it's all right? I caused you enough trouble with that check."

"Forget it. We have worse problems."

Her breath caught, but she didn't want to know more. She glanced down the long corridor. "Wonder where all his drinking buddies are."

"They might think they'd be intruding."

"Maybe he couldn't help himself. Just made that way—like a gator. I always thought I'd like to watch him suffer . . ."

Chapter 67: Rita McKenna

Driving to work for the afternoon shift, she couldn't keep from wallowing in emotion, fighting through pain into anger. She had ignored John's two voicemails. She couldn't speak to him, not until she built up strength to keep her resolve.

His deceptive and controlling nature had surfaced before she became completely tied to him, but she had let down her guard too soon. The claw digging a hole in her stomach was intense. Her sinuses started to fill. She snatched a tissue from the box on the seat and blew her nose. She almost couldn't believe he would make the call. He must have realized he would be going above her authority. Of course, he had watched his mother suffer.

That morning Sunny had given Rita instructions to the new camp, so she could bring the vaccines to the pups the next day—hopefully she hadn't changed her mind. Time to do what had to be done . . . betrayal.

When she opened the door at the shelter, Jackie was at the desk. She looked up with a jolt. "I forgot you were back in town."

"I'm scheduled for the second shift."

Jackie put down her pen. "I had to change that."

"What?"

"I've got a new girl, Jessica, coming in. She's doing an internship."

Rita was miffed. "You could have let me know."

"We won't be requiring your services anymore." She looked down at something on the desk.

Rita stepped up to the desk and crossed her arms. "What's going on? You gave me vacation days."

"It's not that. I can't trust you, Rita. You broke the rules by letting that girl have her dogs back."

The fact jarred her. "It was only the Chihuahua. Nobody would have adopted him with his dermatitis. Denise took the two big ones. Look up the paperwork."

"What about Angel, the Westie? The girl was here, trying to get the dog, and then it disappeared."

Rita tried to remember when she had last seen Angel. "I was out of town."

"Let's go back and talk to Denise," Jackie said.

Rita followed her down the hall. Denise had an Australian terrier on the examination table, expressing his anal glands. "Welcome back, Rita. Meet Dundee." She looked back at her work. "Something wrong?"

Jackie asked her about the two dogs.

"I adopted Rufus and Brindle. Why?"

"What about the Westie?"

Denise looked at Rita. "She disappeared."

"Escaped?"

"She might have had some help."

Jackie looked back and forth between Rita and Denise. "Denise, I thought you had more integrity."

Rita felt heat flowing up her neck.

Denise gave the terrier a pet and picked him up. Her voice was strong. "You're overloaded, with no place to put any more animals. Angel is old and not adoptable. The girl feeds her and loves her."

"Filth, parasites, no vaccinations, litters of unwanted puppies. Yes, it breaks my heart—but she creates the problems, and we get blamed for euthanizing."

Rita leveled her eyes at Jackie. "It's a disease."

"You're enablers." Jackie turned to walk and looked back. "I'm sorry. Your last check will be mailed to you, Rita."

Rita's throat constricted and tears filled in her eyes. She wanted to say goodbye to Denise, but only managed a wave.

Denise called after her. "Rita, wait for me outside so we can talk."

Rita was already halfway down the hall. She ran to her car, evading a smiling volunteer, jumped in and turned on the AC, rested her head on the steering wheel. What was the matter with her? Her choices had seemed worth the risk, but once risk turned into reality, the price was too steep. She had nothing saved, nowhere to go when the rent was due. Nobody. She might as well ask Sunny to share the bus.

She gave in to an outburst. Soon her face was a mess, and she couldn't stop the crying. She started the engine, checked the rearview to be sure Denise wasn't coming through the door, and drove off.

Chapter 68: Bear Hansen

Bear avoided the Spring Waters Inn because of so much bad luck on the last trip, and took Marci to the Holiday Inn in Deland. With her prompting, he got his nerve together to call The Sugar Mill. He sat on the bed and Marci stood watching over him. No Sunny. Already gone for the day and a day off tomorrow. More relief than he could have imagined—another day to endear himself to Marci before the dreaded confrontation. He didn't want to tell her that Sunny had given him directions and he'd lost them. He reminded Marci that they still had five days to get the bus and go back home to ice and snow. "Let's play while we have the time," he told her. "Take a drive to the beach."

Marci suggested that they contact the fellow who wanted to buy the car, and Bear said that he hadn't heard back yet to set up a meeting. "I can always find a dealer in the paper—we need the car to have fun."

Before she could get pissed off, he pulled out the map and pointed out St. Augustine, just an hour up the coast. He'd always wanted to see the fort. Then there was Cape Canaveral, about equidistant the other direction. He lifted Marci off her heels with an enthusiast hug, not off the ground as he had intended. "What do you say?"

She brushed his arms away and looked at the map. "We've never been to EPCOT."

He wasn't thrilled with the idea of fighting crowds at an amusement park, but it was better than tossing a skinny girl out into the woods. "All I want is your pleasure."

His cell phone vibrated on the nightstand, "Freebird" startling him. The area code was local. He picked up, hoping it wasn't Sunny. Marci was alert.

"Mr. Bernard Hansen? This is Rita, a friend of John Wonder's—from the Car Show. Remember, you stepped on my foot?"

Damn. "Are you okay?" All he needed now was a lawsuit.

She said she was fine, and Bear shot Marci a thumbs-up, thinking Rita was calling about the car sale.

"You asked about a girl in a bus. Are you a relative?"

He told her no and shrugged and made wide eyes at Marcy, wondering how to phrase his answer. "I'm a friend."

Rita told him that the girl was in trouble and he might be able to help.

"My wife and I are actually in town to pick up the bus." His stomach was burning, but he agreed to meet at the Sugar Mill Restaurant the next morning and visit Sunny in the woods. He looked at the carpet and tried not to make any facial expressions.

It was settled and Marci accepted the information without questioning the source. If he was really lucky the world might end.

Chapter 69: Sunny Lytle

Sometime after three A.M., Lytle died. With his hand in hers, Sunny thought she would have felt him go, but it took the nurse to notice. Tears didn't come.

Jason walked her back toward camp, the woods black around them except for the dim beam from the flashlight. She played the light up and down the tree trunks, the past pounding in her head. "Remember our first time out here?"

"Most of it. We had a couple beers. Some weed too."

"Was I a virgin?"

"You're asking me?" He smiled. "You seemed to be."

She stopped. "There was blood, wasn't there?"

"I think so."

She leaned against an oak branch. "It could've been my period."

"I guess. I didn't care. I loved you—still do. Sorry. I'm not supposed to say that."

"What if Lytle was the father?"

"What?"

"Of the boy." She let it tumble out. "I hated my father. I thought I made it up or dreamed it, a recurring nightmare, but now I don't know. When he found me at my camp, I was so scared—petrified—beyond normal."

He faced her and put both arms over her shoulders to cradle her head. "Sunny, you're saying . . . when you were in high school?"

"I don't know. When I think back, I have stray memories of things happening in the dark, but I don't know if they were real. The reason . . . when I left . . . I thought he raped me, but maybe I imagined it from guilt or dreamed it up when I was high."

"You stopped doing drugs when we were together."

She put a hand on her forehead. Nothing was clear.

"You would have told me. We didn't have any secrets."

"Get you into a mix-up with him? Doubt it." She hardly remembered who she was back then. "Maybe I made it up for myself, so I could leave you."

He massaged her shoulders. "It doesn't matter now that he's dead."

"It'll always matter."

"I know." He pulled her into a hug. "But it doesn't matter in a practical way."

"It matters if I imagined it and gave away our baby."

"Stop it. We were too young, Sunny. I'm sorry I gave you grief over that." He held her tighter, her cheek to his chest. "Let it go. No more regrets. No more fear."

She buried her face in his shirt and shook, but she wasn't sure what she was crying about, her past or her future. She couldn't outrun the county for long, and soon she might have nothing and no one again.

"I don't know if you're interested in hearing this, but my wife . . . um . . . I'm sleeping in the guest room."

She stepped away and pulled a tissue out of her backpack, keeping her eyes down. "You're splitting up?"

"We have problems. She's a high-powered business woman and I'm a good ole boy."

"She fosters weenie dogs. Doesn't sound so different . . ."

He snickered. "You might've hit on it, Sunny. She's done fostering me, and now it's time to pass me along to a good home."

"That's silly."

"I'm not as upset as I would be if you weren't here."

The breath went out of her. "Don't tell me that!" Now she'd done it. Her body yearned to fall into his arms and let him save her. "I'm not going to talk about this. It's between you and your wife."

She tried to walk away, but he held her back. "It's complicated, but I wanted you to know."

"All right." She motioned with the flashlight. "We'd better keep walking." She started off fast. Buck was waiting for her. Buck was her good guy.

They passed the old spot with its lingering odor of Clorox, and she explained about the move. As they approached the new camp, the dogs started their barking. They stepped into the clearing. Embers were still glowing orange in the campfire. Buck stood and pointed a gun in their direction. Jason stuck out his arm to hold Sunny back. "Whoa, Buck!"

Buck's mouth dropped open and he put the gun to his side. "Fuck! I was up all night protecting this place and you were out on a date?"

"What? No! Jesus! You crazy?" She walked up to him and put her hands on her hips, her eyes on the gun. "My father died. We came from the hospital."

Buck still sounded pissed. "You hate your father."

"I know." She put out her hand for the gun. "Let me see that thing."

He held back for a second, but she stood firm. "Be careful. It's loaded."

He passed it over handle first, aiming it toward the far side. She took a few slow steps closer to the campfire, studying the gun in the firelight. She knew what she had to do. She had a short lead and took off, sprinting into the dark toward the lake.

"What the hell?"

She rounded the bus at top speed and didn't slow until she saw a glimmer of the water's edge a few feet away. Crashing through the scrub, she couldn't tell if he was still chasing her. She stopped fast and gave the gun her best toss. There was a heavy plunk into the thick layer of muck. Buck was beside her in seconds.

"No!" He stomped the ground and flailed his arms. "I can't believe you did that. I had that gun for twenty years!"

"It's dangerous. You could have shot us!"

"Christ! I need it! *We* need it!"

He took her by the shoulders and for a second she thought he was going to shake her. Instead he stared.

She pulled away. "You also think aliens are shooting—it's too scary."

He dropped his arms and turned to the lake. "It's gone. My prized possession."

"You were aiming at us!"

He shook his head, gazing out at the darkness of the lake. "They stopped today, the mags."

"You mean you don't believe in them anymore?"

"No. They stopped. Their power's down. I've been sitting here for hours, trying to figure it out. Either they're giving me a pass or I finished saving the world. 'Course it might not last." He crossed his arms over his head. "My gun . . .

"That's great! No need to worry or waste half the—"

"There's bad news." He sighed. "Let's go back to the fire."

She turned and walked and Buck followed, muttering about the gun.

Jason stood waiting. "I have to work in a couple hours."

Sunny said she had the day off.

Buck wiped a hand over his face. "You're gonna need it when I tell you . . ."

Her eyes went past him to the dogs, down the line, but the light from the fire was dim. She couldn't make out all of them in the shadows. "What's wrong?"

"We have to move again. Especially since you tossed the gun."

Jason stepped closer.

Buck put his arm around Sunny, pulling her a little to the side. "We're too close to the water. Wookie . . . Wookie had an accident."

"What?"

"Got eaten."

She shrieked and broke away from them, ran to Wookie's spot, a pocket of darkness. She closed her eyes and gripped her face, digging in with her fingernails.

Jason and Buck were on each side of her, touching her arm, her shoulder, smoothing her hair, saying things. It was too horrible. It was all her fault.

"Come over to the fire," Buck said. "I'll make you some toast."

She shook her head and stared glazed in his direction.

"She hasn't had anything since lunch," Jason said.

"We have a lot to do today." Buck put his hands on his hips. "You need to eat and sleep."

She didn't respond. She never wanted to do anything again.

There was a kiss on the side of her face. Jason whispered into her ear. "Come with me. You can't stay here with this looney."

She didn't look at him.

He stepped in front of her. "I'd better go. I have to work in a couple hours. I'll tell Patty about your father."

"Thanks," Buck said.

She sensed Jason's steps in the sand as he moved off. How could she have let this happen? Poor, poor Wookie.

Buck's voice took on authority. "You stay right here while I make the toast. He's probably not hungry yet—the gator."

He was trying to scare her, but she didn't care. She didn't want to live. She put her hands over her eyes and cried. Her throat clenched in pain. She wondered if Wookie knew enough to blame her.

Buck took her arm. He pulled her and she stumbled along. She sat in the lounge while he draped a blanket around her shoulders and covered her legs. He handed her a mug of tea and set a plate of toast on her lap. "Lots of honey. Your favorite." He crouched next to her and put his hands on her knees. "Sunny, I'm sorry. I failed you."

She didn't say anything.

He stared at the ground, slumped like a beaten dog. "I'm really sorry. It's my fault—Magnetoids."

She knew it was hard for him to admit. "I picked the spot. If it wasn't for you, it could've been a lot worse." She laid her arm across his thigh and took his hand. "We're beat, Buck. I don't know what to do. Even nature is against us."

She ate a few bites of toast and drank some tea to make Buck feel better. When she finished, she was so tired she could barely sit up. "Can you watch them tonight, Buck? Keep them safe?"

"Promise. I'm ready with my bat. Get some sleep." He pointed away from the bus and the lake. "I'll tie the dogs to a couple trees over there, so I'll have more warning." He walked her to the tent. "I have to tell you though. It's a lot of responsibility. I need to get back to my own camp sometimes." She ducked inside and dropped onto the sleeping bag. Without meaning to, she often put a heavy burden on people who were good to her.

Chapter 70: Jason Cox

Jason wrestled with his intentions and lack of action all the way home. He was still in love with Sunny, and she needed him. It hurt thinking of her molested by Lytle, the secret kept for all those years. As a friend, Jason should have insisted that she come home with him. He could have put her on the couch. It was ridiculous, Sunny living in stench, in danger from alligators, sleeping in a tent with a loony.

The trees were backlit by a red dawn when he pulled into the driveway, and he was dog-tired—more than dog-tired, comparing himself to the weenies, who raced around on three inch legs all day.

He only had an hour before he needed to be at the restaurant. At this point he didn't have the energy to work on saving his marriage. Probably too late anyway. The rules weren't clear, now that he had been moved into the guest room, but he knew he should have called. He'd turned off the cell phone when he saw the sign in the waiting room, and when he remembered to call, it was late. He didn't want to wake Deb.

The porch light was still on. He closed the car door softly. No yapping, but there wasn't a chance that he could creep in without putting the weenies on full alert. Spike would hear the click of the key and let out a sharp note, setting off the explosion of screeching and yapping from Wootsie and the others. He hoped Deb would let the yelling wait until morning.

He turned the key slowly. One click. There it went! Spike and a lightening rip of barks. Nails clicked on the wood floor and the first nose came around the hall corner. He squatted to pet heads and rub butts, let the warm tongues slap across his knuckles. It was all well-intentioned. They were excited to see him. Little snitches that they were, he loved them.

He stood and walked toward the spare room. Deb came flying down the hall, tying her robe, her hair scattered, but her steps sure. She'd been awake. She stopped, leaving a wide space between them. "I didn't know we'd decided the marriage was over—that you'd decided."

"I didn't decide anything." His eyes burned and his face felt unattached, like a plaster mask. He would admit defeat if she'd allow him a five-minute nap, but the nap wasn't an option. She followed him into the guest room.

He opened the dresser drawer. "I have to take a shower and go to work. I'm sorry. I don't have time to discuss this."

"You must be kidding—you think you can spend the whole night out and not say anything?" She followed him to the closet. "You have no respect for me."

"It was an emergency." He gave a brief version of the night at the hospital. "Then I drove her to her camp. That's it."

Deb stopped to digest it, but her face didn't soften. "I don't care. I can't care about Sunny's problems. She has enough to drag the whole world into them. You can go down together, without me."

He took that as her final word and started toward the bathroom, but she grabbed his arm.

"Why didn't you call?"

"Why bother you? I'm sure you were working hard to put food on our—your—table." He removed her hand. "I'm just a guest here."

He shut himself into the bathroom and turned on the shower, wondering why he had come home. He could have slept in his car in the woods and things wouldn't be any worse. Deb didn't need him. Sunny did. He had to figure out something to get her away from the terrible situation before something serious happened, regardless of whether they would ever be a couple again. He knew the best thing he could do was call Animal Control. If Sunny found out, their friendship would end, but he loved her enough to give her up in order to save her life.

Chapter 71: Sunny Lytle

The next morning Buck was missing from his usual chair. The dogs had eaten, but there was no campfire. She wandered past his old tent and through trees, getting no answer to her calls. She rounded the bushes toward the lake, more fearful with each step. No Buck. There wasn't a ripple on the water and no gators she could see.

She leashed up Tulip and Schmeisser. Complaints filled the mist, but she had gotten used to all that. Get done, get going, keep going. If he didn't show soon, she would load the rest of the furniture. They would have to drive on the road to get north of the park, away from the lake, the only safe area left. It was unlike him not to be there on guard. He always kept his word. He might have gone off into the woods for his morning dump, but it had been too long. She had treated him bad, thrown away his gun.

She had saved Pancho for the final group with Peaches and Gus, and it didn't take long for him to start up with his fear of gators. Her words had no effect and her anxiety grew with his. "Stop it! Shut up! I can't take it any more!" She glared at him.

His ears and tail went down, and the little guy stood shaking, his eyes bulging more than usual. Broken-hearted. She knelt and tried to hold him, but he backed into a bush. She lunged to scoop him up, when all three dogs went on alert. Their heads turned back the way they had come, and each let out a woof. Wild barking broke loose from back at the camp.

"God, no!" Tension on the leashes helped to pull her up, and she took off in a run, dragged at a fast-paced stumble through weeds and scrub. Someone else was eaten. She was sure of it. Pancho had smelled the thing coming! She would never forgive herself. Angel or Devo clamped in its teeth . . . She gasped and tears ran down her cheeks. "Please, God, no!"

She tried to stop her past from flashing in front of her eyes, her other family seized in Indiana, the shame she'd felt when Animal Control saw a rotten tooth eaten through the jaw of one of the old shepherds and the swollen wound on a sheepdog's shoulder that she hadn't taken for treatment. She'd never had enough money for vet care, and it wasn't going to change unless she did.

She made a deal. God. Mother Nature. If everyone was all right, she would give it up, the whole damn thing. She would show Rita all the pups, take her advice, do whatever had to be done. Just no more deaths. "Promise. Promise."

By the time she reached the edge of the camp, the noise had calmed. Buck stood by the tent, talking to Rita and Jason. Next to the bus—Bear?

The dogs whined and everyone turned toward Sunny. She let them pull her to the group and shortened their leads so they wouldn't mess up anyone's clean clothes.

"Sunny!" Bear joined them and the dogs barked in recognition, jumping on his legs, licking his hands.

"Is this an intervention?" she asked, trying for a joke.

Nobody answered. She backed off and led the dogs to the bus. It was full of complaints already, tails being stepped on, dry mouths. Everybody was after her. Furs and skins all at once. She pulled the door open a foot and pushed Pancho, Gus, and Peaches, one by one, inside. Bear came around the bus and stood beside her. "Need some help?"

Before she could close the door, Pancho squeezed back out. She stepped on the nylon rope trailing from his collar and tied him to a tree. "We're mostly packed up. How did you all find me?"

"We met up at the restaurant—the waiter led the way."

"Jason?" So now he was on the do-gooder side.

"Was he the guy I sent the check to?"

She felt bad about the money. "I'm sorry. I never thanked you."

"I wasn't hinting. I brought you more."

"I can't take it." She gave him a peck on the cheek. The rest of them were waiting, ready to haul off her family, send her to jail maybe. He grasped her arm. She wasn't sure if he was comforting her or keeping her from running off.

"I see you're still using the camper. I—"

"I won't need it anymore," she told him, keeping her voice strong. "It's over."

He looked at the bus and back to her, shaking his head. His hand went into his pocket and came out with a wad of bills. "You'll need a place to live." He pushed it toward her, holding it low, finally closing her fingers around it. "Put it away somewhere."

"Oh, Bear . . ." He was stiff when she gave him a hug. She stuck the money in her pocket. She walked beside Bear back to Rita and Jason, steadying herself. An older woman came from around a palmetto, closing her cell phone and blowing her nose. Buck was busy stacking firewood on a tarp.

Bear crossed between Sunny and the woman. "This is Marci, my wife." He put his arm around Marci and squeezed.

Marci shook him off. "Pleased to meet you." She put the tissue back under her nose. "Allergies."

Bear toed a stick on the ground.

Sunny looked at Marci. "I'm sorry about the bus—and everything." Heat washed over her face and neck, and she didn't wait for a response. She looked past Marci toward Rita. "We're packed to find a new campsite. This one is too danger—" Her voice caught and she couldn't say it.

Rita took her hand. "I know. Jason told us."

Sunny whispered, "Poor Wookie . . ."

Rita sighed. "A horrible thing."

"It was his time," Jason said. He put his hand on the back of her neck under the braid.

She moved from under his arm and shifted her eyes toward the bus. "It was my fault and they know it. They told me it was dangerous."

Buck dropped a chunk of wood.

"Who did?" Rita asked.

It didn't matter now how crazy they thought she was. "The fur people—Pancho, all of them, old Wookie. They were all afraid—from the smell. They just didn't know to tell me *gators*." She had ignored their fears, just as she had been ignoring every terrible part of their lives. Her arms fell to her sides. "I don't belong in the fur family."

Everyone was staring at her again. Jason took her hand. "Nobody could've done any better."

She pulled away. "You're right, Rita. It's too much for me to handle. I'm too stupid. I'll do what you say." She glanced around the woods for a van or truck. "Am I going to be arrested?"

"Of course not," Rita said. "I have good news."

Sunny crossed her arms and angled her face toward the ground. Good news to Rita, no doubt.

She was smiling. "Doctor Denise called me last night. She's going to open The Haven very soon. We're both invited to be part of it. You can bring your whole family."

Sunny looked up just enough to be polite. It was a good act. They wanted to make sure she went peacefully. "Tell me the truth."

"I am!" Rita's hand moved to Sunny's shoulder and tightened. "You made it happen. She has enough money to start and grant funding on the way."

"I did?" She was trying to remember the woman who called.

Jason pecked her on the cheek. "Cool, huh?"

She leaned against a tree. It was surely a trick, but it didn't matter anymore.

"Neat," Bear said.

"Let's drive over there so you can see the ranch," Rita told her. "Then tomorrow or the next day— when you're ready— we'll return this vehicle, and you can start living in a real home."

Jason beamed a happy "yes" with his eyes. Buck grinned. Sunny motioned toward the packed bus. "Space for everybody?"

"You'll have a nice bedroom to yourself and the fur people will live in clean, dry indoor areas."

"What about Buck?"

Rita frowned. "Maybe he—"

Buck moved next to Sunny and put his hand on her waist. "I'll go back to my own camp."

"You can't." She dropped her voice. "We're soulmates."

Buck glanced at Jason then spoke to Sunny. "I'll visit you, but I miss my camp. I do."

She gave him a sad smile.

"All right then," Rita said. "Let's go to see Denise's, and then I'll help you relocate the bus for tonight."

Sunny felt Jason watching her. She whispered into Buck's ear. "You can share my room—remember, you don't have to live outside."

His mouth was tight. "I can't move into some doctor's house."

"You can camp there. It's a ranch. We can both camp."

He shook his head no, his eyes solid. She felt hurt. She hurt all over.

"Let's get going," Rita said.

Bear motioned to the bus. "There's no rush with this. We can wait a few days."

Marci turned to him and took the tissue from her nose. "Leave it, Barry. We can't *ever* sleep in there."

He took her hand and patted it. "You're right—"

Sunny stepped up to them. "No, Bear . . . Barry. It's your property. I'll clean it up."

Chapter 72: Sunny Lytle

The dogs ripped into crazed barking, and everyone turned to see what they were focused on. A man and a woman in uniform came through the bushes. Animal Control.

"I knew it!" Sunny yelled. "You can't have them!"

Rita shouted to be heard. "Maria, Dave! This case is closed. The animals have a home."

Buck went to quiet the dogs with treats, and the two officers walked up to Rita. "I planned to check with you," Maria said. "We had calls this morning giving us this location. We weren't sure it was the same bus."

"Calls?" Rita frowned.

"I called to report the new campsite," Marci said to Maria. "It was a mistake." Everyone turned to look at her.

"What?" Bear said.

"I phoned the police last week and these people a few minutes ago—before everything was settled."

"Oh, god." Rita blushed dark red.

"Why? How'd you know about the old campsite?" Bear asked.

Marci turned to him. "The directions—in your pants pocket. I was going to report the bus stolen, but then I got scared that the police would lock her up." She turned to Sunny. "You have enough problems."

Bear's jaw dropped. "I can't believe—"

Marci raised her eyebrows.

Sunny turned to Maria. "How many other calls?"

Buck was back, closing a bag of treats. "Sunny, I called. I knew these people could help you."

"Buck . . .you . . .?" She couldn't finish.

Jason raised his hand. "Me, too. I admit it. I did it to save your life."

Sunny twitched. She didn't know what to think.

"Yes," Maria said, "three calls this morning."

"Why?" Sunny knew Jason and Buck hadn't planned it together. Each one had turned her in separately. "Am I too much freaking trouble?" It was true. She backed away, turning to scramble through the bushes to get out of their sight.

Buck grabbed her arm. "It wasn't easy, Sunny. I don't like cops, but after Wookie . . ."

Jason put his hand on her other shoulder. "I know it sounds phoney, like reality TV—but look how many people care about you."

Rita leaned toward her with her arms out. Sunny accepted the hug, but she didn't feel any better.

"I didn't call," Bear said, "but it's all for the good."

Sunny reached into her shorts pocket and brought out the handful of bills. "Bear, you're the best. But I won't need it."

He refused to take it back. Marci looked at him and shook her head. She sneezed and plunged into the brush toward the road.

Bear waved a hand toward the money. "Donation for The Haven." He clomped off through the scrub after Marci.

Sunny moved closer to Rita and offered her wrist, as if it would be handcuffed. "Okay, take me away."

"It'll be great. Denise is counting on you."

Even so, she knew it would be two against one if she tried to fight adoptions, and they would spay and neuter everyone. She looked at Jason and Buck, still silent.

Chapter 73: Rita McKenna

She was desperate to make her apology to John. She told Sunny she'd be right back and ran to catch up with Bear and Marci.

They were standing by their car. "What about the money? You're still keeping secrets! I can't—"

Rita whipped through the scrub, breathing hard. "May I borrow your cell phone?" She felt obliged to explain. "It's an emergency . . . an issue of distrust."

The couple exchanged a grim look, and Bear handed Rita his phone.

"Take as long as you want," Marci told her.

Rita stepped away and punched the numbers, amazed that it worked in the woods since most cells didn't get a signal at her apartment. She was almost hoping to leave a message, so much easier apologizing to a recording.

John picked up.

"This is Rita. Are you busy?"

"No—yes, but I can take a couple of minutes."

"I feel horrible—"

"Oh? What's new?"

He wasn't going to make it easy, and she had no practice at apologizing. She didn't blame him if he wanted to end the relationship. She might not have forgiven him if she had been the one accused of lying. "I know you didn't report Sunny. Bernard Hansen's wife did. In fact, so did two other of Sunny's friends."

"Oh, the car guy—whose cell phone you're using."

"I'm not making excuses, but I remembered giving you the location of her camp, and the call came from out of state—I jumped to a ridiculous conclusion."

"You don't trust me."

She swallowed hard. "I do now. I'm so sorry. I followed my instincts, and they were all wrong. It was fear—I thought I'd fallen for another controlling man."

He chuckled. "You fell for me?"

Her mood lightened. "Flat on my face." She plucked a leaf from a plant and rubbed its velvet between her fingers.

"Rita, I would never turn that poor girl in. I wanted to help you help her."

She pulled the truth up, painfully, from her guts. "I was negligent and couldn't face it. Can you forgive me? Please?"

She hoped for enthusiasm, but he didn't answer. She began to resign herself. Maybe he had already found a California girl, someone younger, without baggage. "I know you gave some start-up money to Denise. You've already helped Sunny." She told him about the plans for the animals. "I'll be working alongside Denise as a vet, under her authority, doing what I love. Even if you never speak to me again, I'll appreciate your part in that."

He didn't speak.

"John, I don't know what else to say." She glanced at the phone. It was the home screen. Either she had lost the connection, or he had hung up on her.

"Free Bird" began to play.

"John? Can you forgive me?"

"Yes, I forgive you. I forgave you the next day. I almost sent you a dozen roses. Twice. But you didn't want me to give you anything else. The car was going to be my excuse for a visit."

"It's waiting for you."

"We'll talk about that later. You need to get your own cell phone, too."

The engine was running, windows up, as she approached the car. She went to the driver's side and Bernard rolled down the window.

"Sorry to keep you waiting." She thanked him, said goodbye, and hurried into the woods. From his demeanor, she could see that the argument hadn't been resolved, but Marci's hand was in Bernard's, resting on his thigh.

On the way to the camp, movement caught her eye. A miniature dinosaur jumped from the weeds and ran on its long back legs across the trail and into the brush. Was she hallucinating? She listened to it scramble through the vegetation, but couldn't catch sight of it again. Crested head, upright posture, leggy stride. It must have been a basilisk, the Jesus Christ lizard that could run on water. Another escapee, like the peacocks that made their rounds through the neighborhood, pythons in the Everglades, iguanas, Nile monitors, and flocks of parrots farther south. The whole state was a battleground of native and invasive species, but she was beginning to like the variety.

Chapter 74: Pancho

Pancho curled up under low fronds. He was tied in shade, but could not sleep. A sound came from the weeds. He strained to see into shadows under the bus. Words of humans close by did not ease his fear. Skin on his back rose as lake scent penetrated his nostrils. The blood and breath and shriek of old Wookie, the snap of jaws was linked to that smell. Lurking upwind on the bank and in the lake, more armored creatures slid teeth first through the weeds and lifted themselves on thick legs to sprint. Pancho recognized himself as meat. He was small and soft, surrounded by the stench of fear in all directions. Only one promising strand of smell remained, the smoky meatness his two-legger called bacon. Freedom was a universe of bacon.

He took the leash into his mouth. The feel of molars sinking again and again into spongy rope soothed him. It did not take long to cut through. He skittered into the scrub.

Chapter 75: Sunny Lytle

She followed Jason with her eyes until he disappeared behind the trees. His confession was a harder punch than Buck's. Buck had gone through plenty—but Jason . . . Had he been looking down from his wonderful life, viewing her as pathetic?

Rita approached from the path. "What can I do to help?"

Sunny looked around. Nothing left on the ground. Buck was carrying the last armload of firewood toward the bus. She only had to put Pancho inside and drive.

"I have a couple of days to get ready for Denise's, right?"

"Let's make it one night, okay? Buck isn't going to let you run off again, so don't even think about that."

"You're in charge. I promised and I mean it." She went to the tree where she had tied the tiny pooch. "Panchy?" She rustled the tall weeds with her foot, peering into the scrub. "Pancho?" She checked the next tree and the next, frantic. She was sure she had tied him right there.

"Sunny! What's the matter?" Buck yelled from inside the bus.

She ran back to the first tree, convinced Pancho was hiding. Her eyes caught the white nylon rope, low around the tree among the weeds. She pulled up the chewed end and recognized tiny teeth marks. "Oh, my god! Buck! Rita!" She ran deeper into the bushes and trees. "Pancho, Pancho! Here, buddy! Here, boy! Where are you?"

Buck jumped down from the bus and stopped dead. "I'll check by the lake." Rita said that she'd go toward the road.

Sunny took off perpendicular to the bus. In between her own yells, she could hear Rita and Buck tramping through brush, calling. She made the second vow of the day, begging God, Mother Nature, even her father, in case he was in a position to help. Neutering, spaying, adopting out—she would go for all of it without a complaint. She would give up the idea of ever trying to create a fur family again.

She held her breath, her childhood means of trying to predict the future, telling herself that if she didn't breathe until she heard

Rita and Buck call Pancho ten times, it was a sign that he would return. She counted eight calls and gasped for air. The next time five.

She went back to the spot where she had tied him and sat in the weeds. At any other time, she couldn't get rid of his feelings. Now nothing. She closed her eyes to concentrate, pleading, sending love. A vision of Pancho, thirsty and scared, filled her, but she couldn't tell if it was telepathy or her imagination.

Rita walked back, still calling.

Sunny pulled herself up. It was hard to ask the question. "You don't think a gator got him, do you?"

"You would have heard something." She had a towel from her car, wiping sweat off her neck. "I looked everywhere between here and the road. He's either hiding or far away. We should get driving before the animals in the bus overheat."

"I know." The complaints from the bus were loud and clear. Norton, the calmest cat, was visible atop a crate, surveying what must have been chaos. "Why is Pancho punishing me like this? Do they all hate me now?"

"You need to stop thinking of animal consciousness being like your own. We don't know if they have the emotion of anger or a conception of good and bad. You're just punishing yourself."

Sunny knew that they had all the emotions, but there was no sense in arguing. "I don't know what to do."

"Everything is going to be better, as soon as you're out of here."

Sunny called to Buck to get ready to go. He loved Pancho and must feel almost as bad as she did. They would have to come back later, and every day, until they found the poor little guy.

Chapter 76: Sunny Lytle

She parked the bus against a thick wall of hollies, strangler figs, and sweet gums for afternoon shade and Buck helped her do a partial unloading, then set up the tent for a nap. Since he'd stopped scouting for Maglatoids, or whatever they were, he had leisure time, and she felt she'd been helpful in talking him out of that craziness.

The way to Denise's was toward Ocala, through an area Sunny didn't know, open fields and stretches of forest. Rita drove past a farm with horses, glossy and well-fed, one flipping its tail in silhouette against a pink sky. A fenced pasture held three miniature horses. "Rita, stop, stop! Let's take a look at those guys."

"These are Denise's neighbors. You can visit any time."

Sunny thought of little Gigolo. Maybe still available. She wondered how many animals could be cared for at The Haven. How many she would really be allowed to keep.

Rita pulled into a long driveway between broad green fields. There were several buildings, including a barn and a white farmhouse. Sunny started to anticipate running water, electricity, and sleeping in a real bed—probably air-conditioning in summer. No more being gnawed on by mosquitoes, chiggers, and ticks, or freezing in a damp sleeping bag. The furs would be protected, too—she could nuzzle their necks again and scratch their behinds.

Walking to the door, she realized it wasn't Buck's kind of place, sturdy brick with frilly curtains, a big picture window. She already missed him.

Deep barking came from inside.

"Oh, my god—Rufus and Brindle. I forgot they'd be here!"

The door opened and Denise stood smiling as the dogs rushed Sunny, licking her arms and legs, wagging their bodies almost in half, pushing into each other, nearly knocking her down. She squatted and put an arm around each neck, feeling nothing but love.

Denise led the way past a large living room with a big screen TV and stuffed sofas and chairs, and into a bright farmhouse kitchen, rustic with wood cabinets, but with sparkling stainless steel sinks and appliances. The dogs settled down, Brindle dropping onto the cool terrazzo next to the wall. Rufus positioned himself to drink from a huge metal dog bowl between his legs.

Denise handed her a tall iced tea, and Sunny sat down at the table, suddenly so sleepy that she could barely hold her head up. It was something about the comfortable temperature of the room and being in a place where she could relax.

Denise offered to show her to her new room and she followed her down a rose-painted hallway. The bedroom was fresh and bright, with walls of smooth light wood and creamy cotton curtains. Light streamed in through the blinds, touching the foot rail of a brass bed, king-size, covered with a leopard print spread and heaped with furry pillows of zebra and cheetah prints. The nightstand held a brass elephant lamp. There was a chest of drawers and a dresser with a lacy doily across it.

Sunny was stunned by the beauty. If Buck wasn't waiting, she'd climb right into bed.

Denise straightened a pillow. "I couldn't resist that bedspread. The furniture is antique. I've been collecting for years."

Sunny hugged her. "I love it so much!" Rita came down the hall and Sunny hugged her, too.

Chapter 77: Pancho

He hid in brush until voices stopped calling and dusk fell, then took up the smoky, fatty, delicious trail. He trotted a long distance, thirsty and tired, but feeling free. He caught a lizard along the way and crunched it, tasting blood and innards. He chewed the hide, still hungry.

By dark, his legs moved slowly. His tongue hung long, wicking saliva into the breeze, but he was afraid to go toward water. A sticker plant caught him on all four legs. He stopped and rolled back on his haunches, lifting a hind leg to chew out burrs between the pads. His chest and feet were crusted in painful prickles. He lay on his side under scrub to clean each foot, teething out the spiny balls and spitting them. His tongue was cut by one that he half swallowed and choked out.

Undergrowth slowed his progress. He walked and scratched and bit stickers until dark, following molecules of scent lingering low to the ground. His pads were raw. He tried holding one foot against his abdomen to trot on three legs, but showing vulnerability made worse fear.

He came to pavement where he could travel faster, but the temperature dropped as the moon rose, too cold for his naked back. Feeding time had passed with no sign of a bowl. He was tired, but there was no secure place to drop down. His nose in charge, he soldiered on, following the bacon trail.

Essence of cat drifted into his radar, unfamiliar feline. The cat had moved on, leaving a rich, nutritious turd. He nosed into the direct line of scent and dug up the morsel. The kind of candy out of reach reach in the bus. He scraped at the dark hardened tidbit, lifted it from the sand with his front teeth onto his tongue, and tossed it back into his jaws, grinding it to paste, swallowing. Divine. It motivated him to push on.

Soon a thick layer of bacon molecules blanketed the grass, leading him to the closed door of a dark building. Intensity peaked. He stood on his hind legs, scratching at the wood, then rested, scratched again, then wandered back under the trees. He found a root to surround his body and lay down, exhausted.

At morning light, a fresh greasy stream aroused his nostrils. He swallowed the rush of juice in his mouth and locked onto the wave, scaring squirrels into trees as he ran, tracking close around the building to the screen door.

Chapter 78: Sunny Lytle

That evening, Sunny brought Pancho's bowls and a can of Kennel Ration Beef Dinner to the old campsite, and Buck carried a jug of water and a six-pack. They walked around calling, and after a while, Sunny sat down in the clearing and Buck joined her. She concentrated, trying to use her telepathy. Clouds blew over the moon.

"How about if I lay on the ground and you get on top of me?" Buck asked. He unbuckled his belt. "I'll wait for the little fart most of the night if there's entertainment."

She didn't feel like making a party out of it, but she hoisted her hips over him, knelt, and sat back on his thighs. "I'm not taking off any clothes. It's too cold."

"What good is that? Just slip off your pants."

"My butt will get bit."

"C'mon. It's our last night under the stars."

"I won't miss them."

"You'll miss it all."

He was right. She would miss the nights when chores were done and Buck made cheese soup, the hours spent talking to him about animals, the background music played by frogs and crickets.

He was a lovable old guy. She stood and pulled off her shoes and jeans and lay flat on top of him, kissing his mouth and eyes, nibbling across his forehead and brushing away the hair to find his ears. Sadness took over, but she didn't let him know.

They left at midnight. In the morning she was running late as usual and Buck volunteered to make another trip back. He promised he would check two or three times every day until Pancho was found.

She hugged him hard. "That could be forever, Buck."

"He's a smart dawg. He knows where his feed is."

He could make her laugh even with tears behind her eyes. "I still love the way you say dog. You never rush over it."

He rolled his eyes and smiled. "Dawg, dawg, dawg. You better get going. Waiting for me to say dawg isn't the greatest excuse for being late."

She tried once more to convince him to move to Denise's with her that evening, but he wouldn't consider it.

The restaurant seemed empty of staff when she walked through the swinging doors. Barbara and Ellen stood behind the counter with their backs toward her, looking into the kitchen.

Barbara turned. "Here she comes!"

Patty called from the kitchen. "Somebody's been looking for you, Sunny." There was a tease in her voice.

Sunny ran past the counter toward the back, and caught a glimpse of them beyond the tall mixer. Pancho cuddled against Jason's chest, taking bits of bacon from his fingers. She rushed to press the tiny face next to her cheek and caress his neck, ignoring the itchiness that came through. He was too busy crunching a mouthful to snuggle or lick or wiggle, and there was no sign that he'd missed her. But it didn't matter.

Jason's eyes shone as he handed over the squirming pooch. Sunny hugged the gritty, bitten, hairless body to her chest. "Bacon breath."

"Could be worse," Patty said.

Chapter 79: Rufus

In the food place, two bowls were filled. Rufus danced the happy dance on back legs with Brindle. They crunched. No others to compete. No small, hot, sticky body, pink testicles, ear-paining shrieks. Nobody to pin or flip. Rufus dropped hips, lay his stomach down on cool wood near Brindle, slept.

A filament of scent wavered in, drew him up. The door opened to a thickness of dung, bacon, and nipper. Nipper launched from the two-legger and landed, scrambling, hopping, licking. His wobble-screech penetrated Rufus' skull. The two-legger patted heads, rubbed chests, kissed noses. Pancho, Pancho, Pancho came to Rufus' ears.

Brindle stood near. Nipper snorted her tender parts, took in the mix of body scents. No longer Rufus' female. Part nipper's.

Rufus sprang, nosed the nipper onto his back, legs up. Nipper stiffened, shook, eyes bulging, breathing hard. Rufus moved one leg at a time, settled next to him.

Chapter 80: Buckaroo

It was a hot, sticky day at the end of April. Buck had been back in his spot on Spring Garden Road for nearly two months. With free time for reading, he'd borrowed *The Call of the Wild* from the library and was finishing the last few chapters, along with a few beers. It had been his favorite book as a boy and still wrenched emotion from deep in his gut. He would like to share the story with Sunny, but she wouldn't feel the beauty, only the sadness. He closed the book, took it into the tent, and brought *Among Grizzlies* out to his chair.

He hadn't seen Sunny for over a week. He'd only spent the night in her room a few times. It still made him nervous to sleep indoors. He was used to hearing the natural night sounds, the frog grunts and the owl hoots, all letting him know that everything was safe. Besides, Sunny insisted on letting Pancho under the covers to rub his scaly dog skin against whatever parts of Buck he happened to curl near. Usually, Tulip, the schnauzer, now in a diaper because of a leakage problem, and Sugar, the fat female terrier with the goatee, piled onto the bed too. The bed was fresh and soft, but there was no room to move. Even Rufus would try to sprawl his 135 pounds between them on the queen mattress. Buck couldn't sleep with hot snoring dogs near his face and between his legs, no matter how lovable they were.

Sunny said she would visit him in the tent, now that she had a car, but so far she hadn't made it. He didn't blame her. She was busy between caring for the animals and working at the restaurant. She liked her jobs, a thing he couldn't understand, but he was happy for her. He had whittled a bust of himself and one of Sunny, a pair to put on her bookcase, and some new animals. She still had the nativity set on her dresser the last time he was there, even though it was April.

Geordie had promised use of the truck on Saturday so Buck could attend a party at The Haven. He didn't look forward to getting dressed up, but Denise was a good cook, and there'd be a huge amount of food. Ribs, he'd been told. He hoped to spend some time with Sunny afterward.

He moved his plastic chair to follow the shade and flipped to the photos in the grizzly book. Lots of bears too close up. "Hulk and Daisy mating." The photographer seemed crazier than Sunny. But then, if she found a grizzly cub, she'd adopt it in a heartbeat. This was his third book on Alaska since he started going to the library. The last frontier was a wild place, like the middle of Florida, but beard-icing, nose-freezing cold in winter. He'd like to see it, do some salmon fishing. Maybe in August when his tent became a sauna and the no-see-ums were trying to make camp under his dreads.

Black clouds rumbled from the east. If rain pooled on the roof, it would drip through, since his waterproofing was pretty much shot. He was thinking he should swap tents with Sunny's newer one. He'd kept it rolled up, dry in a plastic bag, until she was sure she'd fit in over at the ranch. He guessed she was sure by now.

He stowed the grizzly book in a Ziploc with a book on animal communications. He would take that book over to Sunny, see if any of it made sense.

He took a look around, still in the habit. Open sky to the east, but dense thunderheads blowing in from the west, glomming together. These were the kind he used to fear most, the ones with room to hide and plenty of power to harness if you were a Magnetoid.

He'd been trying to remember. Did his final victory occur on the morning of "gator day"? It was sometime around then that he'd smashed a powerful shot into a huge purple-black cumulonimbus. There was a loud bang that he'd taken as lightning, but now he wondered if he'd knocked out some portion of vital equipment. He couldn't be sure if the winning stroke had occurred that morning, but it made sense.

He cracked the last beer in a six-pack. There were still more icy and cold in the cooler and nothing he had to do that day. He took a gulp. He'd finished off the Mags in style, disintegrated the metallic assholes with sheer skill. Pride brought him to his feet. He took a wide stance and whooped.

He stomped out into the open and climbed up on the woodpile so they could see him clearly, the bastards, if any were still alive. "You, motherfuckers!" They should have known better than to fuck with the blond Buccaneer. "Savior of mankind—humankind—furkind!" He struck his chest, raised his beer, and stretched out his arms, tilting his face to the sky. "I got you, didn't I? This bad boy knocked your lights out! Eat me, fuckers! Eat me! Eat me!"

He slugged the rest of the beer and almost slipped off the woodpile, dropping the empty bottle to the sand. From the sound of rain on the leaves, a downpour was traveling toward him through the woods, to reach him in seconds. At that moment his hair stood up from the roots, as if drawn by a vacuum. Sons of bitches! A searing beam nailed his feet to the wood and he whiffed an aroma—grilled pork? His body toppled off the woodpile.

Chapter 81: Sunny Lytle

Rita and Denise had put together a dinner for the people who were helping out and donating auction items for the upcoming fund-raiser. Sunny had introduced Patty to the group, and since Patty knew most everyone in the county, "Friends of the Haven" continued to multiply. Denise cooked up a feast for meat-eaters and vegetarians, and the food was laid out buffet-style on the sideboard. The dining room table and two added tables were filled mostly with new women recruits.

Sunny heaped a plate with salad, corn, and green beans and sat down across from Rita and John, next to Jason. He had poured her a glass of red wine. She realized Buck was missing. She called to Rita across the table. "Buck's not here!"

"He hasn't been around lately, has he?"

"I invited him, but he might've lost track. I've been so busy—I need to drive over to his camp."

"Too late for tonight."

She clicked her tongue. "I feel terrible. Ribs are his favorite. I can take him some tomorrow, but they won't be as good."

Rita winked. "He'll like that."

She felt too good to worry. She picked up a buttery ear of corn and took a big bite. The kernels burst with sweetness.

Jason touched her arm. "I have something to tell you."

Butter ran down her chin and she dabbed it with her napkin.

"My wife took a job in North Carolina."

She put down her corn. "She's gone?"

"Yep. Left yesterday with all of her stuff and two weenie dogs."

"She left you a dog?"

"No, that's all we had. The foster got adopted."

"I'm sorry." She meant about losing the dog, but let him think what he wanted. She sipped the wine. It made her lips pucker. "You're staying here?"

"Sure. Starting computer classes in Deland this summer."

The words she'd yearned to hear, spent so many hours dreaming about, hoping . . . Now the need was gone. "Then what? You'll move up there?"

"I'm staying here where I belong."

He leaned forward to kiss her, aiming for her mouth, but she turned enough to land his lips on her cheek.

By ten the guests had left except for John and Jason. They helped with dishes, put away food, and moved chairs. Sunny let Pancho, Sugar, Tulip, Devo, Rufus, and Brindle out of her room, so they could enjoy the company and have a few scraps. Pancho led the pack into the kitchen.

"They're so well behaved," Rita said. "Never made a peep."

"You mean they never barked," Sunny said. "I heard them all evening. They were terrible, pining for barbequed ribs and smoked brisket."

Nobody said anything, but John stopped rinsing dishes and Jason turned from the refrigerator. Denise looked at Rita.

"Do you all know how Sunny saved the macaw?" Denise asked.

"No," Jason said. "She never mentioned it."

Rita sat down. "You never gave me the details."

Denise put her arm across Sunny's shoulder. "A hyacinth—Smiley, a beautiful, beloved bird—dehydrated, near death." She explained Sunny's diagnosis and the positive outcome. "Without the contribution from his owners, I would never have had the means—or the courage—to start The Haven."

"Way to go, Sunny!" Jason high-fived. John shook her hand.

Denise stroked Sunny's braid. "Many types of animal communication are being studied, but Sunny is way ahead of the research."

Sunny had an inkling that Denise might be poking fun, but it was all among friends.

After everyone else had left or gone to bed, Jason asked Sunny to sit with him in the living room. She turned on the TV, hoping to avoid conversation. Brindle, Tulip, Sugar, and Devo sacked out on the cool floor around the edges of the woven rug. Mitter lay on his back in an overstuffed chair, and Norton was spread atop the bookcase. Contentment and full bellies all around. Jason put an arm around her shoulder and rubbed behind

Rufus' ears with the other hand. Pancho turned round and round and curled in her lap. She drew her finger lightly over his pink nose, across his head, and down the back of his neck, watching his eyes close in ecstasy. She motioned toward the coffee table, the remote. "Can you find *The Dog Whisperer*?"

Jason put his hand on her knee. Instant *déjà vu*. The old days when his parents were sleeping on the other side of the wall. She covered his hand with hers to keep his fingers from wandering farther.

"I'm going to miss seeing you everyday," he said.

She sat up straighter. His hand fell away. "I thought you were staying."

"I'll be in school and only working part-time."

She rolled her eyes. "You'll still see me."

"We can be together at night— to make up the time. Rita told me you're not with Buck anymore."

"I haven't seen him this week, but that doesn't mean . . ."

He took the end of her braid, brushing his chin with the stub and leaned forward, positioning for a kiss.

"You're not divorced."

"My marriage is over."

She took the hand that had crept up her thigh, putting it onto Pancho's back. "There's no rush."

A few months earlier she would have melted over him like cheese, but now her only feeling was fondness. She was just starting to pull her weight and didn't want to end up using him somehow, like Bear and Buck.

"We're both busy. I talked to my mother. She still lives at the address on the letter—has a husband and a muffin business." She hadn't planned to tell him until it was sure. "It's a farm, and I'm invited to visit—two horses, two goats, ten dogs, five cats, and eight chickens."

He tried to act enthusiastic, but she knew him. She thanked him for his help at the hospital and for being a good friend always. "Let's go out to dinner and see a movie sometime. We never did that."

"You always said you'd rather spend the night in the woods."

"Now I want to try civilization." She took his hand and held it. It wasn't time to tell him that her romantic feelings for him were gone.

He massaged her fingers. "I won't be able to keep the house. It's mostly Deb's."

"You don't need that big place." She hoped he wasn't trying for an invitation. He might have guessed that she was supposed to get Lytle's farmhouse. "Everything'll work out."

"One way or another."

"I didn't cause it, the split, did I?"

"No. We had problems for a long time—mostly my fault." She didn't believe him completely. "Give your marriage a chance."

She turned toward the TV, not seeing the screen, but imagining her fur family at Lytle's. After land was sold and bills were paid, there should be a couple of acres left along with the house. But she would keep down the numbers in the fur family so she could make all of them happy. Go slow. No more compulsive decisions.

Chapter 82: Sunny Lytle

Sunny parked on the hill and walked toward the path to the Sugar Mill. Passing a pickup truck reminded her that she had forgotten to deliver the ribs to Buck. She would get them after work and pay him a visit. Life was so much easier having Rita's car. She didn't miss paddling to work.

She walked under the graceful arm of an oak, its Spanish moss draped over a limb like a frosty shawl. She enjoyed trees even more not living under them. She had it good—a nice place to live, human friends, and her fur family. A few of the puppies had gone to homes already, and she was still trying to manage the separation pain. But like Rita said, compromise made the place work.

She had finished serving her first table when Patty met her in the kitchen. "Sunny, take a walk with me—out back."

Bad news. She could tell. Something to knock her down, always. A police officer was standing near the picnic table.

"Have a seat, Sunny," Patty said.

She gripped her hands under the table. The state of Ohio or Indiana had found her.

"This is Sunny Lytle," Patty told the policeman. She stood beside Sunny, touching her elbow. Patty turning her in?

"Hello, Sunny." He put out his hand.

She gave him hers, trying not to tremble.

"Were you acquainted with a Robert Buckholtz?"

"Robert? No."

"He was squatting on Spring Garden Road."

She turned to Patty, saw her expectant look. "Buck?"

"Must be."

The policeman fingered his belt. "He was found yesterday at his camp. I'm sorry."

Sunny's chest went hollow. "Dead?"

"Yes. We got information that he had a friend working here. I came as a courtesy, to let you know before you read it in the newspaper."

She lowered her head and stared at the table. Buck must have told Geordie about her. She wondered . . . his liver . . . but he'd looked fine. She pictured him fallen out of his chair near the camp stove, brown leaves collected by his side from the wind. A tear ran down her cheek.

Patty squeezed her shoulder.

"His possessions will be hauled away in a couple of days. You're welcome to go over and take anything you want."

She wiped her eyes and looked up. "What happened?"

"A probable lightning strike, per the autopsy. It seems that Mr. Buckholtz wasn't found until a few days after his death, and due to unusual circumstances, there's still some question."

"Unusual?"

"The details aren't pretty."

She had known they wouldn't be. "Please, can you tell me?"

"It had to do with . . . the state of his remains."

"Really?" Patty said.

His voice was low. "It sort of looked like spontaneous combustion—but there's no scientific explanation at this point."

Sunny shook her head. "There's no scientific explanation for a lot of things." She knew it—Magnetoids got him. A heavy curtain hung inside of her, like lead separating her from herself. Nothing seemed real.

After work she drove to Buck's camp. The sun was low, creating a view resembling seashore more than sky. Purple peninsulas reached into a pink ocean edged in golden surf, waves breaking on a turquoise beach. They were hiding up there, those Mags, those mother-fuckers that zapped Buck.

She passed a house under construction on the end of Spring Garden Road. It was all property for sale around there, and she guessed it would eventually become another neighborhood, sucking up the space from bears, raccoons, possums, and foxes, ruining the wild jungle that only people like Buck truly appreciated. She parked the car off the edge of the pavement and walked through the short weeds, finding a path between the trailing vines and mix of palmettos, magnolias, and wax myrtle trees.

The tent was still standing, zipped tight, untouched by lightning or Magnetoids. Yellow police tape had fallen to the ground in places, but still surrounded a cleared rectangle with the fire pit, plastic chairs, coolers, and wood pile inside.

Lightning? No way. If only she had let him be, instead of acting like he was nuts and laying on the guilt.

She stepped over the tape, went to the tent, and unzipped it. His cot was there and an orange crate holding his Altoid tin of cigarette butts and a cardboard box of carvings. He always collected his butts for lean days—like when he'd spent all his money on Sunny and her family. She choked up. She wiped her face on her sleeve and sat on the cot. There were Ziploc bags of books sticking out from under the edge. They were library books so she set them next to her to take back.

She reached into the box and pulled out a whittled head, some sort of creature, not human or fur, creepy. Maybe a Magnetoid. The second head made her laugh. It was her, recognizable, the cheekbones, the chipped tooth, the braid. There was a gator and—she reached to the bottom—a bear.

She cupped the last sculpted head in her hand and rubbed her thumb over the smooth forehead, down the nose, over the lips. He had captured his streak of insanity in the wild hair and long beard. The light color of the wood resembled his faded eyes. She felt him, close. "Thank you," she said. It wasn't nearly enough.

A chill brought goose bumps on her arms. The sun was setting and a breeze had kicked up. Shadows of leaves fluttered on the face of the tent, and a low beam of sunlight slanted through the flap. A rustle out in the bushes caught her attention. She placed the carvings back in the box and followed the crackle of dry grass.

A short distance from the clearing, a yellow puppy, too tiny to scamper through the thick brush, lay in the grass near her feet. She crouched to lift it. Holding all four legs together with one hand, she snuggled it against her chest, feeling the delicate bones and frantic heartbeat. The eyes were open, but didn't focus. Maybe only a week old. Her stomach felt hollow with its need, but there was also love. It licked her finger.

She searched the bushes nearby, expecting to find the mother and more pups. Nothing. It seemed impossible that the pup could have survived alone.

She turned it over to check the sex. A boy. What would Rita and Denise say to her bringing home a puppy? They wouldn't believe he had come to her, like magic. They would think she'd adopted him from a litter of farm dogs. She'd been managing to hide one secret kitten in her room, but keeping a puppy this young would never work. The little guy would have to be bottle-fed every few hours.

She tucked her sweatshirt into her jeans and partially unzipped it to place the pup between the layers of warm fabric. He settled against her stomach like it was home. She gathered the plastic bags of books and carvings and took one last look at what was left of Buck's camp. It was a sad sight, but calming in a small way, completion of what had to be.

The pup nudged her stomach, and she peered inside her shirt. Yellow fluff, light blue eyes—lit with mischief? Too much similarity for coincidence. If reincarnation was true, the highest level must be animal.

"Buckaroo? Buccaneer? Buckholtz." She kissed the soft blond head and drew in the rich scent of puppy fur. He wouldn't remember her, but it might be better that way.

Biography

Vicki Hendricks lives in Hollywood, Florida, and teaches writing at Broward College. Her plots and settings reflect participation in adventure sports, such as skydiving and scuba, and knowledge of the Florida environment. Love of animals is also apparent in her earlier noir novels and stories.

Praise for Earlier Books by Vicki Hendricks:

Florida Gothic Stories

"Vicki Hendricks takes us into her Florida, peninsula of dream and steam, full of beautiful, dangerous human beasts. Watch out: something unexpected always lurks in that most Gothic of hiding places, the heart"
—Lynne Barrett, author of *Magpies*.

"This Vicki Hendricks is one wild dame. She goes places the rest of us have never been, don't even know the way to; and she comes back with stories that prove that everyone's lonely, everyone's trying, and everyone's human. Even when they're not" –S.J. Rosan, author of *The Shanghai Moon.*

Noir Novels:

Miami Purity

"A hymn to American trash culture"—*New York Times Book Review.*
"*Miami Purity* cooks white hot . . . An instant redneck idiot savant classic: so gruesome and funny and deadpan outlandish that you wind up baying at the moon like a Florida coondog"—James Ellroy.

Cruel Poetry - Edgar Award Finalist for 2008.

"I loved this book. It's a private ticket into a secret world of desire and sex and the raw edge between them . . . I read it with the fever of the addicted"
—Michael Connelly.

Sky Blues

"I never miss a book by Vicki Hendricks. No one on the current scene is writing supercharged, erotic, real noir novels like these. Think Jack London, James M. Cain, and Colette. *Sky Blues* is another Hendricks' triumph"
     —George Pelecanos, author of *Down by the River Where the Dead Men Go.*

Voluntary Madness

For a writer as fierce as Vicki Hendricks, *Voluntary Madness* is a walk on the tender side of life . . . A bittersweet ending is in the cards, but the ride is exhilarating and endearing as the two misfits sparkle and burn into overdrive" —*Guardian.*

Iguana Love

"In that parallel universe known as noir, Vicki Hendricks has staked her claim—with a spear gun"—*Fort Lauderdale Sun-Sentinel*